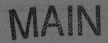

MAIN

The Shadows, Kith and Kin

The Shadows, Kith and Kin

JOE R. LANSDALE

SUBTERRANEAN PRESS 2007

First Edition

ISBN
978-1-59606-081-4

Subterranean Press
PO Box 190106
Burton, MI 48519

www.subterraneanpress.com

F
LAN

617658263

Table of Contents

A Quick Author's Note

When I was a child, very early on, I knew I wanted to be a writer. Pretty much from the beginning, having paper and pencil in hand, I knew it was my calling. The more I read, the more the need to write was fueled. The more I saw stories on TV or in the movies, and especially in comic books, which at that time could do things movies couldn't do—it's a toss up now—the more I wanted to make my living as a freelance writer.

I didn't know what a freelance writer was then, but I knew I wanted to make my living making up stories. So many things influenced me. DC comics had a tremendous impact. *The Iliad* and *The Odyssey*. Fairy tales. Stories of King Arthur's knights. Robin Hood. Folk tales.

The Jungle Book by Kipling dropped on me like an anvil. Edgar Rice Burroughs' novels bumped up against me so hard I'm still bruised. Robert E. Howard tossed a kind of gory glitter in my hair. Edgar Allen Poe creeped me. Bradbury astonished me. Robert Bloch made me wonderfully nervous, and Richard Matheson made me deliciously paranoid. Hemingway sounded neat. Steinbeck touched on things I knew about. He wrote about my people, my parents, their past. Fitzgerald painted beautiful pictures. So many writers. So many different kinds of magic. I also read stories from the bible, which frankly I don't take as a divine word from anyone, but it has lots of good tales full of horror and murder and rapes and incest and heroic deeds. In fact, it's a lot like *The Iliad*, in that it is an adventure story mixed with history and legends and divine intervention. I've always thought it odd that people can't see the connection between the two, or realize that if you can believe in God interacting with man in the bible, then what makes *The Iliad* just an adventure story and the bible divine? They found Troy didn't they, but does that mean the rest of *The Iliad* is true? Does it mean Zeus and Hera are real, the other Greek gods? In the case of the bible they can't even prove the Hebrews were ever held captive in Egypt, let alone that they escaped by parting the Red Sea.

The bottom line is this, telling stories, writing stories, is about telling convincing lies.

Here are my lies. I hope they are convincing. Some of them contain elements of truth, just like *The Iliad* and the bible. I owned mules and I plowed them instead of racing them, but it gave me affection for them, so it's only natural that I would write about them. And I have. Twice. Once in a story called "The Mule Rustlers," a best of the year pick for Otto Penzler's *Best Mystery Stories* and part of the contents for my last collection *Mad Dog Summer and Other Stories*. And now there's "White Mule, Spotted Pig," one of the best stories I've ever written.

"The Shadows, Kith and Kin," which gives the book its title, is based on fact, but is not a factual story. It is about someone not too unlike Charles Whitman, who, when I was young, climbed up in The University of Texas tower in Austin and shot a large number of people with a high powered rifle. I went to school there some years later, and was surprised to find there were still places where the police officer's return shots had chipped away at the tower. I stood where Whitman stood. Shortly thereafter, a young woman, despondent over a love affair or some such thing, jumped from the tower to her death, leaving on the railing her shoes. I came by from class, not knowing about the event, saw men hosing down the ground and hustling about in the bushes. I think they must have been cleaning up the aftermath of her jump. I never found out for sure, but when I got back to the apartment where I lived, I heard about her death, and had a kind of cold chill, and then came a photo in the newspaper of her shoes on the tower railing where she left them just before jumping. It was a startling image. That tower has stayed in my imagination ever since. Back to Charles Whitman. There's a Kinky Friedman song about him that has this line: "There was a rumor of a tumor at the base of his brain." People have been trying to explain these sorts of events for years, but no one has managed to do so convincingly. My story has its own theory.

A side note. Interestingly enough, Kinky Friedman has gone on to run for Governor of Texas. Who would have thunk it? I hope he wins. (He didn't.)

Also included is "Alone" written with Melissa Mia Hall. I want to say right up front that this is more her story than mine. I wrote a few pages of a story that had lain around for ages, but, alas, I couldn't get it to end. Melissa expressed interest in collaborating, and though I'm not a real fan of collaborating, I told her I had this unfinished story, plus another about a woman whose vagina played music, and she wisely chose this one. She did more with it than I could, and gave it a happier ending than I intended, but most likely it is the proper ending.

"Deadman's Road" and "The Gentleman's Hotel" are both about the lead character in *Dead in the West*. "Deadman's Road" is scheduled to appear in *Weird Tales* first. "Gentleman's Hotel" is an original about my cursed reverend, written expressly for this book.

"The Long Dead Day" is a short-short, but I think it has impact, like an ice pick to the brain. It was written in a sudden flush of excitement.

Also included is an oldie but a goodie. A Bram Stoker Award winner that first appeared in *Bestsellers Guaranteed*, a book with a ridiculous dragon cover that had nothing to do with any of the stories in the collection. "The Events Concerning A Nude Fold-Out Found In A Harlequin Romance" won a Bram Stoker and is a favorite of mine, but due to its length, isn't a story that's gotten a lot of replay. I'm proud to have it reprinted here where I hope new readers will discover it.

Also contained here is "Bill, The Little Steam Shovel." I adore this story, and it cooked around inside my head for years before I was able to write it. My son, Keith, is the inspiration. He liked a book about a steam shovel that did all manner of fine things for boys and girls. In fact, there were two books about steam shovels, or diggers, or Digger Dans, as my son called them, and they inspired my idea of a different sort of steam shovel story. I just couldn't quite sit down and write it, though I had written an introduction to it some years before I finally was inspired by Al Sarrantonio's anthology *Flights* to take a serious crack at it. The opening I had written stayed essentially the same, and the rest of it jumped out without problems, having built up its leaping muscles all those years inside my head. I don't do many stories that way, most come at a rush and I discover them as I write. There were discoveries here, the ending for example, but the story was pretty much full blown by the time I sat down to do it, having had the opportunity to let it percolate for so long.

Finally, I hope you like my lies and they give you good entertainment. Bless you all for putting down your hard earned Yankee dollars for this collection. I believe it to be one of my best.

And finally, I dedicate this collection to my good friends Judy and Bill Crider. As fine a people who ever walked the earth, even if Bill did once scoop me on a buy of some very fine old Gold Medal books. He looks like a mild mannered professor. But don't be fooled. He is a ruthless book buyer and he moves with the swiftness of an eagle.

Bless you Judy and Bill. And especially bless you, Judy, as you have to put up with Bill.

Joe R. Lansdale (his ownself)
Nacogdoches, Texas

The Shadows,
Kith and Kin

"...and the soul, resenting it's lot, flies groaningly to the shades."

The Aeneid, by Virgil

There are no leaves left on the trees, and the limbs are weighted with ice and bending low. Many of them have broken and fallen across the drive. Beyond the drive, down where it and the road meet, where the bar ditch is, there is a brown savage run of water.

It is early afternoon, but already it is growing dark, and the fifth week of the storm raves on. I have never seen such a storm of wind and ice and rain, not here in the South, and only once before have I been in a cold storm bad enough to force me to lock myself tight in my home.

So many things were different then, during that first storm. No better. But different.

On this day while I sit by my window, looking out at what the great, white, wet storm has done to my world, I feel at first confused, and finally elated.

The storm. The ice. The rain. All of it. It's the sign I was waiting for.

—◆—

I thought for a moment of my wife, her hair so blonde it was almost white as the ice that hung in the trees, and I thought of her parents, white-headed too, but white with age, not dye, and of our little dog Constance, not white at all, but all brown and black with traces of tan; a rat terrier mixed with all other blends of dog you might imagine.

I thought of all of them. I looked at my watch. There wasn't really any reason to. I had no place to go, and no way to go if I did. Besides, the battery in my watch had been dead for almost a month.

—◆—

Once, when I was a boy, just before night fall, I was out hunting with my father, out where the bayou water gets deep and runs between the twisted trunks and low hanging limbs of water-loving trees; out there where the frogs bleat and jump and the sun don't hardly shine.

We were hunting for hogs. Then out of the brush came a man, running. He was dressed in striped clothes and he had on very thin shoes. He saw us and the dogs that were gathered about us, blue-ticks, long-eared and dripping spit from their jaws; he turned and broke and ran with a scream.

A few minutes later, the Sheriff and three of his deputies came beating their way through the brush, their shirts stained with sweat, their faces red with heat.

My father watched all of this with a kind of hard-edged cool, and the Sheriff, a man dad knew, said, "There's a man escaped off the chain gang, Hirem. He run through here. Did you see him?"

My father said that we had, and the Sheriff said, "Will those dogs track him?"

"I want them to they will," my father said, and he called the dogs over to where the convict had been, where his footprints in the mud were filling slowly with water, and he pushed the dog's heads down toward these shoe prints one at a time, and said, "Sic him," and away the hounds went.

We ran after them then, me and my dad and all these fat cops who huffed and puffed out long before we did, and finally we came upon the man, tired, leaning against a tree with one hand, his other holding his business while he urinated on the bark. He had been defeated some time back, and now he was waiting for rescue, probably thinking it would have been best to have not run at all.

But the dogs, they had decided by private conference that this man was as good as any hog, and they came down on him like heat-seeking missiles. Hit him hard, knocked him down. I turned to my father, who could call them up and make them stop, no matter what the situation, but he did not call.

The dogs tore at the man, and I wanted to turn away, but did not. I looked at my father and his eyes were alight and his lips dripped spit; he reminded me of the hounds.

The dogs ripped and growled and savaged, and then the fat sheriff and his fat deputies stumbled into view, and when one of the deputies saw what had been done to the man, he doubled over and let go of whatever grease-fried goodness he had poked into his mouth earlier that day.

The Sheriff and the other deputy stopped and stared, and the Sheriff, said, "My God," and turned away, and the deputy said, "Stop them, Hirem. Stop them. They done done it to him. Stop them."

My father called the dogs back, their muzzles dark and dripping. They sat in a row behind him, like sentries. The man, or what had been a man, the convict, lay all about the base of the tree, as did the rags that had once been his clothes.

Later, we learned the convict had been on the chain gang for cashing hot checks.

—◆—

Time keeps on slipping, slipping…Wasn't that a song?

— ♦ —

As day comes I sleep, then awake when night arrives. The sky has cleared and the moon has come out, and it is merely cold now. Pulling on my coat, I go out on the porch and sniff the air, and the air is like a meat slicer to the brain, so sharp it gives me a headache. I have never known cold like that.

I can see the yard close up. Ice has sheened all over my world, all across the ground, up in the trees. The sky is like a black velvet back drop, the stars like sharp shards of blue ice clinging to it.

I leave the porch light on, go inside, return to my chair by the window, burp. The air is filled with the aroma of my last meal, canned Ravioli, eaten cold.

I take off my coat and hang it on the back of the chair.

— ♦ —

Has it happened yet, or is it yet to happen.
Time, it just keep on slippin', slippin', yeah it do.

— ♦ —

I nod in the chair, and when I snap awake from a deep nod, there is snow blowing across the yard and the moon is gone and there is only the porch light to brighten it up.

But, in spite of the cold, I know they are out there.
The cold, the heat, nothing bothers them.
They are out there.

— ♦ —

They came to me first on a dark night several months back, with no snow and no rain and no cold, but a dark night without clouds and plenty of heat in the air, a real humid night, sticky like dirty undershorts. I awoke and sat up in bed and the yard light was shining thinly through our window. I turned to look at my wife lying there beside me, her very blonde hair silver in that light. I looked at her for a long time, then got up and went into the living room. Our little dog, who made his bed by the front door, came over and sniffed me, and I bent to pet him. He took to this for a minute, then found his spot by the door again, laid down.

Finally I turned out the yard light and went out on the porch. In my underwear. No one could see me, not with all our trees, and if they could see me, I didn't care.

I sat in a deck chair and looked at the night, and thought about the job I didn't have and how my wife had been talking of divorce, and how my in-laws resented our living with them, and I thought too of how every time I did a thing I failed, and dramatically at that. I felt strange and empty and lost.

While I watched the night, the darkness split apart and some of it came up on the porch, walking. Heavy steps full of all the world's shadow.

I was frightened, but I didn't move. Couldn't move. The shadow, which looked like a tar-covered human-shape, trudged heavily across the porch until it stood over me, looking down. When I looked up, trembling, I saw there was no face, just darkness, thick as chocolate custard. It bent low and placed hand shapes on the sides of my chair and brought its faceless face close to mine, breathed on me; a hot languid breath that made me ill.

"You are almost one of us," it said, then turned, and slowly moved along the porch and down the steps and right back into the shadows. The darkness, thick as a wall, thinned and split, and absorbed my visitor; then the shadows rustled away in all directions like startled bats. I heard a dry crackling leaf sound amongst the trees.

My God, I thought. There had been a crowd of them. Out there.

Waiting.
Watching.
Shadows.
And one of them had spoken to me.

— ◆ —

Lying in bed later that night I held up my hand and found that what intrigued me most were not the fingers, but the darkness between them. It was a thin darkness, made weak by light, but it was darkness and it seemed more a part of me than the flesh.

I turned and looked at my sleeping wife.

I said, "I am one of them. Almost."

— ◆ —

I remember all this as I sit in my chair and the storm rages outside, blowing snow and swirling little twirls of water that in turn become ice. I remember all this, holding up my hand again to look.

The shadows between my fingers are no longer thin.

They are dark.

They have connection to flesh.

They are me.

— ◆ —

Four flashes. Four snaps.

The deed is done.

I wait in the chair by the window.

No one comes.

As I suspected.

The shadows were right.

You see. They come to me nightly now. They never enter the house. Perhaps they can not.

But out on the porch, there they gather. More than one

now. And they flutter tight around me and I can smell them, and it is a smell like nothing I have smelled before. It is dark and empty and mildewed and old and dead and dry.

It smells like home.

—◆—

Who are the shadows?

They are all of those who are like me.

They are the empty congregation. The faceless ones. The failures.

The sad empty folk who wander through life and walk beside you and never get so much as a glance; nerds like me who live inside their heads and imagine winning the lottery and scoring the girls and walking tall. But instead, we stand short and bald and angry, our hands in our pockets, holding not money, but our limp balls.

Real life is a drudge.

No one but another loser like myself can understand that.

Except for the shadows, for they are the ones like me. They are the losers and the lost, and they understand and they never do judge.

They are of my flesh, or, to be more precise, I am of their shadow.

They accept me for who I am.

They know what must be done, and gradually they reveal it to me.

The shadows.

I am one of them.

Well, almost.

—◆—

My wife, my in-laws, every human being who walks this earth, underrates me.

There are things I can do.

I can play computer games, and I can win them. I have created my own characters. They are unlike humans. They are better than humans. They are the potential that is inside me and will never be.

Oh, and I can do some other things as well. I didn't mention all the things I can do well. In spite of what my family thinks of me. I can do a number of things that they don't appreciate, but should.

I can make a very good chocolate milk shake.

My wife knows this, and if she would, she would admit that I do. She used to say so. Now she does not. She has closed up to me. Internally. Externally.

Battened down hatches, inwardly and outwardly.

Below. In her fine little galley, that hatch is tightly sealed.

But there is another thing I do well.

I can really shoot a gun.

My father, between beatings, he taught me that. It was the only time we were happy together. When we held the guns.

— ◆ —

Down in the basement I have a trunk.

Inside the trunk are guns.

Lots of them.

Rifles and shotguns and revolvers and automatics.

I have collected them over the years.

One of the rifles belongs to my father-in-law.

There is lots of ammunition.

Sometimes, during the day, if I can't sleep, while my wife is at work and my in-laws are about their retirement—golf. I sit down there and clean the guns and load them and repack them in the crate. I do it carefully, slowly, like foreplay. And when I finish my hands smell like gun oil. I rub my hands against my face and under my nose, the odor of the oil like some kind of musk.

But now, with the ice and the cold and the dark, with us frozen in and with no place to go, I clean them at night. Not during the day while they are gone.

I clean them at night.

In the dark.

After I visit with the shadows.

My friends.

All the dark ones, gathered from all over the world, past and present. Gathered out there in my yard—my wife's parent's yard—waiting on me. Waiting for me to be one with them, waiting on me to join them.

The only club that has ever wanted me.

—◆—

They are many of those shadows, and I know who they are now. I know it on the day I take the duct tape and use it to seal the doors to my wife's bedroom, to my parents-in-law's bed room.

The dog is with my wife.

I can no longer sleep in our bed.

My wife, like the others, has begun to smell.

The tape keeps some of the stench out.

I pour cologne all over the carpet.

It helps.

Some.

—◆—

How it happened. I'll line it out:

One night I went out and sat and the shadows came up on the porch in such numbers there was only darkness around me and in me, and I was like something scared, but somehow happy, down deep in a big black sack held by hands that love me.

Yet, simultaneously, I was free.

I could feel them touching me, breathing on me. And I knew, then, it was time.

—◆—

Down in the basement, I opened the trunk, took out a well-oiled weapon, a hunting rifle. I went upstairs and did it quick. My wife first. She never awoke. Beneath her head, on the pillow, in the moonlight, there was a spreading blossom the color of gun oil.

My father-in-law heard the shot, met me at their bedroom door, pulling on his robe. One shot. Then another for my mother-in-law who sat up in bed, her face hidden in shadow—but a different shadow. Not one of my shadow friends, but one made purely by an absence of light, and not an absence of being.

The dog bit me.

I guess it was the noise.

I shot the dog too.

I didn't want him to be lonely.

Who would care for him?

—◆—

I pulled my father-in-law into his bed with his wife and pulled the covers to their chins. My wife is tucked in too, the covers over her head. I put our little dog, Constance beside her.

How long ago was the good deed done?

I can't tell.

I think, strangely, of my father-in-law. He always wore a hat. He thought it strange that men no longer wore hats. When he was growing up in the forties and fifties, men wore hats.

He told me that many times.

He wore hats. Men wore hats, and it was odd to him that they no longer did, and to him the men without hats were manless.

He looked at me then. Hatless. Looked me up and down. Not only was I hatless in his eyes, I was manless.

Manless?

Is that a word.

The wind howls and the night is bright and the shadows twist and the moon gives them light to dance by.

They are many and they are one, and I am almost one of them.

—◆—

One day I could not sleep and sat up all day. I had taken to the couch at first, in the living room, but in time the stench from behind the taped doors seeped out and it was strong. I made a pallet in the kitchen and pulled all the curtains tight and slept the day away, rose at night and roamed and watched the shadows from the windows or out on the porch. The stench was less then, at night, and out on the porch I couldn't smell it at all.

—◆—

The phone has rang many times and there are messages from relatives. Asking about the storm. If we are okay.

I consider calling to tell them we are.

But I have no voice for anyone anymore. My vocal cords or hollow and my body is full of dark.

—◆—

The storm has blown away and in a small matter of time people will come to find out how we are doing. It is day break and no car could possibly get up our long drive, not way out here in the country like we are. But the ice is starting to melt.

Can't sleep.

Can't eat.

Thirsty all the time.
Have masturbated till I hurt.

—◆—

Strange, but by nightfall the ice started to slip away and all the whiteness was gone and the air, though chill, was not as cold, and the shadows gathered on the welcome mat, and now they have slipped inside, like envelopes pushed beneath the bottom of the door.

They join me.
They comfort me.
I oil my guns.

—◆—

Late night, early morning, depends on how you look at it. But the guns are well-oiled and there is no ice anywhere. The night is as clear as my mind is now.

I pull the trunk up stairs and drag it out on the porch toward the truck. It's heavy, but I manage it into the back of the pickup. Then I remember there's a dolly in the garage.

My father-in-law's dolly.

"This damn dolly will move anything," he used to say. "Anything."

I get the dolly, load it up, stick in a few tools from the garage, start the truck and roll on out.

—◆—

I flunked out of college.
Couldn't pass the test.
I'm supposed to be smart.
My mother told me when I was young that I was a genius.
There had been tests.
But I couldn't seem to finish anything.
Dropped out of high school. Took the G.E.D. eventually.

Didn't score high there either, but did pass. Barely.

What kind of genius is that?

Finally got into college, four years later than everyone else.

Couldn't cut it. Just couldn't hold anything in my head. Too stuffed up there, as if Kleenex had been packed inside.

My history teacher, he told me: "Son, perhaps you should consider a trade."

— ◆ —

I drive along campus. My mind is clear, like the night. The campus clock tower is very sharp against the darkness, lit up at the top and all around. A giant phallus punching up at the moon.

— ◆ —

It is easy to drive right up to the tower and unload the gun trunk onto the dolly.

My father-in-law was right.

This dolly is amazing.

And my head, so clear. No Kleenex.

And the shadows, thick and plenty, are with me.

— ◆ —

Rolling the dolly, a crowbar from the collection of tools stuffed in my belt, I proceed to the front of the tower. I'm wearing a jump suit. Gray. Workman's uniform. For a while I worked for the janitorial department on campus. My attempt at a trade.

They fired me for reading in the janitor's closet.

But I still have the jump suit.

— ◆ —

The foyer is open, but the elevators are locked.

I pull the dolly upstairs.

It is a chore, a bump at a time, but the dolly straps hold the trunk and I can hear the guns rattling inside, like they want to get out.

—◆—

By the time I reach the top I'm sweating, feeling weak. I have no idea how long it has taken, but some time I'm sure. The shadows have been with me, encouraging me.

Thank you, I tell them.

—◆—

The door at the top of the clock tower is locked.

I take out my burglar's key. The crowbar. Go to work. It's easy.

On the other side of the door I use the dolly itself to push up under the door handle, and it freezes the door. It'll take some work to shake that loose.

—◆—

There's one more flight inside the tower.

I have to drag the trunk of guns.

Hard work. The rope handle on the crate snaps and the guns slide all the way back down.

I push them up.

I almost think I can't make it. The trunk is so heavy. So many guns. And all that sweet ammunition.

—◆—

Finally, to the top, shoving with my shoulder, bending my legs all the way.

The door up there is not locked, the one that leads outside to the runway around the clock tower.

I walk out, leaving the trunk. I walk all around the tower and look down at all the small things there.

Soon the light will come, and so will the people.

Turning, I look up at the huge clock hands. Four o'clock.

I hope time does not slip. I do not want to find myself at home by the window, looking out.

The shadows.

They flutter.

They twist.

The runway is full of them, thick as all the world's lost ones. Thick as all the world's hopeless. Thick, thick, thick, and thicker yet to be. When I join them.

— ◆ —

There is one fine spot at the corner of the tower runway. That is where I should begin.

I place a rifle there, the one I used to put my family and dog asleep.

I place rifles all around the tower.

I will probably run from one station to the other.

The shadows make suggestions.

All good, of course.

I put a revolver in my belt.

I put a shotgun near the entrance to the runway, hidden behind the edge of the tower, in a little outcrop of artful bricks. It tucks in there nicely.

There are huge flower pots stuffed with ferns all about the runway. I stick pistols in the pots.

When I finish, I look at the clock again.

An hour has passed.

— ◆ —

Back home in my chair, looking out the window at the dying night. Back home in my chair, the smell of my family growing familiar, like a shirt worn too many days in a row.

Like the one I have on. Like the thick coat I wear.

I look out the window and it is not the window, but the little split in the runway barrier. There are splits all around the runway wall.

I turn to study the place I have chosen and find myself looking out my window at home, and as I stare, the window melts and so does the house.

The smell.

That does not go with the window and the house.

The smell stays with me.

The shadows are way too close. I am nearly smothered. I can hardly breathe.

—◆—

Light cracks along the top of the tower and falls through the campus trees and runs along the ground like spilt warm honey.

I clutch my coat together, pull it tight. It is very cold. I can hardly feel my legs.

—◆—

I get up and walk about the runway twice, checking on all my guns.

Well oiled. Fully loaded.

Full of hot lead announcements.

Telegram. You're dead.

—◆—

Back at my spot, the one from which I will begin, I can see movement. The day has started. I poke the rifle through the break in the barrier and bead down on a tall man walking across campus.

I could take him easy.

But I do not.

Wait, say the shadows. Wait until the little world below is full.

—◆—

The hands on the clock are loud when they move, they sound like the machinery I can hear in my head. Creaking and clanking and moving along.

The air had turned surprisingly warm.

I feel so hot in my jacket.

I take it off.

I am sweating.

The day has come but the shadows stay with me.

True friends are like that. They don't desert you.

It's nice to have true friends.

It's nice to have with me the ones who love me.

It's nice to not be judged.

It's nice to know I know what to do and the shadows know too, and we are all the better for it.

—◆—

The campus is alive.

People swim across the concrete walks like minnows in the narrows.

Minnows everywhere in there new sharp clothes, ready to take their tests and do their papers and meet each other so they might screw. All of them, with futures.

But I am the future stealing machine.

—◆—

I remember once, when I was a child, I went fishing with minnows. Stuck them on the hooks and dropped them in the wet. When the day was done, I had caught nothing. I violated the fisherman's code. I did not pour the remaining minnows into the water to give them their freedom. I poured them on the ground.

And stomped them.

I was in control.

— ◆ —

A young, beautiful girl, probably eighteen, tall like a model, walking like a dream, is moving across the campus. The light is on her hair and it looks very blonde, like my wife's.

I draw a bead.

The shadows gather. They whisper. They touch. They show me their faces.

They have faces now.

Simple faces.

Like mine.

I trace my eye down the length of the barrel.

Without me really knowing it, the gun snaps sharp in the morning light.

The young woman falls amidst a burst of what looks like plum jelly.

The minnows flutter. The minnows flee.

But there are so many, and they are panicked. Like they have been poured on the ground to squirm and gasp in the dry.

I began to fire. Shot after shot after shot.

Each snap of the rifle a stomp of my foot.

Down they go.

Squashed.

I have no hat, father-in-law, and I am full of manliness.

— ◆ —

The day goes up hot.

Who would have thunk?

I have moved from one end of the tower to the other.

I have dropped many of them.

The cops have come.

I have dropped many of them.

I hear noise in the tower.

I think they have shook the dolly loose.

The door to the runway bursts open.

A lady cop steps through. My first shot takes her in the throat. But she snaps one off at about the same time. A revolver shot. It hits next to me where I crouch low against the runway wall.

Another cop comes through the door. I fire and miss.

My first miss.

He fires. I feel something hot inside my shoulder.

I find that I am slipping down, my back against the runway wall. I can't hold the rifle. I try to drag the pistol from my belt, but can't. My arm is dead. The other one, well, it's no good either. The shot has cut something apart inside of me. The strings to my limbs. My puppet won't work.

Another cop has appeared. He has a shotgun. He leans over me. His teeth are gritted and his eyes are wet.

And just as he fires, the shadows say:

Now, you are one of us.

Deadman's Road

The evening sun had rolled down and blown out in a bloody wad, and the white, full moon had rolled up like an enormous ball of tightly wrapped twine. As he rode, the Reverend Jebidiah Rains watched it glow above the tall pines. All about it stars were sprinkled white-hot in the dead-black heavens.

The trail he rode on was a thin one, and the trees on either side of it crept toward the path as if they might block the way, and close up behind him. The weary horse on which he was riding moved forward with its head down, and Jebidiah, too weak to fight it, let his mount droop and take its lead. Jebidiah was too tired to know much at that moment, but he knew one thing. He was a man of the Lord and he hated God, hated the sonofabitch with all his heart.

And he knew God knew and didn't care, because he knew Jebidiah was his messenger. Not one of the New Testament, but one of the Old Testament, harsh and mean and certain, vengeful and without compromise; a man who would have shot a leg out from under Moses and spat in the face of the Holy Ghost and scalped him, tossing his celestial hair to the wild four winds.

It was not a legacy Jebidiah would have preferred, being the bad man messenger of God, but it was his, and he had earned it through sin, and no matter how hard he tried to lay it down and leave it be, he could not. He knew that to give in and abandon his God-given curse, was to burn in

hell forever, and to continue was to do as the Lord pre-
scribed, no matter what his feelings toward his mean mas-
ter might be. His Lord was not a forgiving Lord, nor was he
one who cared for your love. All he cared for was obedi-
ence, servitude and humiliation. It was why God had
invented the human race. Amusement.

As he thought on these matters, the trail turned and
widened, and off to one side, amongst tree stumps, was a
fairly large clearing, and in its center was a small log house,
and out to the side a somewhat larger log barn. In the cur-
tained window of the cabin was a light that burned orange
behind the flour-sack curtains. Jebidiah, feeling tired and
hungry and thirsty and weary of soul, made for it.

Stopping a short distance from the cabin, Jebidiah leaned
forward on his horse and called out, "Hello, the cabin."

He waited for a time, called again, and was halfway
through calling when the door opened, and a man about
five-foot two with a large droopy hat, holding a rifle, stuck
himself part of the way out of the cabin, said, "Who is it
calling? You got a voice like a bullfrog."

"Reverend Jebidiah Rains."

"You ain't come to preach none, have you?"

"No, sir. I find it does no good. I'm here to beg for a
place in your barn, a night under its roof. Something for my
horse, something for myself if it's available. Most anything,
as long as water is involved."

"Well," said the man, "this seems to be the gathering
place tonight. Done got two others, and we just sat asses
down to eat. I got enough you want it, some hot beans and
some old bread."

"I would be most obliged, sir," Jebidiah said.

"Oblige all you want. In the meantime, climb down
from that nag, put it in the barn and come in and chow.
They call me Old Timer, but I ain't that old. It's cause most

of my teeth are gone and I'm crippled in a foot a horse stepped on. There's a lantern just inside the barn door. Light that up, and put it out when you finish, come on back to the house."

—◆—

When Jebidiah finished grooming and feeding his horse with grain in the barn, watering him, he came into the cabin, made a show of pushing his long black coat back so that it revealed his ivory-handled .44 cartridge-converted revolvers. They were set so that they leaned forward in their holsters, strapped close to the hips, not draped low like punks wore them. Jebidiah liked to wear them close to the natural swing of his hands. When he pulled them it was a movement quick as the flick of a hummingbird's wings, the hammers clicking from the cock of his thumb, the guns barking, spewing lead with amazing accuracy. He had practiced enough to drive a cork into a bottle at about a hundred paces, and he could do it in bad light. He chose to reveal his guns that way to show he was ready for any attempted ambush. He reached up and pushed his wide-brimmed black hat back on his head, showing black hair gone gray-tipped. He thought having his hat tipped made him look casual. It did not. His eyes always seemed aflame in an angry face.

Inside, the cabin was bright with kerosene lamp light, and the kerosene smelled, and there were curls of black smoke twisting about, mixing with gray smoke from the pipe of Old Timer, and the cigarette of a young man with a badge pinned to his shirt. Beside him, sitting on a chopping log by the fireplace, which was too hot for the time of year, but was being used to heat up a pot of beans, was a middle-aged man with a slight paunch and a face that looked like it attracted thrown objects. He had his hat pushed up a bit, and a shock of wheat-colored, sweaty hair hung on his forehead. There was a cigarette in is mouth, half of it ash. He twisted on the chopping log, and Jebidiah saw that his hands were manacled together.

"I heard you say you was a preacher," said the manacled man, as he tossed the last of his smoke into the fireplace. "This here sure ain't God's country."

"Worse thing is," said Jebidiah, "it's exactly God's country."

The manacled man gave out with a snort, and grinned.

"Preacher," said the younger man, "my name is Jim Taylor. I'm a deputy for Sheriff Spradley, out of Nacogdoches. I'm taking this man there for a trial, and most likely a hanging. He killed a fella for a rifle and a horse. I see you tote guns, old style guns, but good ones. Way you tote them, I'm suspecting you know how to use them."

"I've been known to hit what I aim at," Jebidiah said, and sat in a rickety chair at an equally rickety table. Old Timer put some tin plates on the table, scratched his ass with a long wooden spoon, then grabbed a rag and used it as a pot holder, lifted the hot bean pot to the table. He popped the lid of the pot, used the ass-scratching spoon to scoop a heap of beans onto plates. He brought over some wooden cups and poured them full from a pitcher of water.

"Thing is," the deputy said, "I could use some help. I don't know I can get back safe with this fella, havin' not slept good in a day or two. Was wondering, you and Old Timer here could watch my back till morning? Wouldn't even mind if you rode along with me tomorrow, as sort of a backup. I could use a gun hand. Sheriff might even give you a dollar for it."

Old Timer, as if this conversation had not been going on, brought over a bowl with some moldy biscuits in it, placed them on the table. "Made them a week ago. They've gotten a bit ripe, but you can scratch around the mold. I'll warn you though, they're tough enough you could toss one hard and kill a chicken on the run. So mind your teeth."

"That how you lost yours, Old Timer?" the manacled man said.

"Probably part of them," Old Timer said.

"What you say, preacher?" the deputy said. "You let me get some sleep?"

"My problem lies in the fact that I need sleep," Jebidiah said. "I've been busy, and I'm what could be referred to as tuckered."

"Guess I'm the only one that feels spry," said the manacled man.

"No," said, Old Timer. "I feel right fresh myself."

"Then it's you and me, Old Timer," the manacled man said, and grinned, as if this meant something.

"You give me cause, fella, I'll blow a hole in you and tell God you got in a nest of termites."

The manacled man gave his snort of a laugh again. He seemed to be having a good old time.

"Me and Old Timer can work shifts," Jebidiah said. "That okay with you, Old Timer?"

"Peachy," Old Timer said, and took another plate from the table and filled it with beans. He gave this one to the manacled man, who said, lifting his bound hands to take it, "What do I eat it with?"

"Your mouth. Ain't got no extra spoons. And I ain't giving you a knife."

The manacled man thought on this for a moment, grinned, lifted the plate and put his face close to the edge of it, sort of poured the beans toward his mouth. He lowered the plate and chewed. "Reckon they taste scorched with or without a spoon."

Jebidiah reached inside his coat, took out and opened up a pocket knife, used it to spear one of the biscuits, and to scrape the beans toward him.

"You come to the table, young fella," Old Timer said to the deputy. "I'll get my shotgun, he makes a move that ain't eatin', I'll blast him and the beans inside him into that fireplace there."

— ◆ —

Old Timer sat with a double barrel shotgun resting on his leg, pointed in the general direction of the manacled man. The deputy told all that his prisoner had done while he ate. Murdered women and children, shot a dog and a horse, and just for the hell of it, shot a cat off a fence, and set fire to an outhouse with a woman in it. He had also raped women, stuck a stick up a sheriff's ass, and killed him, and most likely shot other animals that might have been some good to somebody. Overall, he was tough on human beings, and equally as tough on livestock.

"I never did like animals," the manacled man said. "Carry fleas. And that woman in the outhouse stunk to high heaven. She ought to eat better. She needed burning."

"Shut up," the deputy said. "This fella," and he nodded toward the prisoner, "his name is Bill Barrett, and he's the worst of the worst. Thing is, well, I'm not just tired, I'm a little wounded. He and I had a tussle. I hadn't surprised him, wouldn't be here today. I got a bullet graze in my hip. We had quite a dust up. I finally got him down by putting a gun barrel to his noggin' half a dozen times or so. I'm not hurt so bad, but I lost blood for a couple days. Weakened me. You'd ride along with me Reverend, I'd appreciate it."

"I'll consider it," Jebidiah said. "But I'm about my business."

"Who you gonna preach to along here, 'sides us?" the deputy said.

"Don't even think about it," Old Timer said. "Just thinking about that Jesus foolishness makes my ass tired.

Preaching makes me want to kill the preacher and cut my own throat. Being at a preachin' is like being tied down in a nest red bitin' ants."

"At this point in my life," Jebidiah said. "I agree."

There was a moment of silence in response to Jebidiah, then the deputy turned his attention to Old Timer. "What's the fastest route to Nacogdoches?"

"Well now," Old Timer said, "you can keep going like you been going, following the road out front. And in time you'll run into a road, say thirty miles from here, and it goes left. That should take you right near Nacogdoches, which is another ten miles, though you'll have to make a turn somewhere up in there near the end of the trip. Ain't exactly sure where unless I'm looking at it. Whole trip, traveling at an even pace ought to take you two day."

"You could go with us," the deputy said. "Make sure I find that road."

"Could," said Old Timer, "but I won't. I don't ride so good anymore. My balls ache I ride a horse for too long. Last time I rode a pretty good piece, I had to squat over a pan of warm water and salt, soak my taters for an hour or so just so they'd fit back in my pants. "

"My balls ache just listening to you," the prisoner said. "Thing is, though, them swollen up like that, was probably the first time in your life you had man-sized balls, you old fart. You should have left them swollen."

Old Timer cocked back the hammers on the double barrel. "This here could go off."

Bill just grinned, leaned his back against the fireplace, then jumped forward. For a moment, it looked as if Old Timer might cut him in half, but he realized what had happened.

"Oh yeah," Old Timer said. "That there's hot, stupid. Why they call it a fire place."

Bill readjusted himself, so that his back wasn't against the stones. He said, "I'm gonna cut this deputy's pecker off, come back here, make you fry it up and eat it."

"You're gonna shit and fall back in it," Old Timer said. "That's all you're gonna do."

When things had calmed down again, the deputy said to Old Timer, "There's no faster route?"

Old timer thought for a moment. "None you'd want to take."

"What's that mean?" the deputy said.

Old Timer slowly lowered the hammers on the shotgun, smiling at Bill all the while. When he had them lowered, he turned his head, looked at the deputy. "Well, there's Deadman's Road."

"What's wrong with that?" the deputy asked.

"All manner of things. Used to be called Cemetery Road. Couple years back that changed."

Jebidiah's interest was aroused. "Tell us about it, Old Timer."

"Now I ain't one to believe in hogwash, but there's a story about the road, and I got it from someone you might say was the horse's mouth."

"A ghost story, that's choice," said Bill.

"How much time would the road cut off going to Nacogdoches?" the deputy asked.

"Near a day," Old Timer said.

"Damn. Then that's the way I got to go," the deputy said.

"Turn off for it ain't far from here, but I wouldn't recommend it," Old Timer said. "I ain't much for Jesus, but I believe in haints, things like that. Living out here in this thicket, you see some strange things. There's gods ain't got nothing to do with Jesus or Moses, or any of that bunch. There's older gods than that. Indians talk about them."

"I'm not afraid of any Indian gods," the deputy said.

"Maybe not," Old Timer said, "but these gods, even the Indians ain't fond of them. They ain't their gods. These gods are older than the Indian folk their ownselfs. Indians try not to stir them up. They worship their own."

"And why would this road be different than any other?" Jebidiah asked. "What does it have to do with ancient gods?"

Old Timer grinned. "You're just wanting to challenge it, ain't you, Reverend? Prove how strong your god is. You weren't no preacher, you'd be a gunfighter, I reckon. Or, maybe you are just that. A gunfighter preacher."

"I'm not that fond of my god," Jebidiah said, "but I have been given a duty. Drive out evil. Evil as my god sees it. If these gods are evil, and they're in my path, then I have to confront them."

"They're evil, all right," Old Timer said.

"Tell us about them," Jebidiah said.

—◆—

"Gil Gimet was a bee keeper," Old timer said. "He raised honey, and lived off of Deadman's Road. Known then as Cemetery Road. That's 'cause there was a graveyard down there. It had some old Spanish graves in it, some said Conquistadores who tromped through here but didn't tromp out. I know there was some Indians buried there, early Christian Indians, I reckon. Certainly there were stones and crosses up and Indian names on the crosses. Maybe mixed breeds. Lots of intermarrying around here. Anyway, there were all manner people buried up there. The dead ground don't care what color you are when you go in, cause in the end, we're all gonna be the color of dirt."

"Hell, " Bill said. "You're already the color of dirt. And you smell like some pretty old dirt at that."

"You gonna keep on, mister," Old Timer said, "and you're gonna wind up having the undertaker wipe your ass." Old Timer cocked back the hammers on the shotgun again. "This here gun could go off accidently. Could happen, and who here is gonna argue it didn't?"

"Not me," the deputy said. "It would be easier on me you were dead, Bill."

Bill looked at the Reverend. "Yeah, but that wouldn't set right with the Reverend, would it Reverend?"

"Actually, I wouldn't care one way or another. I'm not a man of peace, and I'm not a forgiver, even if what you did wasn't done to me. I think we're all rich and deep in sin. Maybe none of us are worthy of forgiveness."

Bill sunk a little at his seat. No one was even remotely on his side. Old Timer continued with his story.

"This here bee keeper, Gimet, he wasn't known as much of a man. Mean-hearted is how he was thunk of. I knowed him, and I didn't like him. I seen him snatch up a little dog once and cut the tail off of it with his knife, just cause he thought it was funny. Boy who owned the dog tried to fight back, and Gimet, he cut the boy on the arm. No one did nothin' about it. Ain't no real law in these parts, you see, and wasn't nobody brave enough to do nothin'. Me included. And he did lots of other mean things, even killed a couple of men, and claimed self-defense. Might have been, but Gimet was always into something, and whatever he was into always turned out with someone dead, or hurt, or humiliated."

"Bill here sounds like he could be Gimet's brother," the deputy said.

"Oh, no," Old Timer said, shaking his head. "This here scum-licker ain't a bump on the mean old ass of Gimet. Gimet lived in a little shack off Cemetery Road. He raised bees, and brought in honey to sell at the community up the road. Guess you could even call it a town. Schow is the way the place is known, on account of a fella used to live up there was named Schow. He died and got ate up by pigs. Right there in his own pen, just keeled over slopping the hogs, and then they slopped him, all over that place. A store got built on top of where Schow got et up, and that's how the place come by the name. Gimet took his honey in there to the store and sold it, and even though he was a turd, he had some of the best honey you ever smacked your mouth around. Wish I had me some now. It was dark and rich, and sweeter than any sugar. Think that's one reason he got away with things. People don't like killing and such, but they damn sure like their honey."

"This story got a point?" Bill said.

"You don't like way I'm telling it," Old Timer said, "why don't you think about how that rope's gonna fit around your neck. That ought to keep your thoughts occupied, right smart."

Bill made a grunting noise, turned on his block of wood, as if to show he wasn't interested.

"Well, now, honey or not, sweet tooth, or not, everything has an end to it. And thing was he took to a little gal, Mary Lynn Twoshoe. She was a part Indian gal, a real looker, hair black as the bottom of a well, eyes the same color, and she was just as fine in the features as them pictures you see of them stage actresses. She wasn't five feet tall, and that hair of hers went all the way down her back. Her daddy was dead. The pox got him. And her mama wasn't too well off, being sickly, and all. She made brooms out of straw and branches she trimmed down. Sold a few of them, raised a little garden and a hog. When all this happened, Mary Lynn was probably thirteen, maybe fourteen. Wasn't no older than that."

"If you're gonna tell a tale," Bill said, "least don't wander all over the place."

"So, you're interested?" Old Timer said.

"What else I got to do?" Bill said.

"Go on," Jebidiah said. "Tell us about Mary Lynn."

Old Timer nodded. "Gimet took to her. Seen her around, bringing the brooms her mama made into the store. He waited on her, grabbed her, and just threw her across his saddle kickin' and screamin', like he'd bought a sack of flour and was ridin' it to the house. Mack Collins, store owner came out and tried to stop him. Well, he said something to him. About how he shouldn't do it, least that's the way I heard it. He didn't push much, and I can't blame him. Didn't do good to cross Gimet. Anyway, Gimet just said back to Mack, 'Give her mama a big jar of honey. Tell her that's for her daughter. I'll even make her another jar or two, if the meat here's as sweet as I'm expecting.'

"With that, he slapped Mary Lynn on the ass and rode off with her."

"Sounds like my kind of guy," Bill said.

"I have become irritated with you now," Jebidiah said. "Might I suggest you shut your mouth before I pistol whip you."

Bill glared at Jebidiah, but the Reverend's gaze was as dead and menacing as the barrels of Old Timer's shotgun.

"Rest of the story is kind of grim," Old Timer said. "Gimet took her off to his house, and had his way with her. So many times he damn near killed her, and then he turned her lose, or got so drunk she was able to get loose. Time she walked down Cemetery Road, made it back to town, well, she was bleeding so bad from having been used so rough, she collapsed. She lived a day and died from loss of blood. Her mother, out of her sick bed, rode a mule out there to the cemetery on Cemetery Road. I told you she was Indian, and she knew some Indian ways, and she knew about them old gods that wasn't none of the gods of her people, but she still knew about them.

"She knew some signs to draw in cemetery dirt. I don't know the whole of it, but she did some things, and she did it on some old grave out there, and the last thing she did was she cut her own throat, died right there, her blood running on top of that grave and them pictures she drawed in the dirt."

"Don't see how that done her no good," the deputy said.

"Maybe it didn't, but folks think it did," Old Timer said. "Community that had been pushed around by Gimet, finally had enough, went out there in mass to hang his ass, shoot him, whatever it took. Got to his cabin they found Gimet dead outside his shack. His eyes had been torn out, or blown out is how they looked. Skin was peeled off his head, just leaving the skull and a few hairs. His chest was ripped open, and his insides was gone, exceptin' the bones in there. And them bees of his had nested in the hole in his chest, had done gone about making honey. Was buzzing out of that hole, his mouth, empty eyes, nose, or where his nose used to be. I figure they'd rolled him over, tore off his pants, they'd have been coming out of his asshole."

"How come you weren't out there with them?" Bill said. "How come this is all stuff you heard?"

"Because I was a coward when it come to Gimet," Old Timer said. "That's why. Told myself wouldn't never be a coward again, no matter what. I should have been with them. Didn't matter no how. He was done good and dead, them bees all in him. What was done then is the crowd got kind of loco, tore off his clothes, hooked his feet up to a horse and dragged him through a blackberry patch, them bees just burstin' out and hummin' all around him. All that ain't right, but I think I'd been with them, knowing who he was and all the things he'd done, I might have been loco too. They dumped him out on the cemetery to let him rot, took that girl's mother home to be buried some place better.

Wasn't no more than a few nights later that folks started seeing Gimet. They said he walked at night, when the moon was
at least half, or full, like it is now. Number of folks seen him,
said he loped alongside the road, following their horses,
grabbing hold of the tail if he could, trying to pull horse and
rider down, or pull himself up on the back of their mounts.
Said them bees was still in him. Bees black as flies, and angry
whirling all about him, and coming from inside him. Worse,
there was a larger number of folks took that road that wasn't
never seen again. It was figured Gimet got them."

"Horse shit," the deputy said. "No disrespect, Old
Timer. You've treated me all right, that's for sure. But a
ghost chasing folks down. I don't buy that."

"Don't have to buy it," Old Timer said. "I ain't trying to
sell it to you none. Don't have to believe it. And I don't
think it's no ghost anyway. I think that girl's mother, she
done something to let them old gods out for awhile, sicked
them on that bastard, used her own life as a sacrifice, that's
what I think. And them gods, them things from somewhere
else, they ripped him up like that. Them bees is part of that
too. They ain't no regular honey bee. They're some other
kind of bees. Some kind of fitting death for a bee raiser, is
my guess."

"That's silly," the deputy said.

"I don't know," Jebidiah said. "The Indian woman may
only have succeeded in killing him in this life. She may not
have understood all that she did. Didn't know she was giving him an opportunity to live again...Or maybe that is the
curse. Though there are plenty others have to suffer for it."

"Like the folks didn't do nothing when Gimet was alive,"
Old Time said. " Folks like me that let what went on go on."

Jebidiah nodded. "Maybe."

The deputy looked at Jebidiah. "Not you too, Reverend.
You should know better than that. There ain't but one true

god, and ain't none of that hoodoo business got a drop of truth to it."

"If there's one god," Jebidiah said, "there can be many. They are at war with one another, that's how it works, or so I think. I've seen some things that have shook my faith in the one true god, the one I'm servant to. And what is our god but hoodoo? It's all hoodoo, my friend."

"Okay. What things have you seen, Reverend?" the deputy asked.

"No use describing it to you, young man," Jebidiah said. "You wouldn't believe me. But I've recently come from Mud Creek. It had an infestation of a sort. That town burned down, and I had a hand in it."

"Mud Creek," Old Timer said. "I been there."

"Only thing there now," Jebidiah said, "is some charred wood."

"Ain't the first time it's burned down," Old Timer said. "Some fool always rebuilds it, and with it always comes some kind of ugliness. I'll tell you straight. I don't doubt your word at all, Reverend."

"Thing is," the deputy said, "I don't believe in no haints. That's the shortest road, and it's the road I'm gonna take."

"I wouldn't," Old Timer said.

"Thanks for the advice. But no one goes with me or does, that's the road I'm taking, provided it cuts a day off my trip."

"I'm going with you," Jebidiah said. "My job is striking at evil. Not to walk around it."

"I'd go during the day," Old Timer said. "Ain't no one seen Gimet in the day, or when the moon is thin or not at all. But way it is now, it's full, and will be again tomorrow night. I'd ride hard tomorrow, you're determined to go. Get there as soon as you can, before dark."

"I'm for getting there," the deputy said. "I'm for getting back to Nacogdoches, and getting this bastard in a cell."

"I'll go with you," Jebidiah said. "But I want to be there at night. I want to take Deadman's Road at that time. I want to see if Gimet is there. And if he is, send him to his final death. Defy those dark gods the girl's mother called up. Defy them and loose my god on him. What I'd suggest is you get some rest, deputy. Old Timer here can watch a bit, then I'll take over. That way we all get some rest. We can chain this fellow to a tree outside, we have to. We should both get slept up to the gills, then leave here mid-day, after a good dinner, head out for Deadman's Road. Long as we're there by nightfall."

"That ought to bring you right on it," Old Timer said. "You take Deadman's Road. When you get to the fork, where the road ends, you go right. Ain't no one ever seen Gimet beyond that spot, or in front of where the road begins. He's tied to that stretch, way I heard it."

"Good enough," the deputy said. "I find this all foolish, but if I can get some rest, and have you ride along with me, Reverend, then I'm game. And I'll be fine with getting there at night."

—◆—

Next morning they slept late, and had an early lunch. Beans and hard biscuits again, a bit of stewed squirrel. Old Timer had shot the rodent that morning while Jebidiah watched Bill sit on his ass, his hands chained around a tree in the front yard. Inside the cabin, the deputy had continued to sleep.

But now they all sat outside eating, except for Bill.

"What about me?" Bill asked, tugging at his chained hands.

"When we finish," Old Timer said. "Don't know if any of the squirrel will be left, but we got them biscuits for you. I can promise you some of them. I might even let you rub one of them around in my plate, sop up some squirrel gravy."

"Those biscuits are awful," Bill said.

"Ain't they," Old Timer said.

Bill turned his attention to Jebidiah. "Preacher, you ought to just go on and leave me and the boy here alone. Ain't smart for you to ride along, cause I get loose, ain't just the deputy that's gonna pay. I'll put you on the list."

"After what I've seen in this life," Jebidiah said, "you are nothing to me. An insect...So, add me to your list."

"Let's feed him," the deputy said, nodding at Bill, "and get to moving. I'm feeling rested and want to get this ball started."

—◆—

The moon had begun to rise when they rode in sight of Deadman's Road. The white cross road sign was sticking up beside the road. Trees and brush had grown up around it, and between the limbs and the shadows, the crudely painted words on the sign were halfway readable in the waning light. The wind had picked up and was grabbing at leaves, plucking them from the ground, tumbling them about, tearing them from trees and tossing them across the narrow, clay road with a sound like mice scuttling in straw.

"Fall always depresses me," the deputy said, halting his horse, taking a swig from his canteen.

"Life is a cycle," Jebidiah said. "You're born, you suffer, then you're punished."

The deputy turned in his saddle to look at Jebidiah. "You ain't much on that resurrection and reward, are you?"

"No, I'm not."

"I don't know about you," the deputy said, "but I wish we hadn't gotten here so late. I'd rather have gone through in the day."

"Thought you weren't a believer in spooks?" Bill said, and made with his now familiar snort. "You said it didn't matter to you."

The deputy didn't look at Bill when he spoke. "I wasn't here then. Place has a look I don't like. And I don't enjoy temptin' things. Even if I don't believe in them."

"That's the silliest thing I ever heard," Bill said.

"Wanted me with you," Jebidiah said. "You had to wait."

"You mean to see something, don't you, preacher?" Bill said.

"If there is something to see," Jebidiah said.

"You believe Old Timer's story?" the deputy said. "I mean, really?"

"Perhaps."

Jebidiah clucked to his horse and took the lead.

—◆—

When they turned onto Deadman's Road, Jebidiah paused and removed a small, fat bible from his saddlebag.

The deputy paused too, forcing Bill to pause as well. "You ain't as ornery as I thought," the deputy said. "You want the peace of the bible just like anyone else."

"There is no peace in this book," Jebidiah said. "That's a real confusion. Bible isn't anything but a book of terror, and that's how God is: Terrible. But the book has power. And we might need it."

"I don't know what to think about you, Reverend," the deputy said.

"Ain't nothin' you can think about a man that's gone loco," Bill said. "I don't want to stay with no man that's loco."

"You get an idea to run, Bill, I can shoot you off your horse," the deputy said. "Close range with my revolver, far range with my rifle. You don't want to try it."

"It's still a long way to Nacogdoches," Bill said.

—◆—

The road was narrow and of red clay. It stretched far

ahead like a band of blood, turned sharply to the right around a wooded curve where it was a dark as the bottom of Jonah's whale. The blowing leaves seemed especially intense on the road, scrapping dryly about, winding in the air like giant hornets. The trees, which grew thick, bent in the wind, from right to left. This naturally led the trio to take to the left side of the road.

The farther they went down the road, the darker it became. By the time they got to the curve, the woods were so thick, and the thunderous skies had grown so dark, the moon was barely visible; its light was as weak as a sick baby's grip.

When they had traveled for some time, the deputy said, obviously feeling good about it, "There ain't nothing out here 'sides what you would expect. A possum maybe. The wind."

"Good for you, then," Jebidiah said. "Good for us all."

"You sound disappointed to me," the deputy said.

"My line of work isn't far from yours, Deputy. I look for bad guys of a sort, and try and send them to hell...Or in some cases, back to hell."

And then, almost simultaneous with a flash of lightning, something crossed the road not far in front of them.

"What the hell was that?" Bill said, coming out of what had been a near stupor.

"It looked like a man," the deputy said.

"Could have been," Jebidiah said. "Could have been."

"What do you think it was?"

"You don't want to know."

"I do."

"Gimet," Jebidiah said.

—◆—

The sky let the moon loose for a moment, and its light spread through the trees and across the road. In the light there were insects, a large wad of them, buzzing about in the air.

"Bees," Bill said. "Damn if them ain't bees. And at night. That ain't right."

"You an expert on bees?" the deputy asked.

"He's right," Jebidiah said. "And look, they're gone now."

"Flew off," the deputy said.

"No...no they didn't," Bill said. "I was watching, and they didn't fly nowhere. They're just gone. One moment they were there, then they was gone, and that's all there is to it. They're like ghosts."

"You done gone crazy," the deputy said.

"They are not insects of this earth," Jebidiah said. "They are familiars."

"What," Bill said.

"They assist evil, or evil beings," Jebidiah said. "In this case, Gimet. They're like a witches black cat familiar. Familiars take on animal shapes, insects, that sort of thing."

"That's ridiculous," the deputy said. "That don't make no kind of sense at all."

"Whatever you say," Jebidiah said, "but I would keep my eyes alert, and my senses raw. Wouldn't hurt to keep your revolvers loose in their holsters. You could well need them. Though, come to think of it, your revolvers won't be much use."

"What the hell does that mean?" Bill said.

Jebidiah didn't answer. He continued to urge his horse on, something that was becoming a bit more difficult as they went. All of the horses snorted and turned their heads left and right, tugged at their bits; their ears went back and their eyes went wide.

"Holy hell," Bill said, "what's that?"

Jebidiah and the deputy turned to look at him. Bill was turned in the saddle, looking back. They looked too, just in time to see something that looked pale blue in the moonlight, dive into the brush on the other side of the road. Black dots followed, swarmed in the moonlight, then darted into the bushes behind the pale, blue thing like a load of buckshot.

"What was that?" the deputy said. His voice sounded as if it had been pistol whipped.

"Already told you," Jebidiah said.

"That couldn't have been nothing human," the deputy said.

"Don't you get it," Bill said, "that's what the preacher is trying to tell you. It's Gimet, and he ain't nowhere alive. His skin was blue. And he's all messed up. I seen more than you did. I got a good look. And them bees. We ought to break out and ride hard."

"Do as you choose," the Reverend said. "I don't intend to."

"And why not?" Bill said.

"That isn't my job."

"Well, I ain't got no job. Deputy, ain't you supposed to make sure I get to Nacogdoches to get hung? Ain't that your job?"

"It is."

"Then we ought to ride on, not bother with this fool. He wants to fight some grave crawler, then let him. Ain't nothing we ought to get into."

"We made a pact to ride together," the deputy said. "So we will."

"I didn't make no pact," Bill said.

"Your word, your needs, they're nothing to me," the deputy said.

At that moment, something began to move through the woods on their left. Something moving quick and heavy, not bothering with stealth. Jebidiah looked in the direction of the sounds, saw someone, or something, moving through the underbrush, snapping limbs aside like they were rotten sticks. He could hear the buzz of the bees, loud and angry. Without really meaning to, he urged the horse to a trot. The deputy and Bill joined in with their own mounts, keeping pace with the Reverend's horse.

They came to a place off the side of the road where the brush thinned, and out in the distance they could see what looked like bursting white waves, frozen against the dark. But they soon realized it was tombstones. And there were crosses. A graveyard. The graveyard Old Timer had told them about. The sky had cleared now, the wind had ceased to blow hard. They had a fine view of the cemetery, and as they watched, the thing that had been in the brush moved out of it and went up the little rise where the graves were, climbed up on one of the stones and sat. A black cloud formed around its head, and the sound of buzzing could be heard all the way out to the road. The thing sat there like a king on a throne. Even from that distance it was easy to see it was nude, and male, and his skin was gray—blue in the moonlight—and the head looked misshapen. Moon glow slipped through cracks in the back of the horror's head and poked out of fresh cracks at the front of its skull and speared out of the empty eye sockets. The bee's nest, visible through the wound in its chest, was nestled between the ribs. It pulsed with a yellow-honey glow. From time to time, little black dots moved around the glow and flew up and were temporarily pinned in the moonlight above the creature's head.

"Jesus," said the deputy.

"Jesus won't help a bit," Jebidiah said.

"It's Gimet, ain't it? He...it...really is dead," the deputy said.

"Undead," Jebidiah said. "I believe he's toying with us. Waiting for when he plans to strike."

"Strike?" Bill said. "Why?"

"Because that is his purpose," Jebidiah said, "as it is mine to strike back. Gird you loins men, you will soon be fighting for your life."

"How about we just ride like hell?" Bill said.

In that moment, Jebidiah's words became prophetic. The thing was gone from the grave stone. Shadows had gathered at the edge of the woods, balled up, become solid, and when the shadows leaped from the even darker shadows of the trees, it was the shape of the thing they had seen on the stone, cool blue in the moonlight, a disaster of a face, and the teeth...They were long and sharp. Gimet leaped in such a way that his back foot hit the rear of Jebidiah's animal, allowing him to spring over the deputy's horse, to land hard and heavy on Bill. Bill let out a howl and was knocked off his mount. When he hit the road, his hat flying, Gimet grabbed him by his bushy head of straw-colored hair and dragged him off as easily as if he were a kitten. Gimet went into the trees, tugging Bill after him. Gimet blended with the darkness there. The last of Bill was a scream, the raising of his cuffed hands, the cuffs catching the moonlight for a quick blink of silver, then there was a rustle of leaves and a slapping of branches, and Bill was gone.

"My God," the deputy said. "My God. Did you see that thing?"

Jebidiah dismounted, moved to the edge of the road, leading his horse, his gun drawn. The deputy did not dismount. He pulled his pistol and held it, his hands trembling. "Did you see that?" he said again, and again.

"My eyes are as good as your own," Jebidiah said. "I saw it. We'll have to go in and get him."

"Get him?" the deputy said. "Why in the name of everything that's holy would we do that? Why would we want to be near that thing? He's probably done what he's done already...Damn, Reverend. Bill, he's a killer. This is just as good as I might want. I say while the old boy is doing whatever he's doing to that bastard, we ride like the goddamn wind, get on out on the far end of this road where it forks. Gimet is supposed to be only able to go on this stretch, ain't he?"

"That's what Old Timer said. You do as you want. I'm going in after him."

"Why? You don't even know him."

"It's not about him," Jebidiah said.

"Ah, hell. I ain't gonna be shamed." The deputy swung down from his horse, pointed at the place where Gimet had disappeared with Bill. "Can we get the horses through there?"

"Think we will have to go around a bit. I discern a path over there."

"Discern?"

"Recognize. Come on, time is wasting."

— ◆ —

They went back up the road a pace, found a trail that led through the trees. The moon was strong now as all the clouds that had covered it had rolled away like wind blown pollen. The air smelled fresh, but as they moved forward, that changed. There was a stench in the air, a putrid smell both sweet and sour, and it floated up and spoiled the freshness.

"Something dead," the deputy said.

"Something long dead," Jebidiah said.

Finally the brush grew so thick they had to tie the horses, leave them. They pushed their way through briars and limbs.

"There ain't no path," the deputy said. "You don't know he come through this way."

Jebidiah reached out and plucked a piece of cloth from a limb, held it up so that the moon dropped rays on it. "This is part of Bill's shirt. Am I right?"

The deputy nodded. "But how could Gimet get through here? How could he get Bill through here?"

"What we pursue has little interest in the things that bother man. Limbs, briars. It's nothing to the living dead."

They went on for a while. Vines got in their way. The vines were wet. They were long thick vines, and sticky, and finally they realized they were not vines at all, but guts, strewn about and draped like decorations.

"Fresh," the deputy said. "Bill, I reckon."

"You reckon right," Jebidiah said.

They pushed on a little farther, and the trail widened, making the going easier. They found more pieces of Bill as they went along. The stomach. Fingers. Pants with one leg in them. A heart, which looked as if it has been bitten into and sucked on. Jebidiah was curious enough to pick it up and examine it. Finished, he tossed it in the dirt, wiped his hands on Bill's pants, the one with the leg still in it, said, "Gimet just saved you a lot of bother and the State of Texas the trouble of a hanging."

"Heavens," the deputy said, watching Jebidiah wipe blood on the leg filled pants.

Jebidiah looked up at the deputy. "He won't mind I get blood on his pants," Jebidiah said. "He's got more important things to worry about, like dancing in the fires of hell. And by the way, yonder sports his head."

Jebidiah pointed. The deputy looked. Bill's head had been pushed onto a broken limb of a tree, the sharp end of the limb being forced through the rear of the skull and out the left eye. The spinal cord dangled from the back of the head like a bell rope.

The deputy puked in the bushes. "Oh, God. I don't want no more of this."

"Go back. I won't think the less of you, cause I don't think that much of you to begin with. Take his head for evidence and ride on, just leave me my horse."

The deputy adjusted his hat. "Don't need the head...And if it comes to it, you'll be glad I'm here. I ain't no weak sister."

"Don't talk me to death on the matter. Show me what you got, boy."

The trail was slick with Bill's blood. They went along it and up a rise, guns drawn. At the top of the hill they saw a field, grown up, and not far away, a sagging shack with a fallen down chimney.

They went that direction, came to the shack's door. Jebidiah kicked it with the toe of his boot and it sagged open. Once inside, Jebidiah struck a match and waved it about. Nothing but cobwebs and dust.

"Must have been Gimet's place," Jebidiah said. Jebidiah moved the match before him until he found a lantern full of coal oil. He lit it and placed the lantern on the table.

"Should we do that?" the deputy asked. "Have a light. Won't he find us?"

"In case you have forgotten, that's the idea."

Out the back window, which had long lost its grease paper covering, they could see tombstones and wooden crosses in the distance. "Another view of the graveyard," Jebidiah said. "That would be where the girl's mother killed herself."

No sooner had Jebidiah said that, then he saw a shadowy shape move on the hill, flitting between stones and crosses. The shape moved quickly and awkwardly.

"Move to the center of the room," Jebidiah said.

The deputy did as he was told, and Jebidiah moved the lamp there as well. He sat it in the center of the floor, found a bench and dragged it next to the lantern. Then he reached in his coat pocket and took out the bible. He dropped to one knee and held the bible close to the lantern light and tore out certain pages. He wadded them up, and began placing them all around the bench on the floor, placing the crumpled pages about six feet out from the bench and in a circle with each wad two feet apart.

The deputy said nothing. He sat on the bench and watched Jebidiah's curious work. Jebidiah sat on the bench beside the deputy, rested one of his pistols on his knee. "You got a .44, don't you?"

"Yeah. I got a converted cartridge pistol, just like you."

"Give me your revolver."

The deputy complied.

Jebidiah opened the cylinders and let the bullets fall out on the floor.

"What in hell are you doing?"

Jebidiah didn't answer. He dug into his gun belt and came up with six silver tipped bullets, loaded the weapon and gave it back to the deputy.

"Silver," Jebidiah said. "Sometimes it wards off evil."

"Sometimes?"

"Be quiet now. And wait."

"I feel like a staked goat," the deputy said.

After a while, Jebidiah rose from the bench and looked out the window. Then he sat down promptly and blew out the lantern.

— ◆ —

Somewhere in the distance a night bird called. Crickets sawed and a large frog bleated. They sat there on the bench, near each other, facing in opposite directions, their silver loaded pistols on their knees. Neither spoke.

Suddenly the bird ceased to call and the crickets went silent, and no more was heard from the frog. Jebidiah whispered to the deputy.

"He comes."

The deputy shivered slightly, took a deep breath. Jebidiah realized he too was breathing deeply.

"Be silent, and be alert," Jebidiah said.

"All right," said the deputy, and he locked his eyes on the open window at the back of the shack. Jebidiah faced the door, which stood halfway open and sagging on its rusty hinges.

For a long time there was nothing. Not a sound. Then Jebidiah saw a shadow move at the doorway and heard the door creak slightly as it moved. He could see a hand on what appeared to be an impossibly long arm, reaching out to grab at the edge of the door. The hand clutched there for a long time, not moving. Then, it was gone, taking its shadow with it.

Time crawled by.

"It's at the window," the deputy said, and his voice was so soft it took Jebidiah a moment to decipher the words. Jebidiah turned carefully for a look.

It sat on the window sill, crouched there like a bird of prey, a halo of bees circling around its head. The hive pulsed and glowed in its chest, and in that glow they could see more bees, so thick they appeared to be a sort of humming smoke. Gimet's head sprouted a few springs of hair, like withering grass fighting its way through stone. A slight turn of its head allowed the moon to flow through the back of its cracked skull and out of its empty eyes. Then the head turned and the face was full of shadows again. The room was silent except for the sound of buzzing bees.

"Courage," Jebidiah said, his mouth close to the deputy's ear. "Keep your place."

The thing climbed into the room quickly, like a spider dropping from a limb, and when it hit the floor, it stayed low, allowing the darkness to lay over it like a cloak.

Jebidiah had turned completely on the bench now, facing the window. He heard a scratching sound against the floor. He narrowed his eyes, saw what looked like a shadow, but was in fact the thing coming out from under the table.

Jebidiah felt the deputy move, perhaps to bolt. He grabbed his arm and held him.

"Courage," he said.

The thing kept crawling. It came within three feet of the circle made by the crumpled bible pages.

The way the moonlight spilled through the window and onto the floor near the circle Jebidiah had made, it gave Gimet a kind of eerie glow, his satellite bees circling his head. In that moment, every aspect of the thing locked itself in Jebidiah's mind. The empty eyes, the sharp, wet teeth, the long, cracked nails, blackened from grime, clacking against the wooden floor. As it moved to cross between two wads of scripture, the pages burst into flames and a line of crackling blue fulmination moved between the wadded pages and made the circle light up fully, all the way around, like Ezekiel's wheel.

Gimet gave out with a hoarse cry, scuttled back, clacking nails and knees against the floor. When he moved, he moved so quickly there seemed to be missing spaces between one moment and the next. The buzzing of Gimet's bees was ferocious.

Jebidiah grabbed the lantern, struck a match and lit it. Gimet was scuttling along the wall like a cockroach, racing to the edge of the window.

Jebidiah leaped forward, tossed the lit lantern, hit the beast full in the back as it fled through the window. The lantern burst into flames and soaked Gimlet's back, causing a wave of fire to climb from the thing's waist to the top of its head, scorching a horde of bees, dropping them from the sky like exhausted meteors.

Jebidiah drew his revolver, snapped off a shot. There was a howl of agony, and then the thing was gone.

Jebidiah raced out of the protective circle and the deputy followed. They stood at the open window, watched as Gimet, flame-wrapped, streaked through the night in the direction of the graveyard.

"I panicked a little," Jebidiah said. "I should have been more resolute. Now he's escaped."

"I never even got off a shot," the deputy said. "God, but you're fast. What a draw."

"Look, you stay here if you like. I'm going after him. But I tell you now, the circle of power has played out."

The deputy glanced back at it. The pages had burned out and there was nothing now but a black ring on the floor.

"What in hell caused them to catch fire in the first place?"

"Evil," Jebidiah said. "When he got close, the pages broke into flames. Gave us the protection of God. Unfortunately, as with most of God's blessings, it doesn't last long."

"I stay here, you'd have to put down more pages."

"I'll be taking the bible with me. I might need it."

"Then I guess I'll be sticking."

— ◆ —

They climbed out the window and moved up the hill. They could smell the odor of fire and rotted flesh in the air. The night was as cool and silent as the graves on the hill.

Moments later they moved amongst the stones and wooden crosses, until they came to a long wide hole in the earth. Jebidiah could see that there was a burrow at one end of the grave that dipped down deeper into the ground.

Jebidiah paused there. "He's made this old grave his den. Dug it out and dug deeper."

"How do you know?" the deputy asked.

"Experience…And it smells of smoke and burned skin. He crawled down there to hide. I think we surprised him a little."

Jebidiah looked up at the sky. There was the faintest streak of pink on the horizon. "He's running out of daylight, and soon he'll be out of moon. For a while."

"He damn sure surprised me. Why don't we let him hide? You could come back when the moon isn't full, or even half full. Back in the daylight, get him then."

"I'm here now. And it's my job."

"That's one hell of a job you got, mister."

"I'm going to climb down for a better look."

"Help yourself."

Jebidiah struck a match and dropped himself into the grave, moved the match around at the mouth of the burrow, got down on his knees and stuck the match and his head into the opening.

"Very large," he said, pulling his head out. "I can smell him. I'm going to have to go in."

"What about me?"

"You keep guard at the lip of the grave," Jebidiah said, standing. "He may have another hole somewhere, he could come out behind you for all I know. He could come out of that hole even as we speak."

"That's wonderful."

Jebidiah dropped the now dead match on the ground. "I will tell you this. I can't guarantee success. I lose, he'll come for you, you can bet on that, and you better shoot those silvers as straight as William Tell's arrows."

"I'm not really that good a shot."

"I'm sorry," Jebidiah said, and struck another match along the length of his pants seam, then with his free hand, drew one of his revolvers. He got down on his hands and knees again, stuck the match in the hole and looked around. When the match was near done, he blew it out.

"Ain't you gonna need some light?" the deputy said. "A match ain't nothin'."

"I'll have it." Jebidiah removed the remains of the bible from his pocket, tore it in half along the spine, pushed one half in his coat, pushed the other half before him, into the darkness of the burrow. The moment it entered the hole, it flamed.

"Ain't your pocket gonna catch inside that hole?" the deputy asked.

"As long as I hold it or it's on my person, it won't harm me. But the minute I let go of it, and the aura of evil touches it, it'll blaze. I got to hurry, boy."

With that, Jebidiah wiggled inside the burrow.

—◆—

In the burrow, Jebidiah used the tip of his pistol to push the bible pages forward. They glowed brightly, but Jebidiah knew the light would be brief. It would burn longer than writing paper, but still, it would not last long.

After a goodly distance, Jebidiah discovered the burrow dropped off. He found himself inside a fairly large cavern. He could hear the sound of bats, and smell bat guano, which in fact, greased his path as he slid along on his elbows until he could stand inside the higher cavern and look about. The last flames of the bible burned itself out with a puff of blue light and a sound like an old man breathing his last.

Jebidiah listened in the dark for a long moment. He could hear the bats squeaking, moving about. The fact that they had given up the night sky, let Jebidiah know daylight was not far off.

Jebidiah's ears caught a sound, rocks shifting against the cave floor. Something was moving in the darkness, and he didn't think it was the bats. It scuttled, and Jebidiah felt certain it was close to the floor, and by the sound of it, moving his way at a creeping pace. The hair on the back of Jebidiah's neck bristled like porcupine quills. He felt his flesh bump up and crawl. The air became stiffer with the stench of burnt and rotting flesh. Jebidiah's knees trembled. He reached cautiously inside his coat pocket, produced a match, struck it on his pants leg, held it up.

At that very moment, the thing stood up and was brightly lit in the glow of the match, the bees circling its skin-stripped skull. It snarled and darted forward. Jebidiah felt its rotten claws on his shirt front as he fired the revolver. The blaze from the bullet gave a brief, bright flare and was gone. At the same time, the match was knocked out of his hand and Jebidiah was knocked backwards, onto his back, the thing's claws at his throat. The monster's bees stung him. The stings felt like red-hot pokers entering his flesh. He stuck the revolver into the creature's body and fired. Once. Twice. Three times. A fourth.

Then the hammer clicked empty. He realized he had already fired two other shots. Six dead silver soldiers were in his cylinders, and the thing still had hold of him.

He tried to draw his other gun, but before he could, the thing released him, and Jebidiah could hear it crawling away in the dark. The bats fluttered and screeched.

Confused, Jebidiah drew the pistol, managed to get to his feet. He waited, listening, his fresh revolver pointing into the darkness.

Jebidiah found another match, struck it.

The thing lay with its back draped over a rise of rock. Jebidiah eased toward it. The silver loads had torn into the hive. It oozed a dark, odiferous trail of death and decaying honey. Bees began to drop to the cavern floor. The hive in Gimet's chest sizzled and pulsed like a large, black knot. Gimet opened his mouth, snarled, but otherwise didn't move.

Couldn't move.

Jebidiah, guided by the last wisps of his match, raised the pistol, stuck it against the black knot, and pulled the trigger. The knot exploded. Gimet let out with a shriek so sharp and loud it startled the bats to flight, drove them out of the cave, through the burrow, out into the remains of the night.

Gimet's claw-like hands dug hard at the stones around him, then he was still and Jebidiah's match went out.

— ♦ —

Jebidiah found the remains of the bible in his pocket, and as he removed it, tossed it on the ground, it burst into flames. Using the two pistol barrels like large tweezers, he lifted the burning pages and dropped them into Gimet's open chest. The body caught on fire immediately, crackled and popped dryly, and was soon nothing more than a blaze. It lit the cavern up bright as day.

Jebidiah watched the corpse being consumed by the biblical fire for a moment, then headed toward the burrow, bent down, squirmed through it, came up in the grave.

He looked for the deputy and didn't see him. He climbed out of the grave and looked around. Jebidiah smiled. If the deputy had lasted until the bats charged out, that was most likely the last straw, and he had bolted.

Jebidiah looked back at the open grave. Smoke wisped out of the hole and out of the grave and climbed up to the sky. The moon was fading and the pink on the horizon was widening.

Gimet was truly dead now. The road was safe. His job was done.

At least for one brief moment.

Jebidiah walked down the hill, found his horse tied in the brush near the road where he had left it. The deputy's horse was gone, of course, the deputy most likely having already finished out Deadman's road at a high gallop, on his way to Nacogdoches, perhaps to have a long drink of whisky and turn in his badge.

The Long Dead Day

She said a dog bit her, but we didn't find the dog anywhere. It was a bad bite, though, and we dressed it
with some good stuff and wrapped it with some bandages,
and then poured alcohol over that, letting it seep in, and,
she, being ten, screamed and cried. She hugged up with her
mama, though, and in a while she was all right, or as all
right as she could be.

Later that evening, while I sat on the wall and looked
down at the great crowd outside the compound, my wife,
Carol, called me down from the wall and the big gun. She
said Ellen had developed a fever, that she could hardly
keep her eyes open, and the bite hurt.

Carol took her temperature, said it was high, and that to
touch her forehead was to almost burn your hand. I went in
then, and did just that, touched her forehead. Her mother
was right. I opened up the dressing on the wound, and was
amazed to see that it had turned black, and it didn't really
look like a dog bite at all. It never had, but I wanted it to,
and let myself be convinced that was just what it was, even
if there had been no dog we could find in the compound. By
this time, they had all been eaten. Fact was, I probably shot
the last one around; a beautiful Shepard, that when it saw
me wagged its tail. I think when I lifted the gun he knew,
and didn't care. He just sat there with his mouth open in
what looked like a dog's version of a smile, his tail beating. I killed him first shot, to the head. I dressed him out

without thinking about him much. I couldn't let myself do that. I loved dogs. But my family needed to eat. We did have the rabbits we raised, some pigeons, a vegetable garden, but it was all very precarious.

Anyway, I didn't believe about the dog bite, and now the wound looked really bad. I knew the real cause of it, or at least the general cause, and it made me sick to think of it. I doctored the wound again, gave her some antibiotics that we had, wrapped it and went out. I didn't tell Carol what she was already thinking.

I got my shotgun and went about the compound, look-ing. It was a big compound, thirty-five acres with a high wall around it, but somehow, someone must have breached the wall. I went to the back garden, the one with trees and flowers where our little girl liked to play. I went there and looked around, and found him sitting on one of the bench-es. He was just sitting. I guess he hadn't been the way he was for very long. Just long enough to bite my daughter. He was about her age, and I knew then, being so lonely, she had let him in. Let him in through the bolted back door. I glanced over there and saw she had bolted it back. I real-ized then that she had most likely been up on the walk around the wall and had seen him down there, not long of turning, looking up wistfully. He could probably still talk then, just like anyone else, maybe even knew what he was doing, or maybe not. Perhaps he thought he was still who he once was, and thought he should get away from the oth-ers, that he would be safe inside.

It was amazing none of the others had forced their way in. Then again, the longer they were what they were, the slower they became, until finally they quit moving alto-gether. Problem with that was, it took years.

I looked back at him, sitting there, the one my daughter had let in to be her playmate. He had come inside, and then he had done what he had done, and now my daughter was sick with the disease, and the boy was just sitting there on the bench, looking at me in the dying sunlight, his eyes black as if he had been beat, his face gray, his lips purple.

He reminded me of my son. He wasn't my son, but he reminded me of him. I had seen my son go down among them, some, what was it, five years before. Go down in a flash of kicking legs and thrashing arms and squirting liquids. That was when we lived in town, before we found the compound and made it better. There were others then, but they were gone now. Expeditions to find others they said. Whatever, they left, we never saw them again.

Sometimes at night I couldn't sleep for the memory of my son, Gerald, and sometimes in my wife's arms, I thought of him, for had it not been such a moment that had created him?

The boy rose from the bench, stumble-stepped toward me, and I shot him. I shot him in the chest, knocking him down. Then I rushed to him and shot him in the head, taking half of it away.

I knew my wife would have heard the shot, so I didn't bother to bury him. I went back across the compound and to the upper apartments where we lived. She saw me with the gun, opened her mouth as if to speak, but nothing came out.

"A dog," I said. "The one who bit her. I'll get some things, dress him out and we'll eat him later."

"There was a dog," my wife said.

"Yes, a dog. He wasn't rabid. And he's pretty healthy. We can eat him."

I could see her go weak with relief, and I felt both satisfied and guilty at the same time. I said, "How is she?"

"Not much better. There was a dog, you say."

"That's what I said, dear."

"Oh, good. Good. A dog."

I looked at my watch. My daughter had been bitten earlier that day, and it was almost night. I said, "Why don't you go get a knife, some things for me to do the skinning, and I'll dress out the dog. Maybe she'll feel better, she gets some meat in her."

"Sure," Carol said. "Just the thing. She needs the protein. The iron."

"You bet," I said.

She went away then, down the stairs, across the yard to the cooking shed. I went upstairs, still carrying the gun.

Inside my daughter's room, I saw from the doorway that she was gray as cigarette ash. She turned her head toward me.

"Daddy," she said.

"Yes, dear," I said, and put the shotgun against the wall by the door and went over to her.

"I feel bad."

"I know."

"I feel different."

"I know."

"Can anything be done? Do you have some medicine?"

"I do."

I sat down in the chair by the bed. "Do you want me to read to you?"

"No," she said, and then she went silent. She lay there not moving, her eyes closed.

"Baby," I said. "She didn't answer."

I got up then and went to the open door and looked out. Carol, my beautiful wife, was coming across the yard, carrying the things I'd asked for. I picked up the shotgun and made sure it was loaded with my daughter's medicine. I thought for a moment about how to do it. I put the shotgun back against the wall. I listened as my wife come up the stairs.

When she was in the room, I said, "Give me the knife and things."

"She okay?"

"Yes, she's gone to sleep. Or she's almost asleep. Take a look at her."

She gave me the knife and things and I laid them in a chair as she went across the room and to the bed.

I picked up the shotgun, and as quietly as I could, stepped forward and pointed it to the back of my wife's head and pulled the trigger. It was over instantly. She fell across the bed on our dead child, her blood coating the sheets and the wall.

She wouldn't have survived the death of a second child, and she sure wouldn't have survived what was about to happen to our daughter.

I went over and looked at Ellen. I could wait, until she opened her eyes, till she came out of the bed, trying for me, but I couldn't stomach that. I didn't want to see that. I took the shotgun and put it to her forehead and pulled the trigger. The room boomed with the sound of shotgun fire again, and the bed and the room turned an even brighter red.

I went outside with the shotgun and walked along the landing, walked all the way around, came to where the big gun was mounted. I sat behind it, on the swivel stool, leaned the shotgun against the protecting wall. I sat there and looked out at the hundreds of them, just standing there, looking up, waiting for something.

I began to rotate and fire the gun. Many of them went down. I fired until there was no more ammunition. Reloaded, I fired again, my eyes wet with tears. I did this for some time, until the next rounds of ammunition were played out. It was like swatting at a hive of bees. There always seemed to be more.

I sat there and tried not to think about anything. I watched them. Their shapes stretched for miles around, went off into the distance in shadowy bulks, like a horde of rats waiting to board a cargo ship.

They were eating the ones I had dropped with the big gun.

After awhile the darkness was total and there were just the shapes out there. I watched them for a long time. I looked at the shotgun propped against the retaining wall. I looked at it and picked it up and put it under my chin, and then I put it back again.

I knew, in time, I would have the courage.

White Mule, Spotted Pig

F rank's papa, the summer of nineteen hundred and nine, told him right before he died that he had a good chance to win the annual Camp Rapture mule race. He told Frank this cause he needed money to keep getting drunk, and he wasn't about to ride no mule himself, fat as he was. If the old man had known he was about to die, Frank figured he would have saved his breath on the race talk and asked for whisky instead, maybe a chaw. But as it was, he said it, and it planted in Frank's head the desire to ride and win.

— ◆ —

Frank hated that about himself. Once a thing got into his head he couldn't derail it. He was on the track then, and had to see it to the end. Course, that could be a good trait, but problem was, and Frank knew it, the only things that normally caught up in his head like that and pushed him were bad ideas. Even if he could sense their badness, he couldn't seem to stop their running forward and dragging him with them. He also thought his mama had been right when she told him once that their family was like shit on shoes, the stink of it followed them wherever they went.

But this idea. Winning a mule race. Well, that had some good sides to it. Mainly money.

He thought about what his papa said, and how he said it, and then how, within a few moments, the old man grabbed the bed sheets, moaned once, dribbled some drool, and was gone to where ever it was he was supposed to go, probably a stool next to the devil at fireside.

He didn't leave Frank nothing but an old run down place with a bit of dried out corn crop, a mule, a horse with one foot in the grave and the other on a slick spot. And his very own shit to clean out of the sheets, cause when the old man let go and departed, he left Frank that present, which was the only kind he had ever given. Something dirty. Something painful. Something shitty.

Frank had to burn the mattress and set fire to the bed clothes, so there really wasn't any really cleaning about it. Then he dug a big hole, and cut roots to do it. Next he had to wrap the old man's naked body in a dirty canvas and put him down and cover him up. It took some work, cause the old man must have weighed three hundred pounds, and he wasn't one inch taller than five three if he was wearing boots with dried cow shit on the heels and paper tucked inside them to jack his height. Dragging him along on his dead ass from the house had damn near caused one of Frank's balls to swell up and pop out.

Finished with the burying, Frank leaned against a sickly sweet gum tree and rolled himself a smoke, and thought: Shit, I should have dragged the old man over here on the tarp. Or maybe hitched him up to the mule and dragged his naked ass face down through the dirt. That would have been the way to go, not pulling his guts out.

But, it was done now, and as always, he had used his brain late in the game.

Frank scratched a match on a thumb nail and lit a rolled cigarette and leaned on a sick sweet gum and smoked and considered. It wasn't that he was all that fond of his old man, but damn if he still didn't in some way want to make him proud, or rather be proud to his memory. He thought: Funny, him not being worth a damn, and me still wanting to please him. Funnier yet, considering the old man used to beat him like a Tom-Tom. Frank had seen him knock mama down once and put his foot on the back of her neck and use his belt to beat her ass while he cussed her for having burned the cornbread. It wasn't the only beating she got, but it was damn sure the champion.

It was shortly after that she decamped with the good horse, a bag of corn meal, some dried meat and a butcher knife. She also managed, with what Frank thought must have been incredible aim, to piss in one of his old man's liquor jugs. This was discovered by the old man after he took a good strong bolt of the liquor. Cheap as the stuff was he drank, Frank was surprised he could tell the difference, that he had turned out to be such a fine judge of shit liquor.

Papa had ridden out after her on the mule but hadn't found her, which wasn't a surprise, because the only thing Papa had been good at tracking was a whisky bottle or some whore, provided she was practically tied down and didn't cost much. He probably tracked the whores he messed with by the stench.

Back from the hunt, drunk and pissed and empty handed, Papa had said it was bad enough Frank's mama was a horse and meal thief, but at least she hadn't taken the mule, and frankly, she wasn't that good a cook anyhow.

The mule's name was Rupert, and he could run like his tail was on fire. Papa had actually thought about the mule as a contender for a while, and had put out a little money to have him trained by Leroy, who though short in many departments, and known for having been caught fucking a goat by a half dozen hunters, was pretty good with mules and horses. Perhaps, it could be said he had a way with goats as well. One thing was certain, none of Leroy's stock had testified to the contrary, and only the nanny goats were known to be nervous.

The night after Frank buried his pa, he got in some corn squeezings, and got drunk enough to imagine weasels crawling out from under the floorboards. To clear his head and to relieve his bladder, he went out to do something on his father's grave that would never pass for flowers. He stood there watering, thinking about the prize money and what he would do with it. He looked at the house and the barn and the lot, out to where he could see the dead corn standing in rows like dehydrated soldiers. The house leaned to the left, and one of the window sills was near on the ground. When he slept at night, he slept on a bed with one side jacked up with flat rocks so that it was high enough and even enough he wouldn't roll out of bed. The barn had one side missing and the land was all rutted from run off, and had never been terraced.

With the exception of the hill where they grazed their bit of stock, the place was void of grass, and all it brought to mind was brown things and dead things, though there were a few bedraggled chickens who wandered the yard like wild Indians, taking what they could find, even eating one another should one of them keel over dead from starvation or exhaustion. Frank had seen a half dozen chickens go at a weak one lying on the ground, tearing him apart with the chicken still cawing, kicking a leg. It hadn't lasted long. About like a dozen miners at a free lunch table.

Frank smoked his cigarette and thought if he could win that race, he would move away from this shit pile. Sell it to some fool. Move into town and get a job that would keep him. Never again would he look up a mule's ass or fit his hands around the handles on a plow. He was thinking on this while looking up the hill at his mule, Rupert.

The hill was surrounded by a rickety rail fence within which the mule resided primarily on the honor system. At the top of the hill was a bunch of oaks and pines and assorted survivor trees. As Frank watched the sun fall down behind the hill, it seemed as if the limbs of the trees wadded together into a crawling shadow, way the wind blew them and mixed them up. Rupert was clearly outlined near a pathetic persimmon tree from which the mule had stripped the persimmons and much of the leaves.

Frank thought Rupert looked quite noble up there, his mule ears standing high in outline against the redness of the sun behind the dark trees. The world seemed strange and beautiful, as if just created. In that moment Frank felt much older than his years and not so fresh as the world seemed, but ancient and worn like the old Indian pottery he had found while plowing through what had once been great Indian mounds. And now, even as he watched, he noted the sun seemed to darken, as if it were a hot wound turning black from infection. The wind cooled and began to whistle. Frank turned his head to the North and watched as clouds pushed across the fading sky. In instants, all the light was gone and there were just shadows, spitting and twisting in the heavens and filling the hard-blowing wind with the aroma of wet dirt.

When Frank turned again to note Rupert, the mule was still there, but was now little more than a peculiar shape next to the ragged persimmon tree. Had Frank not known it was the mule, he might well have mistaken it for a peculiar rise in the terrain, or a fallen tree lying at an odd angle.

The storm was from the north and blowing west. Thunder boomed and lighting cracked in the dirty sky like snap beans, popped and fizzled like a pissed on campfire. In that moment, the shadow Frank knew to be Rupert, lifted its head, and pointed its dark snout toward the sky, as if in defiance. A bolt of lighting, crooked as a dog's hind leg, and accompanied by a bass drum blow of thunder, jumped from the heavens and dove for the mule, striking him a perfect white-hot blow on the tip of his nose, making him glow, causing Frank to think that he had in fact seen the inside of the mule light up with all its bones in a row. Then Rupert's head exploded, his body blazed, the persimmon leaped to flames, and the mule fell over in a swirl of heavenly fire and a cannon shot of flying mule shit. The corpse caught a patch of dried grass a blaze. The flames burned in a perfect circle around the corpse and blinked out, leaving a circle of smoke rising skyward.

"Goddamn," Frank said. "Shit."

The clouds split open, let loose of its bladder, pissed all over the hill side and the mule, and not a drop, not one goddamn drop, was thrown away from the hill. The rain just covered that spot, put out the mule and the persimmon tree with a sizzling sound, then passed on, taking darkness, rain, and cool wind with it.

Frank stood there for a long time, looking up the hill, watching his hundred dollars crackle and smoke. Pretty soon the smell from the grilled mule floated down the hill and filled his nostrils.

"Shit," Frank said. "Shit. Shit. Shit."

Late morning, when Frank could finally drag himself out of bed, he went out and caught up the horse, Dobbin, hitched him to a single tree and some chains, drove him out to where the mule lay. He hooked one of the mule's hind legs to the rigging, and Dobbin dragged the corpse up the hill, between the trees, to the other side. Frank figured he'd just let the body rot there, and being on the other side of the hill, there was less chance of the wind carrying down the smell.

After that, he moped around for a few days, drank enough to see weasels again, and then had an idea. His idea was to seek out Leroy, who had been used to train Rupert. See if he could work a deal with him.

Frank rode Dobbin over to Leroy's place, which was as nasty as his own. More so, due to the yard being full not only of chickens and goats, but children. He had five of them, and when Frank rode up, he saw them right away, running about, raising hell in the yard, one of them minus pants, his little johnson flopping about like a grub worm on a hot griddle. He could see Leroy's old lady on the porch, fat and nasty with her hair tied up. She was yelling at the kids and telling them how she was going to kill them and feed them to the chickens. One of the boys, the ten year old, ran by the porch whooping, and the Mrs., moving deftly for such a big woman, scrambled to the edge of the porch, stuck her foot out, caught him one just above the waist and sent him tumbling. He went down hard. She laughed like a lunatic. The boy got up with a bloody nose and ran off across the yard and into the woods, screaming.

Frank climbed down from Dobbin and went over to Leroy who was sitting on a bucket in the front yard whittling a green limb with a knife big enough to sword fight. Leroy was watching his son retreat into the greenery. As Frank came up, leading Dobbin, Leroy said, "Does that all the time. Sometimes, though, she'll throw something at him. Good thing wasn't nothing lying about. She's got a pretty good throwin' arm on her. Seen her hit a seed salesman with a tossed frying pan from the porch there to about where the road meets the property. Knocked him down and knocked his hat off. Scattered his seed samples, which the chickens ate. Must have laid there for an hour afore he got up and wandered off. Forgot his hat. Got it on my head right now, though I had to put me some newspaper in the band to make it fit."

Wasn't nothing Frank could say to that, so he said, "Leroy, Rupert got hit by lightning. Right in the head."

"The head?"

"Wouldn't have mattered had it been the ass. It killed him deader than a post and burned him up."

"Damn. That there is a shame," Leroy said, and stopped whittling. He pushed the seed salesman's hat up on his forehead to reveal some forks of greasy brown hair. Leroy studied Frank. "Is there something I can do for you? Or you come around to visit?"

"I'm thinking you might could help me get a mule and get back in the race."

"Mules cost."

"I know. Thought we might could come up with something. And if we could, and we won, I'd give you a quarter of the prize money."

"I get a quarter for grooming folks critters in town."

"I mean a quarter of a hundred. Twenty-five dollars."

"I see. Well, I am your man for animals. I got a knack. I can talk to them like I was one of them. Except for chickens. Ain't no one can talk to chickens."

"They're birds."

"That there is the problem. They ain't animal enough."

Frank thought about Leroy and the fucked goat. Wondered what Leroy had said to the goat as way of wooing it. Had he told her something special? I think you got a good-looking face? I love the way your tail wiggles when you walk. It was a mystery that Frank actually wasn't all that anxious to unravel...

"I know you run in the circles of them that own or know about mules," Frank said. "Why I thought you maybe could help me."

Leroy took off the seed salesman's hat, put it on his knee, threw his knife in the dirt, let the whittling stick fall from his hand. "I could sneak up on an idea or two. Old man Torrence, he's got a mule he's looking to sale. And by his claim, it's a runner. He ain't never ridden it himself, but he's had it ridden. Says it can run."

"There's that buying stuff again. I ain't got no real money."

"Takes money to make money."

"Takes money to have money."

Leroy put the seed salesman's hat back on. "You know, we might could ask him if he'd rent out his mule. Race is a ways off yet, so we could get some good practice in. You being about a hundred and twenty-five pounds, you'd make a good rider."

"I've ridden a lot. I was ready on Rupert, reckon I can get ready on another mule."

"Deal we might have to make is, we won the race, we bought the mule afterwards. That might be the way he'd do it."

"Buy the mule?"

"At a fair price."

"How fair?"

"Say twenty-five dollars."

"That's a big slice of the prize money. And a mule for twenty-five, that's cheap."

"I know Torrence got the mule cheap. Fella that owed him made a deal. Besides, times is hard. So they're selling cheap. Cost more, we can make extra money on side bets. Bet on ourselves. Or if we don't think we got a chance, we bet against ourselves."

"I don't know. We lose, it could be said we did it on purpose."

"I can get someone to bet for us."

"Only if we bet to win. I ain't never won nothing or done nothing right in my life, and I figure this here might be my chance."

"You gettin' Jesus?"

"I'm gettin' tired," Frank said.

— ◆ —

There are no real mountains in East Texas, and only a

few hills of consequence, but Old Man Torrence lived at the top of a big hill that was called with a kind of braggarts lie, Barrow Dog Mountain. Frank had no idea who Barrow or Dog were, but that was what the big hill had been called for as long as he remembered, probably well before he was born. There was a ridge at the top of it that overlooked the road below. Frank found it an impressive sight as he and Leroy rode in on Dobbin, he at the reins, Leroy behind him.

It was pretty on top of the hill too. The air smelled good, and flowers grew all about in red, blue and yellow blooms, and the cloudless sky was so blue you felt as if a great lake were falling down from the heavens. Trees fanned out bright green on either side of the path, and near the top, on a flat section, was Old Man Torrence's place. It was made of cured logs, and he had a fine chicken coop that was built straight and true. There were hog pens and a nice barn of thick cured logs with a roof that had all of its roofing slats. There was a sizable garden that rolled along the top of the hill, full of tall bright green corn stalks, so tall they shaded the rows between them. There was no grass between the rows, and the dirt there looked freshly laid by. Squash and all manner of vegetables exploded out of the ground alongside the corn, and there were little clumps of beans and peas growing in long pretty rows.

In a large pen next to the barn was a fifteen hands high chocolate colored mule, prettiest thing Frank had ever seen in the mule flesh department. Its ears stood up straight, and it gave Frank and Leroy a snort as they rode in.

"He's a big one," Leroy said.

"Won't he be slow, being that big?" Frank asked.

"Big mule's also got big muscles, he's worked right. And he looks to have been worked right. Got enough muscles, he can haul some freight. Might be fast as Rupert."

"Sure faster right now," Frank said.

As they rode up, they saw Old Man Torrence on the front porch with his wife and three kids, two boys and a girl. Torrence was a fat, ruddy faced man. His wife was a little plump, but pretty. His kids were all nice looking and they had their hair combed and unlike Leroy's kids, looked clean. As if they might bathe daily. As they got closer, Frank could see that none of the kids looked whacked on. They seemed to be laughing at something the mother was saying. It certainly was different than from his own upbringing, different from Leroy's place. Wasn't anyone tripping anyone, cussing, tossing frying pans, threatening to cripple one another or put out an eye. Thinking on this, Frank felt something twist around inside of him like some kind of serpent looking for a rock to slide under.

He and Leroy got off Dobbin and tied him to a little hitching post that was built out front of the house, took off their hats, and walked up to the steps.

After being offered lemonade, which they turned down, Old Man Torrence came off the porch, ruffling one of his kid's hair as he did. He smiled back at his wife, and then walked with Frank and Leroy out toward the mule pen, Leroy explaining what they had in mind.

"You want to rent my mule? What if I wanted to run him?"

"Well, I don't know," Leroy said. "It hadn't occurred to me you might. You ain't never before, though I heard tell he was a mule could be run."

"It's a good mule," Torrence said. " Real fast."

"You've ridden him?" Frank asked.

"No. I haven't had the pleasure. But my brother and his boys have. They borrow him from time to time, and they thought on running him this year. Nothing serious. Just a thought. They say he can really cover ground."

"Frank here," Leroy said, "he plans on entering, and we would rent your mule. If we win, we could give you a bit of the prize money. What say we rent him for ten, and if he wins, we give you another fifteen. That way you pick up twenty-five dollars."

Frank was listening to all this, thinking: and then I owe Leroy his share; this purse I haven't won is getting smaller and smaller.

"And what if you don't win?" Torrence said.

"You've made ten dollars," Leroy said.

"And I got to take the chance my mule might go lame or get hurt or some such. I don't know. Ten dollars, that's not a lot of money for what you're asking. It ain't even your mule."

"Which is why we're offering the ten dollars," Leroy said.

They went over and leaned on the fence and looked at the great mule, watched his muscles roll beneath his chocolate flesh as he trotted nervously about the pen.

"He looks excitable," Frank said.

"Robert E. Lee has just got a lot of energy is all," Torrence said.

"He's named Robert E. Lee?" Frank asked.

"Best damn general ever lived. Tell you boys what. You give me twenty-five, and another twenty-five if he wins, and you got a deal."

"But I give you that, and Leroy his share, I don't have nothing hardly left."

"You ain't got nothing at all right now," Torrence said.

"How's about," Leroy said, "we do it this way. We give you fifteen, and another fifteen if he wins. That's thirty. Now that's fair for a rented mule. Hell, we might could go shopping, buy a mule for twenty-five, and even if he don't win, we got a mule. He don't race worth a damn, we could put him to plow."

Old Man Torrence pursed his lips. "That sounds good. All right," he said sticking out his hand, "deal."

"Well, now," Frank said, not taking the hand. "Before I shake on that, I'd like to make sure he can run. Let me ride him."

Old Man Torrence withdrew his hand and wiped it on his pants as if something had gotten on his palm. "I reckon I could do that, but seeing how we don't have a deal yet, and ain't no fifteen dollars has changed hands, how's about I ride him for you. So you can see."

Frank and Leroy agreed, and watched from the fence as Torrence got the equipment and saddled up Robert E. Lee. Torrence walked Robert E. Lee out of the lot, and onto a pasture atop the hill, where the overhang was. The pasture was huge and the grass was as green as Ireland. It was all fenced in with barb wire strung tight between deeply planted posts.

"I'll ride him around in a loop. Once slow, and then real fast toward the edge of the overhang there, then cut back before we get there. I ain't got a pocket watch, so you'll have to be your own judge."

— ◆ —

Torrence swung into the saddle. "You boys ready."

"Let'er rip," Leroy said.

Old Man Torrence gave Robert E. Lee his heels. The mule shot off so fast that Old Man Torrence's hat flew off, and Leroy in sympathy, took hold of the brim of the seed salesman's hat, as if Robert E. Lee's lunge might blow it off his head.

"Goddamn," Leroy said. "Look how low that mule is to the ground. He's gonna have the grass touching his belly."

And so the mule ran, and as it neared the barb wire fence, Old Man Torrence gave him a tug, to turn him. But,

Robert E. Lee wasn't having any. His speed picked up, and the barb wire fence came closer.

Leroy said, "Uh oh."

Robert E. Lee hit the fence hard. So hard it caused his head to dip over the top wire and his ass to rise up as if he might be planning a head stand. Over the mule flipped, tearing loose the fence, causing a strand of wire to snap and strike Old Man Torrence, and then Torrence was thrown ahead of the tumbling mule... Over the overhang. Out of sight. The mule did in fact do a headstand, landed hard that way, its hind legs high in the air, wiggling. For a moment, it seemed as if he might hang there, and then, Robert E. Lee lost his headstand and went over after his owner.

"Damn," Leroy said.

"Damn," Frank said.

They both ran toward the broken fence. When they got there Frank hesitated, not able to look. He glanced away, back across the bright green field.

Leroy scooted up to the cliff's edge and took a gander, studied what he saw for a long time.

"Well?" Frank said, finally turning his head back to Leroy.

"Robert E. Lee just met his Gettysburg. And Old Man Torrence is somewhere between Gettysburg and Robert E. Lee...Actually, you can't tell which is which. Mule, Gettysburg, or Old Man Torrence. It's all kind of bunched up."

— ◆ —

When Frank and Leroy got down there, which took some considerable time, as they worked their way down a little trail on foot, they discovered that Old Man Torrence had been lucky in a fashion. He had landed in sand, and the force of Robert E. Lee's body had driven him down deep into it, his nose poking up and out enough to take in air. Robert E. Lee was as dead as a three penny nail, and his tail was stuck up in the air and bent over like a flag that had been broken at the staff. The wind moved the hairs on it a little.

Frank and Leroy went about digging Old Man Torrence out, starting first with his head so he could really breath well. When Torrence spat enough sand out of his mouth, he looked up and said, "You sonsofbitches. This is your fault."

"Our fault?" Leroy said. "You was riding him."

"You goat fucking sonofabitch, get me out of here."

Leroy's body sagged a little. "I knew that was gonna get around good. Ain't nobody keeps a secret. There was only that one time too, and them hunters had to come up on me."

They dug Torrence out from under the mule, and Frank went up the trail and got Old Dobbin and rode to the doctor. When Frank got back with the sawbones, Torrence was none the happier to see him. Leroy had gone off to the side to sit by himself, which to Frank meant the goat had come up again.

Old Man Torrence was mostly all right, but he blamed Frank and Leroy, especially Leroy, from then on. And he walked in a way that when he stepped with his right leg, it always looked as if he were about to bend over and tie his shoe. Even in later years, when Frank saw him, he went out of his way to avoid him, and Leroy dodged him like the small pox, not wanting to hear reference to the goat.

But in that moment in time, the important thing to Frank was simply that he was still without a mule. And the race was coming closer.

— ◆ —

That night, as Frank lay in his sagging bed, looking out from it at the angled wall of the room, listening to the crickets saw their fiddles outside and inside the house, he closed his eyes and remembered how Old Man Torrence's place had looked. He saw himself sitting with the pretty plump wife and the clean, polite kids. Then he saw himself with the wife inside that pretty house, on the bed, and he imagined that for a long time.

It was a pleasant thought, the wife and the bed, but even more pleasant was imagining Torrence's place as his. All that greenery and high growing corn and blooming squash and thick pea and bean vines dripping with vegetables. The house and the barn and the pasture. And in his dream, the big mule, alive, not yet a confusion of bones and flesh and fur, the tail a broken flag.

He thought then of his mother, and the only way he could remember her was with her hair tied back and her face sweaty and both of her eyes blacked. That was how she had looked the last time he had seen her, right before she run off with a horse and some corn meal and a butcher knife. He wondered where she was, and if she now lived in a place where the buildings were straight and the grass was green and the corn was tall.

After a while he got up and peed out the window, and smelled the aroma of other nights drifting up from the ground he had poisoned with his water, and thought: I am better than Papa. He just peed in the corner of the room and shit out the window, splattering it all down the side of the house. I don't do that. I pee out the window, but I don't shit, and I don't pee in the corner. That's a step up. I go out side for the messy business. And if I had a good house, I wouldn't do this. I'd use the slop jar. I'd go to the privy.

That didn't stop him from finishing his pee, thinking about what he would do or ought to do as far as his toilet habits went. Besides, peeing was the one thing he was really good at. He could piss like a horse and from a goodly distance… He had even won money on his ability. It was the one thing his father had been proud of. "My son, Frank. He can piss like a race horse. Get it out, Frank. Show them."

And he would.

But, compared to what he wanted out of life, his ability to throw water from his johnson didn't seem all that wonderful right then.

— ♦ —

Frank thought he ought to call a halt to his racing plans, but like so many of his ideas, he couldn't let it go. It blossomed inside of him until he was filled with it. Then he was obsessed with an even wilder plan. A story he had heard came back to him, and ran round inside his head like a greased pig.

He would find the White Mule and capture it and run it. It was a mule he could have for free, and it was known to be fast, if wild. And, of course, he would have to capture its companion, The Spotted Pig. Though, he figured, by now, the pig was no longer a pig, but a hog, and the mule would be three, maybe four years old.

If they really existed.

It was a story he had heard for the last three years or so, and it was told for the truth by them who told him, his Papa among them. But if drinking made him see weasels oozing out of the floorboards, it might have made Papa see white mules and spotted pigs on parade. But the story wasn't just Papa's story. He had heard it from others, and it went like this:

Once upon a time, there was this pretty white mule with pink eyes, and the mule was fine and strong and set to the plow early on, but he didn't take to it. Not at all. But the odder part of the story was that the mule took up with a farm pig, and they became friends. There was no explaining it. It happened now and then, a horse or mule adopting their own pet, and that was what had happened with the white mule and the spotted pig.

When Frank had asked his Papa, why would a mule take up with a pig, his father had said: "Ain't no explaining. Why the hell did I take up with your mother?"

Frank thought the question went the other way, but the tale fascinated him, and his Papa was just drunk enough to be in a good mood. Another pint swallowed, he'd be kicking his ass or his mama's. But he pushed while he could, trying to get the goods on the tale, since outside of worrying about dying corn and sagging barns, there wasn't that much in life that thrilled him.

The story his papa told him was the farmer who owned the mule, and no one could ever put a name to who that farmer was, had supposedly found the mule wouldn't work if the pig wasn't around, leading him between the rows. The pig was in front, the mule plowed fine. The pig wasn't there, the mule wouldn't plow.

This caused the farmer to come up with an even better idea. What would the mule do if the pig was made to run? So the farmer got the mule all saddled, and had one of his boys put the pig out front of the mule and swat it with a knotted plow line, and away went the pig and away went the white mule. The pig pretty soon veered off, but the mule, once set to run, couldn't stop, and would race so fast that the only way it halted was when it was tuckered out. Then it would go back to the start, and look for its pig. Never failed.

One night the mule broke loose, kicked the pig's pen down, and he and the pig, like Jesse and Frank James, headed for the hills. Went into the East Texas greenery and wound in amongst the trees, and were lost to the farmer. Only to be seen after that in glimpses and in stories that might or might not be true. Stories about how they raided corn fields and ate the corn and how the mule kicked down pens and let hogs and goats and cattle go free.

The White Mule and The Spotted Pig. Out there. On the run. Doing whatever it was that white mules and spotted pigs did when they weren't raiding crops and freeing critters.

Frank thought on this for a long time, saddled up Dobbin and rode over to Leroy's place. When Frank arrived, Leroy was out in the yard on his back, unconscious, the seed sales man hat spun off to the side and was being moved around by a curious chicken. Finding Leroy like this didn't frighten Frank any. He often found Leroy that way, cold as a wedge from drink, or the missus having snuck up behind him with a stick of stove wood. They were rowdy, Leroy's bunch.

The missus came out on the porch and shook her fist at Frank, and not knowing anything else to do, he waved. She spat a stream of brown tobacco off the porch in his direction and went inside. A moment later one of the kids bellowed from being whapped, and there was a sound like someone slamming a big fish on flat ground. Then silence.

Frank bent down and shook Leroy awake. Leroy cursed, and Frank dragged him over to an overturned bucket and sat him up on it, asked him, "What happened?"

"Missus come up behind me. I've got so I don't watch my back enough."

"Why'd she do it?"

"Just her way. She has spells."

"You all right?"

"I got a headache."

Frank went straight to business. "I come to say maybe we ain't out of the mule business."

"What you mean?"

Frank told him about the mule and the pig, about his idea.

"Oh, yeah. Mule and pig are real. I've seen em once myself. Out hunting. I looked up, and there they were at the end of a trail, just watching. I was so startled, I just stood there looking at them."

"What did they do?"

"Well, Frank, they ran off. What do you think? But it was kind of funny. They didn't get in no hurry, just turned and went around the trail, showing me their ass, the pig's tail curled up and a little swishy, and the mule swatting his like at flies. They just went around that curve in the trail, behind some oaks and blackberry vines, and they was gone. I tracked them a bit, but they got down in a stream and walked it. I could find their tracks in the stream with my hands, but pretty soon the whole stream was brown with mud, and they come out of it somewhere I didn't find, and they was gone like a swamp fog come noon."

"Was the mule really white?"

"Dirty a bit, but white. Even from where I was standing, just bits of light coming in through the trees, I could see he had pink eyes. Story is, that's why he don't like to come out in day much, likes to stay in the trees, and do his crop raiding at night. Say the sun hurts his skin."

"That could be a drawback."

"You act like you got him in a pen somewhere."

"I'd like to see if I could get hold of him. Story is, he can run, and he needs the pig to do it."

"That's the story. But stories ain't always true. I even heard stories about how the pig rides the mule, and that the mule is stump broke, and the pig climbs up on a stump and diddles the mule in the ass. I've heard all manner of tale, and ain't maybe none of it got so much as a nut of truth in it. Still, it's one of them ideas that kind of appeals to me. Course, you know, we might catch that mule and he might not can run at all. Maybe all he can do is sneak around in the woods and eat corn crops."

"Well, it's all the idea I got, " Frank said, and the thought of that worried Frank more than a little. He considered on his knack for clinging to bad notions like a rutting dog hanging onto a fella's leg. But, like the dog, he was determined to finish what he started.

"So what you're saying here," Leroy said, "is you want to capture the mule, and the pig, so the mule has got his help mate. And you want to ride the mule in the race?"

"That's what I said."

Leroy paused for a moment, rubbed the knot on the back of his noggin. "I think we should get Nigger Joe to help us track him. We want him, that's the way we do it. Nigger Joe catches him, and we'll break him, and you can ride him."

Nigger Joe was part Indian and part Irish and part Negro. His skin was somewhere between brown and red and he had a red cast to his kinky hair and strawberry freckles and bright green eyes. But the black blood named him, and he himself went by the name, Nigger Joe.

He was supposed to be able to track a bird across the sky, a fart across the yard. He had two women that lived with him and he called them his wives. One of them was a Negro, and the other one was part Negro and Cherokee. He called the black one Sweetie, the red and black one Pie.

When Frank and Leroy rode up double on Dobbin, and stopped in Nigger Joe's yard, a rooster was fucking one of the hens. It was a quick matter, and a moment later the rooster was strutting across the yard like he was ten foot tall and bullet proof.

They got off Dobbin, and no sooner had they hit the ground, then Nigger Joe was beside them, tall and broad shouldered with his freckled face.

"Damn, man," Frank said, "where did you come from?"

Nigger Joe pointed in an easterly direction.

"Shit," Leroy said, "coming up on a man like that could make him bust a heart."

"Want something?" Nigger Joe asked.

"Yeah," Leroy said. "We want you to help track the White Mule and the Spotted Pig, cause Frank here, he's going to race him."

"Pig or mule?" Nigger Joe asked.

"The mule," Leroy said. "He's gonna ride the mule."

"Eat the pig?"

"Well," Leroy said, continuing his role as spokesman, "not right away. But there could come a point."

"He eats the pig, I get half of pig," Nigger Joe said.

"If he eats it, yeah," Leroy said. "Shit, he eats the mule, he'll give you half of that."

"My women like mule meat," Nigger Joe said. "I've eat it, but it don't agree with me. Horse is better," and to strengthen his statement, he gave Dobbin a look over.

"We was thinking," Leroy said, "we could hire you to find the mule and the pig, capture them with us."

"What was you thinking of giving me, besides half the critters if you eat them?"

"How about ten dollars?"

"How about twelve?"

"Eleven."

"Eleven-fifty."

Leroy looked at Frank. Frank sighed and nodded, stuck out his hand. Nigger Joe shook it, then shook Leroy's hand.

Nigger Joe said, "Now, mule runs like the rock, that ain't my fault. I get the eleven-fifty anyway."

Frank nodded.

"Okay, tomorrow morning," Nigger Joe said, "just before light, we'll go look for him real serious and then some."

"Thing does come to me," Frank said, "is haven't other

folks tried to get hold of this mule and pig before? Why are you so confident."

Nigger Joe nodded. "They weren't Nigger Joe."

"You could have tracked them before on your own," Frank said. "Why now?"

Nigger Joe looked at Frank. "Eleven-fifty."

— ◆ —

In the pre-dawn light, down in the swamp, the fog moved through the trees like someone slow-pulling strands of cotton from cotton boles. It wound its way amongst the limbs that were low down, along the ground. There were wisps of it on the water, right near the bank, and as Frank and Leroy and Nigger Joe stood there, they saw what looked like dozens of sticks rise up in the swamp water and move along briskly.

Nigger Jim said, "Cottonmouth snakes. They going with they heads up, looking for anything foolish enough to get out there. You swimming out there now, pretty quick you be bit good and plenty and swole up like old tick. Only you burst all over and spill green poison, and die. Seen it happen."

"Ain't planning on swimming," Frank said.

"Watch your feet," Nigger Joe said. "Them snakes is thick this year. Them cottons and them copperheads. Cottons, they always mad."

"We've seen snakes," Leroy said.

"I know it," Nigger Joe said, "but where we go, they are more than a few, that's what I'm trying to tell you. Back there where mule and pig hides, it's thick in snakes and blackberry vines. And the trees thick like the wool on a sheep. It a goat or a sheep you fucked?"

"For Christsakes," Leroy said. "You heard that too?"

"Wives talk about it when they see you yesterday. There the man who fuck a sheep, or a goat, or some such. Say you ain't a man can get pussy."

"Oh, hell," Leroy said.

"So, tell me some," Nigger Joe said. "Which was it, now."

"Goat," Leroy said.

"That is big nasty," Nigger Joe said, and started walking, leading them along a narrow trail by the water. Frank watched the cotton mouth snakes swim on ahead, their evil heads sticking up like some sort of water devil erections.

The day grew hot and the trees held the hot and made it hotter and made it hard to breathe, like sucking down wool and chunks of flannel. Frank and Leroy sweated their clothes through and their hair turned to wet strings. Nigger Joe, though sweaty, appeared as fresh as a virgin in spring.

"Where you get your hat?" Nigger Joe asked Leroy suddenly, when they stopped for a swig from canteens.

"Seed salesman. My wife knocked him out and I kept the hat."

"Huh, no shit?" Nigger Joe took off his big old hat and waved around. "Bible salesman. He told me I was gonna go to hell, so I beat him up, kept his hat. I shit in his bible case."

"Wow, that's mean," Frank said.

"Him telling me I'm going to hell, that make me real mad. I tell you that to tell you not to forget my eleven-fifty. I'm big on payment."

"You can count on us, we win," Frank said.

"No. You owe me eleven-fifty win or lose." Nigger Joe said this, putting his hat back carefully on his head, looking at the two smaller men like a man about to pick a hen for neck wringing and Sunday dinner.

"Sure," Frank said. "Eleven-fifty, win or lose. Eleven-fifty when we get the pig and the mule."

"Now that's the deal as I see it," Nigger Joe said. "I tell women it's eight dollars, that way I make some whisky money. Nigger Joe didn't get up yesterday. No he didn't.

And when he gets up, he got bible salesman's hat on."

—◆—

They waded through the swamp and through the woods for sometime, and just before dark, Nigger Joe picked up on the mule's unshod tracks. He bent down and looked at them. He said, "We catch him, he's gonna need trimming and shoes. Not enough rock to wear them down. Soft sand and swamp. And here's the pig's tracks. Hell, he's big. Tracks say, three hundred pounds. Maybe more."

"That's no pig," Leroy said. "That's a full blown hog."

"Damn," Frank said. "They're real."

"But can he race?" Leroy said. "And will the pig co-operate?"

They followed the tracks until it turned dark. They threw up a camp, made a fire, and made it big so the smoke was strong, as the mosquitoes were everywhere and hungry and the smoke kept them off a little. They sat there in the night before the fire, the smoke making them cough, watching it churn up above them, through the trees. And up there, as if resting on a limb, was a piece of the moon.

They built the fire up big one last time, turned into their covers, and tried to sleep. Finally, they did, but before morning, Frank awoke, his bladder full, his mind as sharp as if he had slept well. He got up and stoked up the fire, and walked out a few paces in the dark and let it fly. When he looked up to button his pants, he saw through the trees, across a stretch of swamp water, something moving.

He looked carefully, because whatever it was had stopped. He stood very still for a long time, and finally what he had seen moved again. He thought at first it was a deer, but no. There was enough light from the early rising sun knifing through the trees that he could now see clearly what it was.

The White Mule. It stood between two large trees, just looking at him, its head held high, its tall ears alert. The mule was big. Fifteen hands high, like Robert E. Lee, and it was big chested, and its legs were long. Something moved beside it.

The Spotted Pig. It was big and ugly, with one ear turned up and one ear turned down. It grunted once, and the mule snorted, but neither moved.

Frank wasn't sure what to do. He couldn't go tearing across the stretch of swamp after them, since he didn't know how deep it was, and what might be waiting for him. Gators, snakes and sink holes. And by the time he woke up the others, the mule and hog would be gone. He just stood there instead, staring at them. This went on for a long time, and finally the hog turned and started moving away, behind some thicket. The mule tossed its head, turned and followed.

My God, thought Frank. The mule is beautiful. And the hog, he's a pistol. He could tell that from the way it had grunted at him. He had some strange feelings inside of him that he couldn't explain. Some sensation of having had a moment that was greater than any moment he had had before.

He thought it strange these thoughts came to him, but he knew it was the sight of the mule and the hog that had stirred them. As he walked back to the fire and lay down on his blankets, he tried to figure the reason behind that, and only came up with a headache and more mosquito bites.

He closed his eyes and slept a little while longer, thinking of the mule and the hog, and the way they were free and beautiful. And then he thought of the race, and all of that went away, and when he awoke, it was to the toe of Nigger Joe's boot in his ribs.

"Time to do it," Nigger Joe said.

Frank sat up. "I saw them."

"What?" Leroy said, stirring out of his blankets.

Frank told them what he had seen, and how there was nothing he could do then. Told them all this, but didn't tell them how the mule and the hog had made him feel.

"Shit," Leroy said. "You should have woke us."

Nigger Joe shook his head. "No matter. We see over there where they stood. See what tracks they leave us. Then we do the sneak on them."

— ◆ —

They worked their way to the other side of the swamp, swatting mosquitoes and killing a cotton mouth in the process, and when they got to where the mule and the hog stood, they found tracks and mule droppings.

"You not full of shit, like Nigger Joe thinking," Nigger Joe said. "You really see them."

"Yep," Frank said.

Nigger Joe bent down and rubbed some of the mule shit between his fingers, and smelled it. "Not more than a couple hours old."

"Should have got us up," Leroy said.

"Easier to track in the day," Nigger Joe said. "They got their place they stay. They got some hide out."

The mosquitoes were not so bad now, and finally they came to some clear areas, marshy, but clear, and they lost the tracks there, but Nigger Joe said, "The two of them, they probably cross here. It's a good spot. Pick their tracks up in the trees over there, on the soft ground."

When the crossed the marshy stretch, they came to a batch of willows and looked around there. Nigger Joe was the one who found their tracks.

"Here they go," he said. "Here they go."

They traveled through woods and more swamp, and from time to time they lost the tracks, but Nigger Joe always found them. Sometimes Frank couldn't even see what Nigger Joe saw. But Nigger Joe saw something, because he kept looking at the ground, stopping to stretch out on the earth, his face close to it. Sometimes he would pinch the earth between finger and thumb, rub it about. Frank wasn't sure why he did that, and he didn't ask. Like Leroy, he just followed.

Mid-day, they came to a place that amazed Frank. Out there in the middle of what should have been swamp, there was a great clear area, at least a hundred acres. They found it when they came out of a stretch of shady oaks. The air was sweeter there, in the trees, and the shadows were cooling, and at the far edge was a drop of about fifty feet. Down below was the great and natural pasture. A fire, brought on by heat or lightning, might have cleared the place at some point in time. It had grown back without trees, just tall green grass amongst a few rotting, ant-infested stumps. It was surrounded by the oaks, high up on their side, and low down on the other. The oaks on the far side stretched out and blended with sweetgums and black jack and hickory and bursts of pines. From their vantage point they could see all of this, and see the cool shadow on the other side amongst the trees.

A hawk sailed over it all, and Frank saw there was a snake in its beak. Something stirred again inside of Frank, and he was sure it wasn't his last meal. "You're part Indian," Frank said to Nigger Joe. "That hawk and that snake, does it mean something?"

"Means that snake is gonna get et," Nigger Joe said. "Damn trees. Don't you know that make a lot of good hard lumber…Go quiet. Look there."

Coming out of the trees into the great pasture was the mule and the hog. The hog lead the way, and the mule followed close behind. They came out into the sunlight, and pretty soon the hog began to root and the mule began to graze.

"Got their own paradise," Frank said.

"We'll fix that," Leroy said.

They waited there, sitting amongst the oaks, watching, and late in the day the hog and the mule wandered off into the trees across the way.

"Ain't we gonna do something besides watch?" Leroy said.

"They leave, tomorrow they come back," Nigger Joe said. "Got their spot. Be back tomorrow. We'll be ready for them."

—◆—

Just before dark they came down from their place on a little trail and crossed the pasture and walked over to where the mule and the hog had come out of the trees. Nigger Joe looked around for some time, said, "Got a path. Worked it out. Always the same. Same spot. Come through here, out into the pasture. What we do is we get up in a tree. Or I get in tree with my rope, and I rope the mule and tie him off and let him wear himself down."

"He could kill himself, thrashing," Frank said.

"Could kill myself, him thrashing. I think it best tie him to a tree, folks."

Frank translated Nigger Joe's strange way of talking in his head, said, "He dies, you don't get the eleven fifty."

"Not how I understand it," Nigger Joe said.

"That's how it is," Frank said, feeling as if he might be asking for a knife in his belly, his guts spilled. Out here, no one would ever know. Nigger Joe might think he could do that, kill Leroy too, take their money. Course, they didn't have any money. Not here. There was fifteen dollars buried in a jar out back of the house, eleven fifty of which would go to Nigger Joe, if he didn't kill them.

Nigger Joe studied Frank for a long moment. Frank shifted from one foot to the other, trying not to do it, but unable to stop. "Okay," Nigger Joe said. "That will work up good enough."

"What about Mr. Porky?" Leroy asked.

"That gonna be you two's job. I rope damn mule, and you two, you gonna rope damn pig. First, we got to smell like dirt."

"What?" Frank said.

— ◆ —

Nigger Joe rubbed himself down with dark soil. He had Frank and Leroy rub themselves down with it. Leroy hated it and complained, but Frank found the earth smelled like incoming rain, and he thought it pleasant. It felt good on his skin, and he had a sudden strange thought, that when he died, he would become one and the same as the earth, and he wondered how many dead animals, maybe people, made up the dirt he had rubbed onto himself. He felt odd thinking that way. He felt odd thinking in anyway.

They slept for awhile, then Nigger Joe kicked him and Leroy awake. It was still dark when they rolled dirty out of their bed clothes.

"Couldn't we have waited on the dirt," Leroy said, climbing out of his blankets. "It's all in my bed roll."

"Need time for dirt to like you good, so you smell like it," Nigger Joe said. "We put some more on now, rub in the hair good, then get ready."

"It's still dark," Frank said. "They gonna come in the dark? How you know when they're gonna come?"

"They come. But we gotta be ready. They have a good night in farmer's corn fields, they might come real soon, full bellies. Way ground reads, they come here to stand and to wallow. Hog wallows all time, way ground looks. And they shit all over. This their spot. They don't get corn and peas and such, they'll be back here. Water not far from spot, and they got good grass. Under the trees, hog has some acorns.

Hogs like acorns. Wife, Sweetie, makes sometimes coffee from acorns."

"How about I make some regular coffee, made from coffee?" Leroy said.

"Nope. We don't want a smoke smell. Don't want our smell. Need to piss or shit, don't let free here. Go across pasture there. Far side. Dump over there. Piss over there. Use the heel of your shoe to cover it all. Give it lots of dirt."

"Walk all the way across?" Leroy said.

"Want hog and mule," Nigger Joe said. "Walk all the way across. Now, eat some jerky, do your shit over on other side. Put more dirt on. And wait."

— ◆ —

The sun rose up and it got hot, and the dirt on their skins itched, or at least Frank itched, and he could tell Leroy itched, but Nigger Joe, he didn't seem to. Sat silent. And when the early morning was eaten up by the heat, Nigger Joe showed them places to be, and Nigger Joe, with his lasso, climbed up into an oak and sat on a fat limb, his feet stretched along it, his back against the trunk, the rope in his lap.

The place for Frank and Leroy to be was terrible. The dirt they smeared on themselves came from long scoops they made. Then they lay down in the scoops with their ropes, and Nigger Joe, before he climbed the tree, tossed leaves and sticks and dirt and bits of mule and hog shit over them. The way they lay, Frank and Leroy were twenty feet apart, on either side of what Nigger Joe said was a trail the hog and mule traveled. It wasn't much of a trail. A bit of ruffled oak leaves, some wallows the hog had made.

The day crawled forward and so did the worms. They were all around Frank, and it was all he could do not to jump up screaming. It wasn't that he was afraid of them. He had put a many of them on hooks for fishing. But to just lay there and have them squirm against your arm, your neck. And there was something that bit. Something in the hog shit was Frank's thought.

Frank heard a sound. A different sound. Being close to the ground it seemed to move the earth. It was the slow careful plodding of the mule's hooves, and another sound. The hog, maybe.

They listened and waited and the sounds came closer, and then Frank, lying there, trying not to tremble with anticipation, heard a whizzing sound. The rope. And then there was a bray, and a scuffle sound.

Frank lifted his head slightly.

Not ten feet from him was the great white mule, the rope around its neck, the length of it stretching up into the tree. Frank could see Nigger Joe. He had wrapped the rope around the limb and was holding onto it, tugging, waiting for the mule to wear itself out.

The hog was bounding about near the mule, as if it might jump up and grab the rope and chew it in two. It actually went up on its hind legs once.

Frank knew it was time. He burst out of his hiding place, and Leroy came out of his. The hog went straight for Leroy. Frank darted in front of the leaping mule and threw his rope and caught the hog around the neck. It turned instantly and went for him.

Leroy dove and grabbed the hog's hind leg. The hog kicked him in the face, but Leroy hung on. The hog dragged Leroy across the ground, going for Frank, and as his rope become more slack, Frank darted for a tree.

By the time Frank arrived at the tree trunk, Leroy had managed to put his rope around the hog's hind leg, and now Frank and Leroy had the hog in a kind of tug of war.

"Don't hurt him now some," Nigger Joe yelled from the

tree. "Got to keep him up for it. He's the mule leader. Makes him run."

"What the hell did he say?" Frank said.

"Don't hurt the goddamn pig," Leroy said.

"Ha," Frank said, tying off his end of the rope to a tree trunk. Leroy stretched his end, giving the hog a little slack, and tied off to another tree. Nearby the mule leaped and kicked.

Leroy made a move to try and grab the rope on the mule up short, but the mule whipped as if on a Yankee dollar, and kicked Leroy smooth in the chest, launching him over the hog and into the brush. The hog would have had him then, but the rope around its neck and back leg held it just short of Leroy, but close enough a string of hog spittle and snot was flung across Leroy's face.

"Goddamn," Leroy said, as he inched farther away from the hog.

For a long while, they watched the mule kick and buck and snort and snap its large teeth.

It was near nightfall when the mule, exhausted, settled down on its front knees first, then rolled over on its side. The hog scooted across the dirt and came to rest near the great mule, its snout resting on the mule's flank.

"I'll be damned," Leroy said. "The hogs girlie or something."

It took three days to get back, because the mule wasn't co-operating, and the hog was no pushover either. They had to tie logs on either side of the hog, so that he had to drag them. It wore the hog down, but it wore the men down too, because the logs would tangle in vines and roughs, and constantly had to be removed. The mule was hobbled loosely, so that it could walk, but couldn't bolt. The mule was lead by Nigger Joe, and fastened around the mule's waist was a rope with two rope lines leading off to the rear.

They were in turn fastened to a heavy log that kept the mule from bolting forward to have a taste of Nigger Joe, and to keep him, like the hog, worn down.

At night they left the logs on the critters, and built make-do corrals of vines and limbs and bits of leather straps.

By the time they were out of the woods and the swamp, the mule and the hog were covered in dirt and mud and such. The animals heaved as they walked, and Frank feared they might keel over and die.

They made it though, and they took the mule up to Nigger Joe's. He had a corral there. It wasn't much, but it was solid and it held the mule in. The hog they put in a small pen. There was hardly room for the hog to turn around. Now that the hog was well placed, Frank stood by the pen and studied the animal. It looked at him with a feral eye. This wasn't a hog who had been slopped and watered. This was an animal who early on had escaped into the wild, as a pig, and had made his way to adulthood. His spotted hide was covered in scars, and though he had a coating of fat on him, his body was long and muscular, and when the hog flexed its shoulders to startle a fly, those muscles rolled beneath its skin like snakes beneath a tight-stretched blanket.

The mule, after the first day, began to perk up. But he didn't do much. Stood around mostly, and when they walked away for a distance, it began to trot the corral, stopping often to look out at the hog pen, at his friend. The mule made a sound, and the hog made a sound back.

"Damn, if I don't think they're talking to one another," Leroy said.

"Oh yeah. You can bet. They do that all right," Nigger Joe said.

— ◆ —

The race was coming closer, and within the week, Leroy and Nigger Joe had the mule's hooves trimmed, but no shoes. Decided he didn't need them, as the ground was soft this time of year. They got him saddled. Leroy got bucked off and kicked and bitten once, a big plug was out of his right elbow.

"Mean one," Nigger Joe said. "Real bastard, this mule. Strong. He got the time, he eat Leroy."

"Do you think he can run?" Frank asked.

"Time to see soon," Nigger Joe said.

That night, when the saddling and bucking was done, the mule began to wear down, let Nigger Joe stay on his back. As a reward, Nigger Joe fed the mule well, but with only a little water. He fed the hog some pulled up weeds, a bit of corn, watered him.

"Want mule strong, but hog weak," Nigger Joe said. "Don't want hog strong enough to do digging out of pen that's for some sure."

Frank listened to this, wondering where Nigger Joe had learned his American.

Nigger Joe went in for the night, his two wives calling him to supper. Leroy walked home. Frank saddled up Dobbin, but before he left, he led the horse out to the corral and starred at the mule. There in the starlight, the beams settled around the mule's head, and made it very white. The mud was gone now and the mule had been groomed, cleaned of briars and burrs from the woods, and the beast looked magnificent. Once Frank had seen a book. It was the only book he had ever seen other than the bible, which his mother owned. But he had seen this one in the window of the General Store downtown. He hadn't opened the book, just looked at it through the window. There on the cover was a white horse with wings on its back. Well, the mule didn't look like a horse, and it didn't have wings on its back, but it certainly had the bearing of the beast on the book's cover. Like maybe it was from somewhere else other than here; like the sky had ripped open and the mule had ridden into this world through the tear.

Frank led Dobbin over to the hog pen. There was nothing beautiful about the spotted hog. It stared up at him, and the starlight filled its eyes and made them sharp and bright as shrapnel.

As Frank was riding away, he heard the mule make a sound, then the hog. They did it more than once, and were still doing it when he rode out of earshot.

—◆—

It took some doing, and it took some time, and Frank, though he did little but watch, felt as if he were going to work every day. It was a new feeling for him. His Old Man often made him work, but as he grew older he had quit, just like his father. The fields rarely got attention, and being drunk became more important than hoeing corn and digging taters. But here he was not only showing up early, but staying all day, handing harness and such to Nigger Joe and Leroy, bringing out feed and pouring water.

In time Nigger Joe was able to saddle up the mule with no more than a snort from the beast, and he could ride about the pen without the mule turning to try and bite him or buck him. He even stopped kicking at Nigger Joe and Leroy, who he hated, when they first entered the pen.

The hog watched all of this through the slats of his pen, his beady eyes slanting tight, its battle torn ears flicking at flies, its curly tail curled even tighter. Frank wondered what the hog was thinking. He was certain, whatever it was, was not good.

Soon enough, Nigger Joe had Frank enter the pen, climb up in the saddle. Sensing a new rider, the mule threw him.

But the second time he was on board, the mule trotted him around the corral, running lightly with that kind of rolling barrel run mules have.

"He's about ready for a run, he is," Nigger Joe said.

—◆—

Frank led the mule out of the pen and out to the road, Leroy following. Nigger Joe led Dobbin. "See he'll run that way. Not so fast at first," Nigger Joe said. "Me and this almost dead horse, we follow and find you, you ain't neck broke in some ditch somewheres."

Cautiously, Frank climbed on the white mule's back. He took a deep breath, then settling himself in the saddle, he gave the mule a kick.

The mule didn't move.

He kicked again.

The mule trotted down the road about twenty feet, then turned, dipped its head into the grass that grew alongside the red clay road, and took a mouthful.

Frank kicked at the mule some more, but the mule wasn't having any. He did move, but just a bit. A few feet down the road, then across the road and into the grass, amongst the trees, biting leaves off of them with a sharp snap of his head, a smack of his teeth.

Nigger Joe trotted up on Dobbin.

"You ain't going so fast."

"Way I see it too," Frank said. "He ain't worth a shit."

"We not bring the hog in on some business yet."

"How's that gonna work? I mean, how's he gonna stay around and not run off."

"Maybe hog run off in goddamn woods and not see again, how it may work. But, nothing else, hitch mule to plow or sell. You done paid me eleven fifty."

"Your job isn't done," Frank said.

"You say, and may be right, but we got the one card, the hog, you see. He don't deal out with an ace, we got to call him a joker, and call us assholes, and the mule, we got to make what we can. We have to, shoot and eat the hog. Best, keep him up a few more days, put some corn in him, make him better than what he is. Fatter. The mule, I told you ideas. Hell, eat mule too if nothing other works out."

— ◆ —

They let the hog out of the pen.

Or rather Leroy did. Just picked up the gate, and out came the hog. The hog didn't bolt. It bounded over to the mule, on which Frank was mounted. The mule dipped its head, touched noses with the hog.

"I'll be damn," Frank said, thinking, he had never had a friend like that. Leroy was as close as it got, and he had to watch Leroy. He'd cheat you. And if you had a goat, he might fuck it. Leroy was no real friend. Frank felt lonesome.

Nigger Joe took the bridle on the mule away from Frank, and led them out to the road. The hog trotted beside the mule.

"Now, story is, hog likes to run," Nigger Joe said. "And when he run, mule follows. And then hog, he falls off, not keeping up, and mule, he got the arrow-sight then, run like someone put turpentine on his nut sack. Or that the story as I hear it. You?"

"Pretty close," Frank said.

Frank took the reins back, and the hog stood beside the mule. Nothing happened.

"Gonna say go, is what I'm to do here now. And when I say, you kick mule real goddamn hard. Me, I'm gonna stick boot in hog's big ass. Hear me now, Frank?"

"I do."

"Signal will be me shouting when kick the hog's ass, okay?"

"Okay."

"Ready some."

"Ready."

Nigger Joe yelled, "Git, hog," and kicked the hog in the ass with all his might. The hog did a kind of hop, and bolted. A hog can move quick for its size for a short distance, haul some serious freight, and the old spotted hog, he was really fast, hauling the whole freight line. Frank expected the hog to dart into the woods, and be long gone. But it didn't. The hog bounded down the road running for all it was worth, and before Frank could put his heels to the mule, the mule leaped. That was the only way to describe it. The mule did not seemed cocked to fire, but suddenly it was a white bullet, lunging forward so fast Frank nearly flew out of the saddle. But he clung, and the mule ran, and the hog ran, and after a bit, the mule ducked its head and the hog began to fade. But the mule was no longer following the hog. Not even close. It snorted, and its nose appeared to get long and the ears laid back flat. The mule jetted by the fat porker and stretched its legs wider, and Frank could feel the wind whipping cool on his face. The body of the mule rolled like a barrel, but man, my God, thought Frank, this sonofabitch can run.

There was one problem. Frank couldn't turn him. When he felt the mule had gone far enough, it just kept running, and no amount of tugging led to response. That booger was gone. Frank just leaned forward over the mule's neck, hung on, and let him run.

Eventually the mule quit, just stopped, dipped its head to the ground, then looked left and right. Trying to find the hog, Frank figured. It was like the mule had gone into a kind of spell, and now he was out of it and wanted his friend.

He could turn the mule then. He trotted it back down the road, not trying to get it to run anymore, just letting it trot, and when it came upon Nigger Joe and Leroy, standing in the road, the hog came out of the woods and moseyed up beside the mule.

As Nigger Joe reached up and took the mule's reins, he said, "See that there. Hog and him are buddies. He stays around. He don't want to run off. Wants to be with mule. Hog a goddamn fool. Could be long gone, out in the woods. Find some other wild hog and fuck it. Eat acorns. Die of old age. Now he gonna get et sometime."

"Dumb shit hog," Leroy said.

The mule tugged at the reins, dipped its head. The hog and the mule's noses came together. The mule snorted. The hog made a kind of squealing sound.

—◆—

They trained for several days the same way. The hog would start, and then the mule would run. Fast. They put the mule up at night in the corral, hobbled, and the hog, they didn't have to pen him anymore. He stayed with the mule by choice.

One day, after practice, Frank said, "He seems pretty fast."

"Never have seen so fast," Nigger Joe said. "He's moving way good."

"Do you think he can win?" Leroy said.

"He can win, they let us bring hog in. No hog. Not much on the run. Got to have hog. But there's one mule give him trouble. Dynamite. He runs fast too. Might can run faster."

"You think?"

"Could be. I hear he can go lickity split. Tomorrow, we find out, hey?"

—◆—

The world was made of men and mules and dogs and one hog. There were women too, most of them with parasols. Some sitting in the rows of chairs at the starting line, their legs tucked together primly, their dresses pulled down tight to the ankles. The air smelled of early summer morning and hot mule shit and sweat and perfume, cigar smoke, beer and farts. Down from it all, in tents, were other women who smelled different and wore less clothes. The women with parasols would not catch their eye, but some of the men would, many when their wives or girls were not looking.

Frank was not interested. He couldn't think of anything but the race. Leroy was with him, and of course, Nigger Joe. They brought the mule in, Nigger Joe leading him. Frank on Old Dobbin, Leroy riding double. And the hog, loose, on its own, strutting as if he were the one throwing the whole damn shindig.

The mules at the gathering were not getting along. There were bites and snorts and kicks. The mules could kick backwards, and they could kick out sideways like cattle. You had to watch them.

White Mule was surprisingly docile. It was as if his balls had been clipped. He walked with his head down, the pig trotting beside him.

As they neared the forming line of mules, Frank looked at them. Most were smaller than the white mule, but there was one that was bigger, jet black, and had a roaming eye, as if he might be searching for victims. He had a big hard on and it was throbbing in the sunlight like a fat cotton mouth.

"That mule there, big dicked one, " Nigger Joe said pausing. "He the kind get a hard on he gonna race or fight, maybe quicker than the fuck, you see. He's the one to watch. Anything that like the running or fighting better than pussy, him, you got to keep the eye on."

"That's Dynamite," Leroy said. "Got all kinds of mule muscle, that's for sure."

White Mule saw Dynamite, lifted his head high and threw back his ears and snorted.

"Oh, yeah," said Leroy. "There's some shit between them already."

"Somebody gonna outrun somebody or fuck other in ass, that's what I tell you for sure. Maybe they fight some too. Whole big blanket of business here."

White Mule wanted to trot, and Nigger Joe had to run a little to keep up with him. They went right through a clutch of mules about to be lined up, and moved quickly so that White Mule was standing beside Dynamite. The two mules looked at one another and snorted. In that moment, the owner of Dynamite slipped blinders on Dynamite's head, tossing off the old bridal to a partner.

The spotted hog slid in between the feet of his mule, stood with his head poking out beneath his buddy's legs, looking up with his ugly face, flaring his nostrils, narrowing his cave-dark eyes.

Dynamite's owner was Levi Crone, one big gent in a dirty white shirt with the sleeves ripped out. He had a big red face and big fat muscles and a belly like a big iron wash pot. He wore a hat you could have bathed in. He was as tall as Nigger Joe, six foot two or more. Hands like hams, feet like boats. He looked at the White Mule, said, "That ain't the story mule is it?"

"One and the same," Frank said, as if he had raised the white mule from a colt.

"I heard someone had him. That he had been caught. Catch and train him?"

"Me and my partners."

"You mean Leroy and the nigger?"

"Yeah."

"That the hog in the stories, too, I guess?"

"Yep," Frank said.

"What's he for? A step stool?"

"He runs with the mule. For a ways."

"That ain't allowed."

"Where say can't do it, huh?" Nigger Joe asked.

Crone thought. "Nowhere, but it stands to reason."

"What about rule can't run with the dick hard," Nigger Joe said, pointing at Dynamite's member.

"Ain't no rule like that," Crone said. "Mule can't help that."

"Ain't no rule about goddamn hog none either," Nigger Joe said.

"It don't matter," Crone said. "You got this mule from hell, given to you by the goddamn red-assed devil his ownself, and you got the pork chop there too from the same place, it ain't gonna matter. Dynamite here, he's gonna outrun him. Gets finished, he'll fuck your mule in the ass and shit a turd on him."

"Care to make a bet on the side some?" Nigger Joe said.

"Sure," Crone said. "I'll bet you all till my money runs out. That ain't good enough, I'll arm wrestle you or body wrestle you or see which of us can shoot jack-off the farthest. You name it speckled nigger."

Nigger Joe studied Crone as if he might be thinking about where to make all the prime cuts, but he finally just grinned, got out ten of the eleven-fifty he had been paid. "There mine. You got some holders?"

"Ten dollars. I got sight of it, and I got your word, which better be good," Crone said.

"Where's your money?" Leroy said.

Crone pulled out a wad from his front pocket, presented it with open palm as if he might be giving a teacher an apple. He looked at Leroy, said, "You gonna trade a goat? I hear you like goats."

"Okay," Leroy said. "Okay. I fucked a goddamn goat. What of it?"

Crone laughed at him. He shook the money at Nigger Joe. "Good enough?"

"Okay," Nigger Joe said.

"Here's three dollars," Frank said, dug in his pocket, held it so Crone could see.

Crone nodded.

Frank slipped the money back in his pocket.

"Well," Leroy said. "I ain't got shit, so I just throw out my best wishes."

"You boys could bet the mule," Crone said.

"That could be an idea," Leroy said.

"No," Frank said. "We won't do that."

"Ain't we partners?" Leroy said, taking off his seed salesman hat.

"We got a deal," Frank said, "but I'm the one paid Nigger Joe for catching and training. So, I decide. And that's about as partner as we get."

Leroy shrugged, put the seed salesman's hat back on.

—◆—

The mules lined up and it was difficult to make them stay the line. Dynamite, still toting serious business on the undercarriage, lined up by White Mule, stood at least a shoulder above him. Both wore blinders now, but they turned their heads and looked at one another. Dynamite snapped at the white mule, who moved quickly, nearly throwing Frank from the saddle. White Mule snapped back at Dynamite's nose, grazing him. He threw a little kick sideways that made Dynamite shuffle to his right.

There was yelling from the judges, threats of disqualification, though no one expected that. The crowd had already figured this race out. White Mule, the forest legend, and Dynamite, of the swinging big dick, they were the two to watch.

Leroy and Nigger Joe had pulled the hog back with a rope, but now they brought him out and let him stand in front of his mule. They had to talk to the judges on the matter, explain. There wasn't any rule for or against it. One judge said he didn't like the idea. One said the hog would get trampled to death anyway. Another said, shit, why not. Final decision, they let the hog stay in the race.

—◆—

So the mules and the hog and the riders lined up, the hog just slightly to the side of the white mule. The hog looked over its shoulder at Nigger Joe standing behind him. By now the hog knew what was coming. A swift kick in the ass.

Frank climbed up on the white mule, and a little guy with a face like a timber axe, climbed up on Crone's mule, Dynamite.

Out front of the line was a little bald man in a loose shirt and suspenders holding up his high-water pants, showing his scuffed and broken-laced boots. He had a pistol in his hand. He has a voice loud as Nester on the Greek line.

"Now, we got us a mule race today, ladies and gentleman. And there will be no cheatin', or there will be disqualification, and a butt-beating you can count on to be remembered by everyone, 'specially the cheater. What I want now, line of mules and riders, is a clean race. This here path is wide enough for all twenty of you, and you can't fan too much to the right or left, as we got folks all along the run watching. You got to keep up pretty tight. Now, there might be some biting and kicking, and that's to be expected. From the mules. You riders got to be civil. Or mostly. A little out of line is all right, but no knives or guns or such. Everyone understand and ain't got no questions, let up a shout."

A shout came from the line. The mules stirred, stepped back, stepped forward.

"Anybody don't understand what I just said? Anyone not speak Texan or 'Merican here that's gonna race?"

No response.

"All right, then. Watch women and children, and try not to run over the men or the whores neither. I'm gonna step over there to the side, and I'm gonna raise this pistol, and when you hear the shot, there you go. May the best mule and the best rider win. Oh, yeah. We got a hog in the race too. He ain't supposed to stay long. Just kind of lead. No problems with that from anybody, is there?"

There were no complaints.

"All right, then."

The judge stepped briskly to the side of the road and raised his old worn .36 Navy at the sky and got an important look on his face. Nigger Joe removed the rope from the pig's neck and found a solid position between mules and behind the hog. He cocked his foot back.

The judge fired his pistol. Nigger Joe kicked the hog in the ass. The mule line charged forward.

The hog, running for all it was worth surged forward as well, taking the lead even. White Mule and Dynamite ran dead even. The mules ran so hard a cloud of dust was thrown up. The mules and the men and the hog were swallowed by it. Frank, seeing nothing but dust, coughed and cursed and lay tight against the white mule's neck, and squinted his eyes. He feared, without the white mule being able to see the hog, he might bolt. Maybe run into another mule, throw him into a stampede, get him stomped flat. But as they ran the cloud moved behind them, and when Frank came coughing out of the cloud, he was amazed to see the hog was well out in front, running as if he could go like that all the way to Mexico.

To his right, Frank saw Dynamite and his little axe-faced

rider. The rider looked at him and smiled with gritty teeth. "You gonna get run into a hole, shit breath."

"Shitass," Frank said. It was the best he could come up with, but he threw it out with meaning.

Dynamite was leading the pack now, leaving the white mule and the others behind, throwing dust in their face. White Mule saw Dynamite start to straighten out in front of him, and he moved left, nearly knocking against a mule on that side. Frank figured it was so he could see the hog. The hog was moving his spotted ass on down the line.

"Git him, White Mule," Frank said, and leaned close to the mule's left ear, rubbed the side of the mule's neck, then rested his head close on his mane. The white mule focused on the hog and started hauling some ass. He went lower and his strides got longer and the barrel back and belly rolled. When Frank looked up, the hog was bolting left, across the path of a dozen mules, just making it off the trail before taking a tumble under hooves. He fell, rolled over and over in the grass.

Frank thought: Shit, White Mule, he's gonna bolt, gonna go after the hog. But, nope, he was true to the trail, and closing on Dynamite. The spell was on. And now the other mules were moving up too, taking a whipping, getting their sides slapped hard enough Frank could hear it, thing it sounded like Papa's belt on his back.

"Come on, White Mule. You don't need no hittin', don't need no hard heels. You got to outrun that hard dick for your own sake."

It was as if White Mule understood him. White Mule dropped lower and his strides got longer yet. Frank clung for all he was worth, fearing the saddle might twist and lose him.

But no, Leroy, for all his goat-fucking and seed salesman hat stealing, could fasten harness and belly bands better than anyone that walked.

The trail became shady as they moved into a line of oaks on either side of the road. For a long moment the shadows were so thick they ran in near darkness. Then there were patches of lights through the leaves and the dust was lying closer to the ground and the road was sun-baked and harder and showing clay the color of a poison-ivy rash.

Scattered here and there along the road were viewers. A few in chairs. Most standing.

Frank ventured a look over his shoulder. The other mules and riders were way back, and some of them were already starting to falter. He noticed a couple of the mules were rid-erless, and one had broken rank with its rider and was off trail, cutting across the grass, heading toward the creek that twisted down amongst a line of willow trees.

As White Mule closed on Dynamite, the mule took a snapping bite at Dynamite's tail, jerking its head back with teeth full tail hair.

Dynamite tried to turn and look, but his rider pulled his head back into line. White Mule lunged forward, going even lower than before. Lower than Frank had ever seen him go. Lower than he thought he could go. Now White Mule was pulling up on Dynamite's left. Dynamite's rider jerked Dynamite back into the path in front of White Mule. Frank wheeled his mount to the right side of Dynamite. In mid-run, Dynamite wheeled and kicked, hit White Mule in the side hard enough there was an explosion of breath that made Frank think his mule would go down.

Dynamite pulled ahead.

White Mule was not so low now. He was even stagger-ing a little as he ran.

"Easy, boy," Frank said. "You can do it. You're the best goddam mule ever ran a road."

White Mule began to run evenly again, or as even as a

mule can run. He began to stretch out again, going low. Frank was surprised to see they were closing on Dynamite again.

Frank looked back.

No one was in sight. Just a few twists of dust, a ripple of heat waves. It was White Mule and Dynamite, all the way.

As Frank and White Mule passed Dynamite, Frank noted Dynamite didn't run with a hard-on anymore. Dynamite's rider let the mule turn its head and snap at White Mule. Frank, without really thinking about it, slipped his foot from the saddle and kicked the mule in the jaw.

"Hey," yelled Dynamite's rider. "Stop that."

"Hey, shitass," Frank said. "You better watch…that limb."

Dynamite and his rider had let White Mule push them to the right side of the road, near the trees, and a low hanging hickory limb was right in line with them. The rider ducked it by a half inch, losing only his cap.

Shouldn't have told him, thought Frank. What he was hoping was to say something smart just as the limb caught the bastard. That would have made it choice, seeing the little axe-faced shit take it in the teeth. But he had outsmarted his own self.

"Fuck," Frank said.

Now they were thundering around a bend, and there were lots of people there, along both sides. There had been a spot of people here and there, along the way, but now they were everywhere.

Must be getting to the end of it, thought Frank.

Dynamite had lost a step for a moment, allowing White Mule to move ahead, but now he was closing again. Frank looked up. He could see that a long red ribbon was stretched across in front of them. It was almost the end.

Dynamite lit a fuse.

He came up hard and on the left, and begin to pass. The

axe-faced rider slapped out with the long bride and caught Frank across the face.

"You goddamn turd," Frank said, and slashed out with his own bridal, missing by six inches. Dynamite and axe-face pulled ahead.

Frank turned his attention back to the finish line. Thought: this is it. White Mule was any lower to the ground he'd have a belly full of gravel, stretched out any farther, he'd come apart. He's gonna be second. And no prize.

"You done what you could," Frank said, putting his mouth close to the bobbing head of the mule, rubbing the side of his neck with the tips of his fingers.

White Mule brought out the reinforcements. He was low and he was stretched, but now his legs were moving even faster, and for a long, strange moment, Frank thought the mule had sprung wings, like that horse he had seen on the front of the book so long ago. There didn't feel like there was any ground beneath them.

Frank couldn't believe it. Dynamite was falling behind, snorting and blowing, his body lathering up as if he were soaped.

White Mule leaped through the red ribbon a full three lengths ahead to win.

Frank let White Mule run past the watchers, on until he slowed and began to trot, and then walk. He let the mule go on like that for some time, then he gently pulled the reins and got out of the saddle. He walked the mule a while. Then he stopped and unbuttoned the belly band. He slid the saddle into the dirt. He pulled the bridle off of the mule's head.

The mule turned and looked at him.

"You done your part," Frank said, and swung the bridle gently against the mule's ass. "Go on."

White Mule sort of skipped forward and began running

down the road, then turned into the trees. And was gone.

Frank walked all the way back to the beginning of the race, the viewers amazed he was without his mule.

But he was still the winner.

"You let him go?" Leroy said. "After all we went through, you let him go?"

"Yep," Frank said.

Nigger Joe shook his head. "Could have run him again. Plowed him. Ate him."

Frank took his prize money from the judges and side bet from Crone, paid Leroy his money, watched Nigger Joe follow Crone away from the race's starting line, on out to Crone's horse and wagon. Dynamite, his head down, was being led to the wagon by axe-face.

Frank knew what was coming. Nigger Joe had not been paid, and on top of that, he was ill tempered. As Frank watched, Nigger Joe hit Crone and knocked him flat. No one did anything.

Black man or not, you didn't mess with Nigger Joe.

Nigger Joe took his money from Crone's wallet, punched the axe-faced rider in the nose for the hell of it, and walked back in their direction.

Frank didn't wait. He went over to where the hog lay on the grass. His front and back legs had been tied and a kid about thirteen was poking him with a stick. Frank slapped the kid in the back of the head, knocking his hat off. The kid bolted like a deer.

Frank got Dobbin and called Nigger Joe over. "Help me."

Nigger Joe and Frank loaded the hog across the back of Dobbin as if he were a sack of potatoes. Heavy as the porker was, it was accomplished with some difficulty, the hog's head hanging down on one side, his feet on the other. The hog seemed defeated. He hardly even squirmed.

"Misses that mule," Nigger Joe said.

"You and me got our business done, Joe," Frank asked.
Nigger Joe nodded.

Frank took Dobbin's reins and started leading him away.

"Wait," Leroy said.

Frank turned on him. "No. I'm through with you. You and me. We're quits."

"What?" Leroy said.

Frank pulled at the reins and kept walking. He glanced back once to see Leroy standing where they had last spoke, standing in the road looking at him, wearing the seed salesman's hat.

— ◆ —

Frank put the hog in the old hog pen at his place and fed him good. Then he ate and poured out all the liquor he had, and waited until dark. When it came he sat on a large rock out back of the house. The wind carried the urine smell of all those out the window pees to his nostrils. He kept his place.

— ◆ —

The moon was near full that night and it had risen high above the world and its light was bright and silver. Even the old ugly place looked good under that light.

Frank sat there for a long time, finally dozed. He was awakened by the sound of wood cracking. He snapped his head up and looked out at the hog pen. The mule was there. He was kicking at the slats of the pen, trying to free his friend.

Frank got up and walked out there. The mule saw him, ran back a few paces, stared at him.

"Knew you'd show," Frank said. "Just wanted to see you one more time. Today, buddy, you had wings."

The mule turned its head and snorted.

Frank lifted the gate to the pen and the hog ran out. The

hog stopped beside the mule and they both looked at Frank.

"It's all right," Frank said. "I ain't gonna try and stop you."

The mule dipped its nose to the hog's snout and they pressed them together. Frank smiled. The mule and the hog wheeled suddenly, as if by agreed signal, and raced toward the rickety rail fence near the hill.

The mule, with one beautiful leap, jumped the fence, seemed pinned in the air for a long time, held there by the rays of the moon. The way the rays fell, for a strange short instant, it seemed as if he were sprouting gossamer wings.

The hog wiggled under the bottom rail and the two of them ran across the pasture, between the trees and out of sight. Frank didn't have to go look to know that the mule had jumped the other side of the fence as well, that the hog had worked his way under. And that they were gone.

When the sun came up and Frank was sure there was no wind, he put a match to a broom's straw and used it to start the house afire, then the barn and the rotten out-buildings. He kicked the slats on the hog pen until one side of it fell down.

He went out to where Dobbin was tied to a tree, saddled and ready to go. He mounted him and turned his head toward the rail fence and the hill. He looked at it for a long time. He gave a gentle nudge to Dobbin with his heels and started out of there, on down toward the road and town.

Bill, the Little Steam Shovel

Bill the Little Steam Shovel was very excited. He was getting a fresh coat of blue paint from Dave the Steam Shovel Man in the morning, and the thought of that made him so happy he secreted oil through his metal. He had been sitting idle in the big garage since he had been made and he was ready to go out into the world to do his first job.

The first of many.

He was going to move big mounds of dirt and big piles of rocks. He was going to make basements for schools and hospitals. He was going to clear land for playgrounds so good little boys and good little girls would have a place for swings and merry-go-rounds and teeter-totters. He was going to move big trees and flatten hills so farmers could grow good food for the good little boys and girls to eat. He was going to clear land for churches and synagogues and cathedrals and mosques and buildings for the worship of Vishnu, Voudan, and such.

He was so happy.

So eager.

He hoped he wouldn't fuck up.

At night, all alone in the big garage, he thought about a lot of things. The work he wanted to do. How well he wanted to do it. The new coat of paint he was going to get. And sometimes he slept and had the dreams. Thinking about the dreams made his metal turn cold and his manifold blow leaky air.

What was happening to him on those long nights in the dark corner of the garage, waiting for his coat of paint and his working orders, was unclear to him. He knew only that he didn't like it and the dreams came to him no matter how much he thought about the good things, and the dreams were about falling great distances and they were about the dark. A dark so black, stygian was as bright as fresh-lit candle. One moment he seemed to be on solid support, the next, he was in mid-air, and down he would go, sailing through the empty blackness, and when he hit the ground, it was like, suddenly, he was as flexible as an accordion, all his metal wadded and crunched, his steam shovel knocked all the way back to his ass end. Dave, The Steam Shovel Man, crunched in the cab, was squirting out like a big bag of busted transmission fluid.

Then he would pop awake, snapping on his head beams, disturbing others in the garage, and from time to time, Butch The Big Pissed-Off Steam Shovel would throb his engine and laugh.

"You just a big Tinker Toy," Butch would say.

Bill wasn't sure what a Tinker Toy was, but he didn't like the sound of it. But he didn't say anything, because Butch would whip his ass. Something Butch would remind him of in his next wheezing breath.

"I could beat you to a pile of metal flakes with my shovel. You just a big Tinker Toy."

There was one thing that Bill thought about that helped him through the long nights, even when he had the dreams. And that was Miss Maudie. The little gold steam shovel with the great head beams that perked high and the little tail pipe that looked so...Well, there was no other way he could think of it...So open and inviting, dark and warm and full of dismissed steam that could curl around your dip stick like...No. That was vulgar and Miss Maudie would

certainly not think of him that way. She was too classy. Too fine. Bill thanked all the metal in Steam Shovel Heaven that she was made the way she was.

Oh, but Heaven Forbid, and in the name of Jayzus, The Steam Shovel Who Had Died For His Sins and all Steam Shovel's sins by allowing himself to be worked to a frazzle and ran off a cliff by a lot of uncaring machines of the old religion, in his name, he shouldn't think such things.

He was a good little steam shovel. Good little steam shovels didn't think about that sort of business, about dipping their oil sticks down good, little, girl, steam shovel's, tail pipes, even if it probably felt damn good. The Great Steam Shovel in The Sky on The Great Expanse of Red Clay, and Jayzus and The Holy Roller Ghost, would know his thoughts, and it would be a mark against him, and when it was his time to be before the door of the Big Garage in the Sky, he would not meet his maker justified, but would be sent way down there to the scrap heap where flames leaped and metal was scorched and melted, twisted and crushed, but never died.

Besides, why would anyone as neat and bright with such big head beams and that fine tail pipe think of him? He didn't even have his coat of paint yet. Here he was, brand new, but not painted. He was gray as a storm cloud and just sitting, having never done work before. And he was a cheap machine at that, made from cheap parts: melted toasters, vacuums, refrigerators and such.

Maudie looked to be made from high quality steel, like Butch, who eyed her and growled at her from time to time and made her flutter. Happily or fearfully, Bill could not determine. Perhaps both.

But Bill was just a cheap little machine made to do good hard work for all the good little children in the world, and the men and women who made him—

Then Bill saw his Dave.

—◆—

Dave came into the building, slid the door way open to let in the morning air, went to a corner of the garage, moved something on the front of his pants and took out his little poker and let fly with steaming water, going, "Oooooooh, yeah, the pause that refreshes, the envy of all race horses."

Now I know why it stinks in here, Bill thought. Hadn't seen that before, but now I have. He's letting juice out of himself. Smells worse than transmission fluid, oil, or windshield cleaner. Don't the Daves get an oil change?

Dave went out again, came back with a paint gun and a big canister of blue paint fastened to it. He started right in on Bill.

"How's that, Bill?" Dave said, "How's that feel?"

Bill cranked his motor and purred.

"Oh, yeah, now you're digging it," Dave said.

Dave used several canisters, and soon Bill was as blue as the sky. Or, at least he's always heard that the sky was

blue when the pollution was light. He spent all his time in the garage, where he was built and where he had set for months, listening to the other steam shovels and diggers and such, so, he didn't know blue from green. He was just a little machine with an eager engine and a desire to do good, and Dave had promised to paint him blue, so he figured the color on him, the paint coming out of the sprayer, must be blue, and it must be the color of the sky.

When Dave finished with the paint, he brought out a big hand held dryer and went over Bill with that. The dryer felt warm on Bill's metal, and when that was done, Dave took a long bristly device and poked it down his steam pipe and made Bill jump a little.

"Easy, boy. You'll get used to this."

The bristle worked inside to clean him, but Bill knew he wasn't dirty. This made him wonder about Dave, him doing this, smiling while he did, poking fast as he could in the ole pipe. But, then again, it did feel pretty good.

When Dave finished, he said, "When you go to work, little fella, make me proud."

On the way out, Dave stopped by Miss Maudie, bent looked up her tail pipe, said, "Clean. Really clean," and departed.

—◆—

That day, because of the new coat of paint, the finishing touch, Bill thought he would be sent to work. Dave had said so. But no. The day went by and the other steam shovels, including Miss Maudie, went out to do their work, but he remained inside, fresh and blue and unused.

That night, when the steam shovels returned, he was still in his place, and they, tired, weaving their shovels and dragging their treads, were hosed down by the other Daves, rubbed with rags and oiled and put away for the night.

What was wrong with him? thought Bill.

Why are they not using me to build roads and schools and churches and synagogues and all that shit?

What's up with that?

Night came and shadows fell through the windows and made the barn dark. Bill squatted on his treads in the gloom and tried not to cry. He was so disappointed. And with the night, he was scared.

He hated the dark. And he hated the dreams, and he knew if he slept they would come.

But if he didn't sleep, how would that be?

What if they called him out tomorrow? He'd be too tuckered to shovel. He had to sleep. Had to.

And he tried.

And did...

—◆—

Down in the motor functions where the oil squeezed slow and the little rotors turned and the fans hummed and the coals burned, down there, way down there in the constantly fed nuclear pellet fire, Bill dreamed.

And the dream was a blossom of blackness, and he was falling, fast, so fast. Then he hit and his engine screamed. His lights popped on. Then Butch's lights popped on, and there was a hum of Butch's motor, and a clunk of treads, and pretty soon, Butch, was beside him.

"You just a big Tinker Toy, and you starting to make me really mad, little squirt. You wrecking Butch's sleep. And Butch, he don't like it. He don't like it some at all, you diggin' on that, Tinker Toy? Well...No, you don't dig at all, do you, little friend? You sit and sit and soon rust and rust. If you live that long. You scream that engine again, you gonna wake up with a crowd of mechanics around you. Understand?"

"Yes, sir," Bill said.

"Good. Now..." and to emphasize, Butch lifted his shovel and rubbed it against Bill's side, made a scratch that ran all the way from Bill's cab to his treads..."there's a little taste of what may be the appetizer to a big ole dinner. Dig? Oh, wrong term for you. You don't dig at all. You're too little."

"I may be little, but I'm willing to work," Bill said. "I want to build schools and churches and—"

"Shut the fuck up, Billy. Hear me, little bitty Billy. You just a big tinker toy."

"I..."

"Hear me?"

"Yes, sir."

"That's better, oil squirt."

"Lebe em alone, ya ole clunk of paper clips."

Lights were coming toward them, along with a rattling sound, like loose bolts and creaky hinges in a bucket, and soon, close up, Bill saw that it was Gabe, the Wise Old Steam Shovel. His paint had gone gray and his shovel wobbled and leaned a bit to the left, and his treads were frayed, but his head beams were still bright.

"You talking to me, Four Cylinder?," Butch said. "If that many work."

"Gid the fug away from him," Gabe said, "or I'll slap duh gohtdamn steam out of ya."

Butch laughed.

"You do any slapping, old shovel, your shovel will come off. You barely running on treads now, you greasy box of parts."

"Kizz muh ass," Gabe said.

"Won't poison myself with that idea," Butch said. "Gonna let you go cause you so old you make the stone wheel look like it a modern invention. You do, you know."

Chuckling under the roar of his engine, Butch motored off.

Gabe lifted up on one tread and let fly a steam fart that sounded like a howitzer.

"Thad's whad you can do wid yer gohtdamn stone wheel, ya big hunk of bolt-suckin', leakin' steamin' pile of—"

"Please," Bill said. "There's a lady nearby." Bill rolled his headlamps toward Miss Maudie, who sat with her beams on, awakened by the commotion.

"Oh," Gabe said. "Sorry, girlie. Gid a liddle worked up sometimes."

"Excuse us for the bother," Bill said to Miss Maudie.

"That's all right," she said, and the sound of her motor made Bill feel a tightening in his joints and a gurgle in his transmission fluid. She blinked her head lights, then shut them down, with, "But I do need the sleep."

"Sure," Bill said. "Of course." And he could feel a tingling in his lines and parts that wasn't just fluid circulation.

"Yah ain't eben giddin' none, and you done exhaust-whipped," Gabe said.

"Sshhhhhh," Bill said, letting out a soft puff of steam. "You'll embarrass her...And me...And Butch will come back and scratch me again, or beat me....But thanks. Thanks for taking up for me."

"Ain't nuthin'. Jes wand to sleep muhself. So shud up. 'sides, don't like to see some medal-assed whipper-snapper bullyin' a liddle steam fard like yerself. Now, go to sleep."

"Sure," Bill said, and smiled. "Thanks again."

"Nothin' to id," Gabe said. "And kid, you're habbin' dreams, right? I hear ya moanin' yer engine."

"I am. The same dream."

"Whad is id?"

Bill told him.

"Huuummmm," Gabe said. "Pud my thinker on thad one. I'm a preddy smart fugger, say so myself...But in the meantime, ya want to git them dreams outta yer head, least a lidde, what ya do, ya close yer eyes, and ya think of yerself ridin' Miss Maudie's tail pipe like yer trying to climb a gohtdamn straid up incline without any treads. Gid me? That'll put yer liddle nut of a fire in a gohtdamn happy place, thad's whad I'm tryin' to tell ya."

"Don't say that."

"Done said."

And with that, Gabe chuckled dryly and rattled off to leave Bill with the shadows and his dreams.

—◆—

Inside Bill the little nuclear pellet fed the fire that fed the coals that heated the water and fed the steam, and once again, Bill dreamed.

He first dreamed of a fine warm place with soft light and he dreamed of mounting Maudie, his dip stick out, riding her tailpipe like he was going up a steep incline. It was a good dream, and he felt a kind of release, as if all his steam had been blown out and all his oils and fluids had been sucked from him. It was a feeling like he could collapse into a heap of smoking metal, and it felt good, this dream, but when it was over, he dreamed of falling again, and falling from way up and down fast, striking the ground, going to pieces, squashing Dave this way and that. And when he awoke, panting heavy through his steam pipe, he found that in his sleep, during the dream about Maudie, he had squirted transmission fluid all over the floor.

(Or had it happened out of fear?)

He was glad it was dark. He was so embarrassed.

Bill looked about, but in the dark all he could see were the shapes of the other shovels. He glanced where Maudie's shape was, and she was still and her lights were shut up tight behind their shields.

Near the wall, where Butch stayed, he heard Butch snoring, the air blowing up through his steam pipe in a loud masculine way. The big bruiser even snored like a thug.

Rest of the night Bill tried to stay awake, to neither have the bad dream or to think of Maudie, but think of her he did, but this time, differently, not mounting her tailpipe as if trying to push up an incredible incline, but side by side with her, motoring along, the two of them blowing a common tune through their whistles, her turning her shovel to him, lifting it, and underneath, her bright red rubber bumper was parting to meet with his...and kiss.

But that wasn't going to happen.

He was never going to kiss Maudie or mount her tail pipe.

And, the way it looked now, he was never going to build schools and churches and such for all those children, and what did he care?

Little bastards. They didn't need that stuff anyway.

Then daylight came through the windows of the garage and turned the floor bright, like a fresh lube spill, and for a moment, Bill was renewed and hopeful and willing.

—◆—

A bunch of Daves came into the garage and each of them climbed onto a steam shovel, and Bill, hoping, hoping so hard he thought he might just start his own engine and drive out of there, saw his Dave approaching.

His Dave climbed inside his little cabin and touched the controls and Bill's motor roared. Bill felt his pistons throbbing with excitement, felt oil growing warm and coursing through his tubes and wetting up his machinery. When

Dave turned him around and drove him out of the garage, he was so proud he thought he might blow a gasket.

Outside he saw sunlight shining bright off his blue shovel and he could feel the ground and gravel crunching beneath his treads, and to his left and right were the others, rolling along in line, off to work.

His dream had come true.

—◆—

They motored to the site and begin to dig. It was a location that would provide space for a large apartment complex, and it was next to another large apartment complex, right across from two other large apartment complexes and a row of fast food joints, out of which came a steady stream of Daves who didn't drive steam shovels.

The site was currently a patch of woods, a bunch of beautiful trees full of happy singing birds and squirrels at play. But fuck that. Bill and his fellow shovels were at work.

The steam shovels rode in and pushed that shit down, dug up the roots and pushed it in a pile to burn. Birds flew away and squirrels scampered for safety. Eggs in fallen bird's nest were crunched beneath their treads.

The machines dug deep and pushed the dirt until anything that was rich with natural compost was completely scraped up and mounded, revealing clay beneath, red as a scraped wound. Half of the patch of woods was scratched away in short time, and Bill was scraping with the rest as hard as he could, knocking some of his bright blue paint off on roots and rocks. But he didn't mind. Those were battle scars.

In the cockpit he heard Dave say, "Now we're talking. Lookin' good. Fucking trees. Goddamn birds. Shitting squirrels."

About noon they stopped so the Daves could climb

down and gather up and eat food and drink from the little black boxes they carried.

Bill, parked by Gabe, said, "Gabe. What about all the birds and squirrels and little animals? What about them?"

"Fug em," said Gabe. "They're all gone, who'll gib a shit? Can't fret over somethin' ain't around, can ya kid? 'Sides, whad's them fuggers ever done fer ya?"

"Well…"

"Nothin'. Not a gohtdamn thang."

"Well, yeah, I guess…But, gee, Gabe, what happens when all the world is scraped down, and they don't need us?

"Aw, we'll push down old buildings, scrape em down red to the clay, and they'll build some new shit. Always somethin' fer us to fug up so stuff can be built again. Don't fret, kid."

"But, don't the children need trees for shade, and don't trees help make the air fresh…"

"Don't believe thad shit. Tree is a tree is a tree. Them liddle children, shit, them fuggers can wear a hat and breathe through an oxygen mask for all I care…Hey, saw yer greasy spot when you rolled out this mornin'. Kinda had ya one of em night time squirdaramas, didn't ya?"

Bill felt embarrassed. "Well, I…"

"Fug it. It's normal. Thinkin' about thad liddle cuddie over there, weren't ya, son?"

Bill looked where Maudie was at rest, next to the last line of trees. She looked bright and gold and even with dirt and clay on her shovel, she had a kind of charm, a sweetness. And a nice tail pipe.

"Well, said Gabe, "ya was thinking 'bout it, wadn't you? That's why ya squirded yer juice."

"I suppose."

"Gohtdamn, boy. Ain't no suppose to it. Thad's all right. Thad's natural. Ought to try and talk ya up some of thad, thad's what I'm trying to tell ya. Was younger, ya can bet I'd be sportin' around her, throbbin' my engine, whippin' muh shovel. Muh old dipstick pokin' up under muh hood. Hell, all I can do these days is use id to check muh oil."

"I was wondering about that, Gabe. If the dipstick is under the hood, and the...well, you know, the ladies tail pipe is where tail pipes are...How does that work, Gabe?"

Gabe laughed. "Ya kiddin', ain't ya? Naw, gohtdamnit, ya ain't. Well, son, on the old underbelly is another panel, and ya get stiff and pokey, it hits the hood, but when ya want to do the deed, ya see, ya led thad little section underneath ya pop open, stick lowers, and, well, son, ya'll figure it out. Promise. Figured out in ya sleep, didn't ya? Old parts and lines knew whad to do without no thinkin' on yer part."

"I didn't say I was going to do anything—"

"—shit, boy. Ain't nothin' wrong wid wantin' a piece of tail pipe. Oh, and I been thinkin' on yer dream, and I know someone might be able to help ya on that. Can figure it...But later. Here come duh Daves. Time to gid wid it."

They went back to work, and pretty soon Dave said to Bill, "Bill, we got a big old stubborn tree that just won't go, and we got to push it down so we can scrape the clay. I think you're ready for it. Am I right? Are you ready?"

Bill rumbled his engine and whistled air through his steam pipe in response.

"All right, you little shovel, let's do er."

And away they went. Bill lifted his shovel and poked it out and Dave guided him to the tree. It was a big old tree and round enough that four men with their hands linked couldn't have surrounded it. Must have been hundreds of years old, but Bill, he was determined it wasn't going to get a day older.

He put out his shovel and began to push. He pushed hard, giving it all he had. He revved up his engine and whistled his steam and dug in with his treads and...

The tree didn't move.

He revved up higher and pushed and pushed and…

Nothing.

He might as well have had his engine turned off and be sitting in the garage with a tread up his exhaust.

He pushed harder, and.

He cut one. A big one. It came out of his exhaust with a kind of blat-blat-blat sound.

Bill couldn't believe it. He had cut a fart to end all farts, and right in front of Dave and all the other steam shovels. He turned one of his head beams slowly, looked to his right, and there was Maudie. She was so shocked the split in her front bumper hung open showing her gear-cog teeth (all perfect and shiny), and Bill, he wanted to just run off a cliff. But there weren't any cliffs. Just that big tree standing upright in front of him, and he hadn't done any more than crack a little bark.

"Well," said Bill's Dave, "this is just too much for you. We'll have to get a bigger and better machine. One that can do the job. And we might want to cut back on that cheap transmission fluid, boy."

Dave backed Bill off from the tree, stood up in the cab and called out, "You better bring in Butch. This is a job for a real steam shovel."

Bill felt his body droop on its treads. His shovel hit the ground with a thud.

He was not only a weakling and a farter, he was being beat out by his worst enemy.

Butch revved his engine and threw out his shiny shovel and went up against the tree, and at first Bill thought: Well, he won't do it either.

The tree stood firm, not moving, and then, suddenly, it began to lean and lean and lean, and there was a cracking sound, then a cry of roots and timber like the sound of something being jerked from its womb, and the great tree went down, the roots popping up, clay flying from them in red clunks.

Butch backed off, lifted his shovel, and with a sort of slide, treaded back to the center of the work force.

Bill saw Maudie turn and look to him, and her bumper was split wide again. But this time, she was smiling.

—◆—

Back in the barn, Bill sat alone as the windows turned dark. Gabe came rolling over.

"Ya all right, son?"

"I guess."

"Damn, boy. Can't believe ya farded. Thad one knocked a bird out of a tree, gabe us all an oil stink ya wouldn't believe. A fard like that, ya must hab passed into another dimension for awhile. Yer gohtdamn headbeams crossed, you cut wind so hard."

"Gee, thanks."

"Ah, don't led it bother you. I led fards all the time. And sometime on purpose…Big ole tree like thad, it ain't for a kid. I couldn't do it. Well, in my day I could."

"Young as me?"

"Oh, yeah. Damn, what a fard."

"Please, Gabe. Don't mention it anymore."

"All right. But, son, it was a champion."

Bill sighed.

"Ya know, I told ya I had someone could tell ya 'bout them dreams yer always having?"

"Yes."

"Well, I'm gonna bring him over. Sid tight."

Gabe rolled away, and a moment later, Bill saw him return with an old gray steam shovel who had steam coming up from between his bumpers. When he got closer, Bill saw that it wasn't steam at all, he was smoking a metal pipe stuffed with old oily shop rags.

"This is Professor Zoob," Gabe said.

"Ah, how are you ma boy?"

"Fine…I guess. Why haven't I seen you before?"

"I am in the back of the garage, yes. I hang there and do little jobs. Push garbage about. But I am old and they do not call me out much. I would think, soon, I will be for the scrap machine, yes. I have been around for many years, I have, and was driven by a student of much psychology. He studied in my cockpit during his breaks, yes. And when he did, he read aloud from his books, and I listened. I learned much. I learned much about dreams, I did."

"Really?"

"Yes. And before we analyze them, might I say, that I heard about today, about your trouble with the tree and the tremendous fart."

"From Gabe, I suppose."

"Oh, from everyone. It was quite some joke, it was."

"Grand."

"But, if you will tell me your dreams, let me consider on it, maybe I can help you understand."

"I don't know."

"Sure. Sure. Try me."

"Well, there's only one that concerns me, really scares me.

Zoob puffed his pipe faster, sending up a haze of smoke.

"That really stinks," Bill said. "And isn't that bad for you?"

"Of course, but at my age, why would I give a shit? I use a seven percent solution of oil and transmission fluid. The rags burn slower, and in their haze, I think big thinks, I do. And could it stink any worse than the whopper you cut lose with today, huh?"

"I'll never live that down, will I?"

"Won't be easy," Gabe said.

"The dream?" Zoob said.

—◆—

Bill told him about the dream, about the darkness and the falling and the smashing, and Zoob said, "When you are falling. What is it you smell?"

"Smell?"

"Yes. Do you smell anything? Hear anything? Taste anything?"

"Why no. It's a dream."

"Ah, but there are dreams where one can hear or smell or taste. Have you not had the dreams about the lady steam shovels, and how that feels and smells and tastes, with the after bite of steam on the tail pipe, huh, have you not?"

"I...I suppose."

"Yes, of course, you can. You can smell things in a dream if there is something to smell."

"Hope ya can't smell thad fard in one," Gabe said. "Thad would peel duh paint right off."

"That's enough," Bill said.

"Well, then, my little friend, think this, do you remember anything in the darkness of your dream? Anything at all? Anything in the shadows?"

"No."

"Ah, then we must resort to the hypnotism."

"What?"

"Hypnotism. Now," Zoob said rolling back a pace. "I'm going to swing my shovel back and forth, and I want you to watch, listen only to the sound of my voice, and watch the shovel please. There is a small silver spot scraped near the center of it, and that's what I want you to concentrate on...Ready?"

—◆—

Bill watched the shovel swing back and forth and Zoob said soothing things and no one mentioned the fart and pretty soon Bill was feeling sleepy, a little dizzy, as if he might fall over, then he felt like he was in a tunnel, and the only light in the tunnel was the shiny spot on Zoob's shovel, and the tunnel was swaying, and then it went still, and there was just the spot before him, like a beacon, and, Zoob's voice, easy and soft and suggestive.

"Now, Little Bill, you are in the dream. All dark. Tell me now, what is happening in this falling dream? Tell me."

"Well, let me see. It's dark…That's it. It's dark."

"Listen carefully, Little Bill. You are in this bad dream. And it's dark—"

"And you're in there wid thad fard," Gabe said, and chuckled.

"Silence, Gabe," Zoob said. "No more with the fart… Now, you are in the bad dream, in the dark, and you are falling. Are you there, Little Bill?"

"Yes," Bill said. And he was in the dream all right. And it was dark. No little scrape of light visible. And he was falling. And he felt the old fear rise up out of the darkness and come over him in a rush.

"Shit," Bill said.

"Now," said Zoob, "you are falling, and you are feeling the shit feeling, and I want you to slow this fall, and I want you to look about you…It's all right. You'll be all right. You should not be scared this time. We have control over this dream, you and I, and you are falling slow and you can take the time to look about. You look about you now, and you listen, and you tell Zoob what it is you see and hear, or smell. You tell me everything, Little Bill, yes."

"Yes…I…I am falling, and it's dark, and I'm scared and I can see to my right that there's a shape."

"What is this shape?"

"I...I don't know."

"Yes. Yes, you do. We stop the fall. You hang in mid-air. You study the shape and it is...?"

"It's a...It's a Dave."

"A Dave, huh? Ah hah. Go on, Little Bill."

"He's standing in the shadows...He's getting around fine in the dark—"

"He familiar with the place," Zoob said.

"Yes, it's his home. There are all kinds of machines and gadgets there."

"Like what?"

"A refrigerator, and there's a little light. I guess I didn't notice it before. The Dave is opening the refrigerator and taking something out and the light is coming from there."

"The refrigerator light," Zoob said. "He's getting food. They are always with the food, which is why, over the years, you got the same driver, his ass gets heavy. It makes them blow up like a hot valve. But, go on, Little Bill."

"He's turning, his elbow is hitting something... Something on the stove, and it's falling off."

"What is it?"

"I don't know."

"Take yourself some closer."

"I don't want to."

"It is quite all right, Little Bill. Go closer."

"It's a waffle iron."

"No shit?"

"Yes, sir."

"It is a waffle iron. Now that is some confusing business...Ah, ah...Okay, what else do you see, Little Bill?"

"Nothing. It's All gone black."

"Wake up."

—◆—

Bill opened his head lamps.

"Wow," he said.

"Ain't that some shit?" Zoob said. "One time, in the mirror, I hypnotize myself into thinking I am one big chicken. Tried to roost on top of the garage, but ended up pushing down the wall. Oh, the Daves were mad that day."

"But…What about me?"

"You are the waffle iron."

"Beg pardon."

"The waffle iron and many things. Old metals. Busted parts. They were melted down to make you, and the memories of before, they are in the metal. Are at least certain memories. Like the fall. That was traumatic, and the memory, a little metal ghost, it stayed with the metal. The waffle iron, it must have become part of the mainframe that holds your memories. That is it, Little Bill. You remember the fall, and therefore, you dream of it and you fear it."

"But I'm not the waffle iron. And now that I know, it'll go away. Right?"

"Nah. You have to work through it."

"How do I do that?"

"Don't know."

"But you're the professor."

"Well, I call myself that. But this, this is up to you, Little Bill. You have to sort of cinch up the old transmission and deal with it. And yes, knowing the source. That will help. You must overcome your fears, and when you do, the dreams will stop."

Professor Zoob turned and rumpled away on his treads. Gabe said, "See, told ya he could help you…How about thad? Yer a sissy cause ya got a mashed waffle iron inside ya. Ain't thad some shit? I'm glad I was made from good metal. Well, going to gid a lube job, if you know what I mean, so, hang tight, kid, and good luck."

"Thanks, Gabe, I think," Bill said, and Gabe went away.

—◆—

Sitting alone in the corner, his shovel dipped, his head beams to the wall, Bill was surprised to feel a soft metallic touch. He turned, and there was Maudie.

"I know you were embarrassed today, Bill, but I want you to know, it's only natural. A lot of fluid in the system, exertion. I wouldn't feel too bad."

"Well, I do…And you were laughing."

"Yeah. Well, it was funny. On the outside, anyway. From your point of view, not so funny. It was just so loud and long, and that look on your face…I wasn't laughing because I think you're a loser. I mean, a fart like that, it kind of embarrasses everyone, and you're always glad it's the other guy, but, don't feel too bad. I puked once. Oil all over the place, and there was a big chunk of rust in it. I was so humiliated."

"Really?"

"Really."

"Was it before I came here?"

"I was here a few days before you, and yes, it was."

"Did everyone see it?"

"No. Only me, but I was still embarrassed."

"That's not exactly the same."

"No. Yours was more humiliating, I admit, but, still, I was embarrassed, if just to myself. I mean yours was right out in front of God and everybody…"

"Yes. I know. Maudie, I'm going to go right to it. Is there anyway, you and me could get together?"

"You mean, together together?"

"I just want to get to know you. I like you. I'm not a bad guy…"

"I like you too."

"Really?"

"Sure. Everyone in the barn, except Butch says your nice."

"No, shit?"

"No, shit."

"Well, that's swell, Maudie. Maybe, you know, some-time, after work, we could get together in the far corner of the garage. Maybe get our oil changed or something. Watch a little TV in the rec room afterwards. There's a car chase movie on, the big new one about car wrecks and the fire department, LOTS OF CARS AND A DOZEN HOSES."

"Oh, those cars. I've seen previews. They're so sexy. So are the fire trucks. That's some metal the cars are built from, isn't it?"

"Actually, I don't know cars and steam shovels go together—"

"Ah, jealous already and we haven't even had our first date."

"I guess...A little. I mean, how do you compete with movie cars?"

"That's cute...Long as it doesn't get out of hand. And listen, those movie cars, they're always being remade and rebuffed and they don't really run as fast as they show in the movie. I'm looking for the real deal, and you're the real deal, I think. I'd sure like to find out for sure."

"Gee, Maudie. That's swell."

"Remember, about the tree. That was a big one. It would take someone like Butch to push it over. For heavens' sake, Bill, he's three times your size. It's not your fault."

"Yeah...Yeah, you're right."

"You might want to drink a little less transmission fluid, though, you're gonna be straining that hard. I mean...You know?"

"Sure. Of course. Good advice."

"See you later."

"Tomorrow? After work?"

"It's a date."

—◆—

That night Bill slept and he dreamed, but it was not the dream about falling. Zoob had really helped him, and probably had no idea how much. In his dream he thought of Maudie. And it was a good dream, and they were warm and close and friendly, and spent quality time together, watching T.V., having their oil changed, and, in the end, he mounted her like he was climbing an incline to a Rocky Mountain trailer park entrance.

But just as he was about to finish, he cut another one.

He awoke in a sweat.

He had swapped one bad dream for another.

He wasn't falling anymore, but now he was afraid he was going to cut a big one at an inopportune moment.

But, hell, he had about as much chance of mounting Maudie, having any kind of relationship with her, as a bird had of finding a tree in a Taco Bell parking lot.

—◆—

Morning came, and Bill tried to put a good face on it, smiled his rubber bumpers wide when he saw the beautiful Maudie being driven out of the barn. She waved her radio antennae at him, and he waved his back, and she was gone, out into the sunlight.

For a long moment, Bill feared he was not going to get another chance. Steam shovel after steam shovel was rolled outside, and still he set. No Dave to drive him.

But then, finally, his Dave showed up.

Dave came and climbed up on him. Bill cranked the engine without giving Dave time to do it.

"Wow, you're raring to go," Dave said. "Sorry, I was late. Wife felt frisky. Since that happens about once every six months, had to take advantage of it."

They rolled outside and the sun was bright against the concrete. The team of shovels went past where they had worked before, started motoring along the road, puffing steam, cracking gravel under their treads.

They rolled along until the road rose up and the mountains gathered around them, and still they went up. Bill felt a strain in his motor, and he took a deep breath of steam, squirted it out, hunkered down and dug in with his treads. Up he went, carrying his Dave high and deep into the mountains along the concrete road. Bill tried not to look to his right, toward the edge of the road and the great fall that was there. The feelings he had in the dreams came back when he did. His insides trembled like a piston was blown. His nuclear pellets, his gas and oil engine, his back up steam engine, all seemed to miss a beat as the went up. And up. And up.

The road narrowed, and finally they came to where the road turned to clay, then ended up against the mountain.

Bill realized this was a spot where other shovels had been working. It was wide here. You could put four steam shovels across, digging. Digging open the mountain so the road could keep going up and Daves and their Sallys could ride in their cars carrying all their little Daves and Sallys.

Bill was not first in line, but well behind the first four that went to work, Butch and Maudie among them. Dave pulled him in line with three other shovels, and killed his motor. Bill watched Maudie as she worked, the way the sun hit the metal of her shiny ass, the way her tail pipe wiggled, and he was amazed and grateful for her fine construction.

He watched Butch dig and toss the dirt, and was impressed in spite of himself. What a powerful machine.

He liked the way the cables rolled under his metal skin and the way he could lay back on the rear of his treads and lift himself up. And he liked the way Butch cussed as he worked, digging, insulting the mountain.

He looked around him and saw Gabe working alongside the road, on little jobs, like making the road wider for more concrete to be laid. He thought of Zoob, back in the barn. Did he wish he was out here, digging?

Most likely.

It was the dream of every good construction shovel.

The digging went on and the day got hotter. His metal grew warm and he could feel the oils, the liquids inside of him, starting to grow warm and loose. He lifted his head beams and looked at the sky. A single bird soared against it, and the blue of the sky faded as a cloud of pollution, the sign of progress, rolled across it, gray as cobwebbed garage corner. He thought: if I could shoot a rifle, like a Dave, I bet I could pop that goddamn bird.

Then Dave started his motor again.

Now Bill and three others took the place of the four who had been in line. As Maudie rolled past him, she winked a headlight. Then Butch rolled past him, said, "You just a Tinker Toy."

Bill gritted his gears and went up against the mountain with the other three, and he began to dig. He thought: Dig, boy, dig. And don't cut one. Die before you do that. Dig. Dig this mountain down. Dig like you want to flatten the entire earth. Which, actually, seemed like a fairly noble ambition. Making all the world flat and covered in concrete.

But then what would he do?

Why, tear up the concrete, of course. Like Gabe had said. It had to wear out, crack and buckle. Tear it up and scrape it into piles and let them put down more concrete. Oh, yes, Gabe was right. This was the life. Fuck the earth.

Fuck the wildlife. Fuck it all. To dig was to live.

And so he dug and he dug, then, suddenly, Dave was wheeling him about. He thought at first he had done something wrong, but realized he was growing low on power. That he had to pull back, like the first four. Maybe get a new pellet to refire the steam. That was it. He had done fine.

He smiled as he clattered tiredly back through the line and another four moved up.

—◆—

So the day went, three rows of four, taking turns, twelve steam shovels working against the mountain, and Gabe working the side of the road. And finally, mid-day, the Daves pulled back all the shovels and stopped, had them set alongside the road.

The Daves went about checking oil and fluids and such, and old Gabe, he was sent up to the front to shovel the bits of dirt that remained, scraping it down to the clay, which was a job that made him happy.

Then, the mountain came down.

It came down with a slight rumble, then a big rumble, and Bill looked up and saw Gabe look up, and the mountain went over Gabe and Bill could hear the sound of metal bending, then there was nothing but a great dust cloud.

Butch, who was behind him now, rolled forward suddenly, without benefit of his Dave, said, "Man, did you see that shit there. Old Gabe, he done fucked now. One less old geezer in the garage. And that ain't bad."

Bill wheeled. He swung his shovel and hit Butch with everything he had. And Butch, well, it didn't bother him much.

Butch swung his shovel too, and just as it hit Bill, making Bill slide back on his treads, Bill heard Maudie's voice.

"You got to get Gabe out from under there, boys. You got to."

"Ain't gonna dig him out unless I got to," said Butch. "He nothing to me, he ain't."

"You're right, Maudie" said Bill, and he hummed up his engine and rolled forward. His Dave tried to work the controls, to make Bill do what he wanted, but Bill ignored him. I got free will, he thought. I can do what I want, and he went at the dirt and began to dig. He dug and he dug, and eventually he saw a bit of scarred metal, and he dug faster, and finally, finally, there was Gabe.

Or what was left of him. He was squashed and his old shovel had been knocked completely off. Oil dribbled all over the earth.

"Gabe!" Bill said.

Weak as a busted oil line, Gabe said, "Thanks, boy. But ain't no use. I'm a gonner. Fugged from bucket to ass end."

And he was.

They brought in a wrecker and took Gabe away, down the hill. That night when they rolled back in the garage, Bill found that Gabe had been dismantled and stacked. Tomorrow, he went to the furnace to be melted down, and reformed.

"It's another life," Maudie said. "He'll be melted into some other kind of machinery. It's not over for him."

"It won't be him," Bill said.

"And there's his soul, it's gone to the sky. That can't be changed. Can't be taken away from him. A residues remains. Isn't it in the manual that residuals can remain?"

Bill thought about the ghost inside him, the residual of the waffle iron. And then he thought about heaven.

"What's heaven like, Maudie? What do you think it's like?"

"Flat. Lots of concrete. But everyday, new hills pop up, and new trees, and they have to be taken down. And we'll be there, just like all the others that have gone before us and will come after us."

"Will Butch be there?"

"I don't think so. I think he gets the other place."

"Gabe was just an old guy," Bill said. "A good old guy."

"I know. Don't look at him anymore."

Zoob rolled up. He said, "I am sorry, Bill. He was good, he was. I miss him already."

"Me too," Bill said.

"I wish you the best of a night you could have," Zoob said. "Gabe, he is all through with the pain. The ache in the bolts and the hinges. Maybe he's lucky. I think maybe I could wish it was me, you see."

"No way," Bill said.

"Thank you. And I wish you, and the lady, good night."

"Goodnight," Bill and Maudie said in unison.

They rolled away together, went to the dark shadows on the far side of the garage. Maudie swung her shovel so that it draped over Bill's back. Her bumper parted and pressed to his, and they kissed. And kissed again. Soon they were holding each other, stroking metal, and then, heaven above and flatten all earth, he was behind her, and down came the oil stick, and then came the loving.

Afterward, they set low on their treads together in the shadows and slid open their side traps and dropped their oil tubes into a fine vat of thirty weight, sucked it up together.

"I...I don't know what happened there..." Bill said.

"What happened was wonderful," Maudie said. "I haven't felt that good since...Well, I haven't felt that good."

"Neither have I," he said.

That night, Bill did not have the bad dreams.

—◆—

Next morning the Daves came and rolled out all the steam shovels, drove them back up into the mountains. Today, Bill was not as aware of the heights. He felt strong and wanted at the mountain.

They came to where they had stopped working, where Gabe had been crushed, and spread into groups of four. He was in the first group. To his left was Maudie, to her left, Glen, an older steam shovel. And to Bill's right, Butch, who was next to the ledge that fell away into what seemed like eternity.

"I gonna show you how to work today, Tinker Toy," said Butch. "Gabe, he done gone now. Ain't here to take up for you. Not that it mattered none, but who wants to beat up an old steam shovel?"

"You don't mind threatening to beat up a smaller shovel than you," Bill said, with a kind of new found bravado, thinking, getting tail pipe made you crazy, made you brave. "I was your size, you might not be so tough."

Butch narrowed his head lamps.

"You pushing, little Tinker Toy. I gonna show you how to work. And, I may show you a thing or two other than that, you hear me?"

"Like I give an oil squirt."

Butch said, "I think maybe you been getting a little business, a little of the golden steam shovel's tail business, and it's making you think you a man, little Tinker Toy, you know what I mean? You ain't no man. You just a Tinker Toy."

Bill shoved Butch. It was sudden. Butch was actually knocked to the side a pace, near the mountains edge.

"Hey," Butch said.

"Stop it," Bill's Dave said. "I came here to work. What are you shovels doing?"

"I remember that you did that, Tinker Toy," Butch said.

"Hope you do," Bill said.

—◆—

They began to dig and everything went well. The mountain moved for them. The dirt was mounded to the side away from the ledge, and some of it was put behind them and carried down the hill and away by other shovels. Zoob was working the edges of the road, doing the soft jobs, the way Gabe had been, though even more slowly.

They worked on and on and the sun rose high and grew hot and made their metal warm and finally very warm, and then hot as the top of a stove. Their metal shined like a newly minted coin in the sunlight, and their well-oiled shovels and treads worked beautifully and tore apart the mountain, and somewhere, inside the mountain, as if the mountain had had enough, a vein of rock that ran all the way to the summit quivered and quaked and let go, and the huge tip of the mountain, like a peaked hat knocked over by a high wind, tumbled down on the four working shovels below.

One moment there was the sun, then there was the darkness. Bill could feel the pressure of the dirt and the rocks pushing down on him. Then, below him the ground moved, and he went down into it. Amazingly, he slipped down at an angle, and down, down, down, as he slid into a weak place in the mountain, a natural tunnel filled with soft dirt. He began to slide back into that. And a rock, dislodged, shot out and stuck in front of him, stopped the progress of falling rock from above.

It gave Bill a bit of space.

He could move his shovel, like a Dave might move his elbow if he were inside a tow sack. He moved the shovel and some dirt shook. He began to move it back and forth. More dirt shifted. Finally he grabbed the great rock and gave it all he had. The rock moved and dirt came in, but Bill rocked back on his treads and the dirt flowed around him like black water.

He kept working that shovel, and it made a sound like it was trying to let go of clotted oil in the lines. Still, Bill shoveled, lifting it a bit up and down, a little from side to side. Finally, he had traction, and he was moving the dirt. And he was going up that incline, climbing it the way he'd climbed the sweet golden Maudie the night before. He put that image in his head and kept at it, and pretty soon the image was as tight in his head as a screwed down bolt.

Up he went. Up. And finally there was light.

And he realized his Dave was gone. Probably washed away in the rock and dirt, covered up and crushed like an aluminum oil can.

—◆—

On the surface, he found the shovels and the Daves digging at the mountain, furiously. As he rose out of the ground like a metal mole, the Daves cheered and the engines revved their motors.

He lifted his shovel high.

But it was a short lived triumph.

He saw that the mountain had come down in such a way that it had covered Maudie and Butch.

Glen had survived it all. His shovel had been knocked off and one of his treads was slightly dislodged, but already a huge wrecker had come for him and he was being hooked up even as Bill looked.

As Bill watched the wrecker take Glen away, he realized he didn't feel so good and his vision was blurry. There was dirt inside of his busted right head lamp, and it was partially covering his line of vision. Inside, way down deep, he felt as if a bag of bolts and gears had been randomly mixed and tossed into a paint shaker. When he moved, he squeaked and clanked and he hurt near the right hinge of his shovel like a Dave had been at him with a welding torch.

Bill hunkered down on his treads and tore at the mountain. Tried to dig where he had last seen Maudie, but he couldn't be sure she was there. Maybe, like him, she had been washed down into a soft part of the ground. He dug and he dug, and finally he saw metal. He revved his engine and other shovels came. They dug and dug and pretty soon they saw the shiny gold metal of the beautiful Maudie, less beautiful now. Dented and scratched gray in strips, her shovel dangling by one bolt.

Bill hooked his shovel around her and pulled her out. And as he did, he saw behind her was a roof of rocks supported by a wall of rock slabs, and in there, crushed down, but alive (he could see the headlights blinking) was Butch. When Maudie came out, the dirt went down. Butch went out of sight.

Bill sighed air through his manifold.

Maybe he was dead. The bastard.

The shovels were slowing down behind him. They had Maudie out, and no one was working that hard for Butch, and Bill could understand that....

But, damn it, Butch was a steam shovel. He was a worker. And he had been caught in the storm of the mountain fall while on the job. And though Bill thought it might be nice to just let the mountain crush him, he just couldn't do it. That wasn't the way it was in the manual. Machines helped machines. Machines helped the Daves.

Bill went at it again, digging, digging, and pretty soon the other shovels were helping, and the dirt began to move.

When it was clear enough, they could see Butch in there. He was much shorter than before, his metal rippled in the center, and above him, supported on two wobbly slabs of rock, was a much bigger slab of rock. It looked as if it were large enough to build a subdivision on.

Bill moved in close and tried to pull Butch out, but it was like trying to work a greasy bolt out of an engine with a coat hanger tipped with chewing gum. Touch and go.

Butch was moaning with pain as the tugging tore at his metal.

"I've lost my crankshaft," he said. "And my oil pan's loose. I can feel it sliding around in side."

"Don't move," Bill said. He dug a space close to the edge of the mountain, and within a short time he found he could scrunch in there. One tread was hanging halfway over the edge, and he could hear rock tumbling down the side of the mountain, and feel it sliding out from under his treads. He felt himself slipping a little. For a moment, the old dream came back, flashed before his inner head lamps, and he was falling, and he was scared.

He shook it off.

He looked out and he saw Maudie. She was banged up, but she was going to be okay. Nothing a few tools, a blow torch and paint couldn't fix. She looked at him and her lights came on and her bumper parted in a smile, showing that pretty gear work inside, slightly dusty. It gave him strength. He scrunched back farther. Being smaller, he could fit right in beside Butch.

"What in the world will you be doing, my boy?"

It was old Zoob. He had slid up close to the opening. The old steam shovel bent down on its creaky treads and eyed Bill with his head lamps.

"Why are you in there, my boy? Let the rock crush this one, the big hunk of scrap metal."

"He was on the job," Bill said. "He's one of us."

"I think he's not worth it some at all, that is what I think."

"You may be right," Bill said.

"Hey," Butch said. "I'm right here."

Bill brought his shovel up and touched the great slab above him. He hunkered down on his treads and flexed his metal, and lifted with the shovel.

And the great rock moved.

Shovel God in Heaven, and praise Jayzus, but Bill felt strong. He pushed. And he pushed with his shovel, and he felt the bolts that hinged it go tight as a pair of vice grips, but he pushed up anyway.

And that rock moved some more.

"Pull...him....out," Bill said.

They came forward, two big steam shovels, and they reached in and got hold of Butch, started pulling.

Bill, looking at Maudie, suddenly felt weak. He could feel his hydraulic fluid starting to eek out, could hear it hissing as it erupted through the tubes.

"Oh, shit," Bill said.

Then there was pain.

Sharp. Quick.

And he was flying along through darkness, and ahead of him was a great tunnel lit by a white light. He could see himself flying along, treads working, but touching nothing, and a flock of birds and scampering squirrels and insects and fish and snakes and possums and raccoons and bears, and all manner of wild life, was rushing along beside him, as well as a flying waffle iron.

And he felt good and happy and fulfilled.

He rushed faster and the light grew brighter, and the animals and insects were sucked forward as if by a vacuum cleaner, and then, just as he was about to go into the brightest and warmest part of the light—

He saw Gabe.

Gabe was blocking his path.

Gabe rammed up against him.

"Gohtdamnit, boy. Not yet. Id's not yer time just now. Ain't far off. But not yet. Got to finish whad yer doin', son."

There was a rush of wind and light as Bill fled back along the tunnel and the light went dark. Then he was standing there, with that great slab of rock on his shovel, and he saw Maudie, looking at him, and that look in her eye was worth all the agony in his shovel, worth the tubes he was splitting, the fluids he was draining.

The shovels tugged at Butch, and, slowly, he came free.

Bill couldn't see him now. Couldn't see much of anything. Maudie and Zoob, the other shovels, they were a blur.

"Is…he…out?" Bill asked.

"He is," Maudie said.

"I love you, Maudie," Bill said.

"And I love you. Oh, no, Bill. Hold on. We'll prop it up and pull you out."

"Too late. I'm…a hero…aren't I?"

"You are," Maudie said. "Oh, no, Bill. Hold on."

"You'll always remember me?"

Oil slipped from between the edges of her head lamps, rolled down her metal face, over her rubber mouth, as she said, "I will."

"So will I," said Butch. "You ain't no tinker toy, after all. You a better man than me. Than anyone I know."

"Nice knowing you some, kid," said Zoob.

And the great slab of rock came down.

—◆—

It was like an explosion when it hit. Bill felt himself being crushed, washed sideways over the side of the cliff. For a moment he felt the old fear, and it was a fear worth having now, for, in fact, he was falling.

But he didn't keep the fear. Didn't hold onto it.

He was a gonner. He knew it. But he was a hero too. And as he fell, he looked up, saw the shadow of the great rock slab falling after him. He chuckled deep inside his gears, yelled, "Geronimo!"

Then he hit the ground. His shovel, which was hanging by a strand of metal, came completely off and spun away.

His head lamps went out. There was darkness.

Along with the sound of the great rock falling, a sound like wind through what was left of the world's pines.

"One, one thousand," Bill said, counting the fall of the rock. "Two, one thousand."

Of course, he never heard it when it struck, but—

—◆—

—down that long black tunnel he went again, and it gave up its blackness to a warm light, and there in the light, fleeing along with him, were more birds and insects and snakes and all manner of wildlife whose homes he had destroyed, and that damn waffle iron, whose soul had been caught up inside him, and he thought, shit, that wasn't good of me, doing that to the birds and the squirrels and such, but here I go anyway, because this must be heaven, it feels so good, so bright and warm, and he could see Gabe up ahead, beckoning him forward with his shovel.

Then he realized Gabe was whole again. He hadn't thought about that before. In fact, Bill thought, I'm whole again. Bright and shiny with paint blue as the sky.

Now Gabe was beside him. They flowed forward.

Gabe said, "Ya know, stuff I told ya aboud all dem Gohtdamn birds and such?"

"Yeah," Bill said.

"I was wrong. But The Shovel Ghawd, he don't gib a shit. We is his, and he is ours. He knows what kind of fuel pump is in a good machine's chest, and boy, you and me, we got good ones."

Then, they were sucked into the total light of paradise.

Alone

(WITH MELISSA MIA HALL)

The smooth silver rockets stood against the sky, silent sentinels piercing the night. Waiting for something or someone, those spaceships reminded him of those big, old stone faces down on the ridge outside of Mud Creek. He never knew rightly how they got there but their open mouths and wide eyes turned ever skyward seemed connected somehow, since the rockets never rusted and the moss never grew over the expectant stone features. They were always bright with the morning light or copper red with the dying sun. He liked them best when they glowed silver in the moonlight or burned like white gold when the moon vanished blindly behind clouds.

And though the rockets seemed ready for take-off at any time of day or night, there was no one to ride in them. And no one had anything to do with them except him, James Leroy Carver, the self-appointed guardian of the town and the rockets—although what he did wouldn't pass for much and there was never anyone to pat him on the back and say, "Good job, Jim; good job!"

For that matter, there was hardly anyone left at all. There was Sleepy Sam who worked the fields with the help of his son, Cranky Dan'l, and Issy, a big spotted hound dog, two cows, a goat, two hogs and some chickens. They lived in a farmhouse that used to be white but was now faded into mottled gray. They also had a barn with a tin roof and some pitiful outbuildings they took care of just about as good as they took care of the vegetable garden that was surrounded by barbed wire—fair-to-middling. There used to be a horse but it died of old age. They gave Jim eggs, carrots, onions and potatoes when he helped out. He had to barter for anything else.

Behind and beyond the spaceships, the trees had started to come back, and Jim realized he had lived practically his entire life (how long that was he had no expert opinion) watching them return. First, they'd just been scorched sprouts, but somehow their roots had survived and given bloom to new life. Gradually, they inched up until they were almost taller than Jim. Lately, they'd grown as big as one of the sheds at Sleepy Sam's. It amazed him. Didn't seem quite right. Were trees supposed to grow that fast?

The world was coming back green, and he felt like there was nothing much left but the green. His parents were long dead now. The Revolution had taken them.

Back in the before time, the bad times when he was really small, he hid more than anything. The people who survived the fighting didn't seem much interested in him. Sometimes someone would take him in and feed him. Sometimes he'd just steal food. He stole so little, no one much minded. One time an ugly man, an outsider who talked funny tried to take him outside of town on his bike but Jim cut him with his knife and bit him for good measure and escaped. And then Sleepy Sam had killed him after a poker game went wrong and the man refused to hand over his bike. Jim never knew the drifter's name. He hadn't been a regular in Mud Creek and certainly not on his street.

Part of the street sign had broken off so he couldn't quite remember the whole name of the street. *Something* Heights. His mom had had a book called *Wuthering Heights* that she liked a lot. "Nobody ever wrote a book as good as *Wuthering Heights*." Funny how things stuck in a person's head. Jim took to calling his place "Wuthering Heights" although most of the house had burned down during the Revolution when his parents ran off and left him or were killed. He couldn't remember anything. Seemed his life began one day when he woke up in the back seat of the SUV, head on his plaid backpack, sucking his thumb and holding on to his old brown teddy and his blue *bankie* and his crackers. He loved his warm sleeping space in the family's unworkable SUV that was parked in what was left of the garage. He had been old enough then to survive.

And, in time, there was no one really hunting boy meat anymore, or anybody doing much of anything. Sleepy Sam said the cannibals focused on the still crowded cities, not on the dead little towns or out here on the fringe—that's what Sleepy Sam said. Jim thought that suited him just fine out here by the rockets. And as far as it went, he was okay. Cannibals didn't like rockets, he guessed. Can't eat rockets. And they didn't seem to like any meat but human meat. Animal meat must seem too tame.

"Stay here and keep your nose clean," Sleepy Sam said. He had a generator so he had electricity when the lights went out and stayed out a few years ago.

Most people left the little town during the Revolution or were killed by the monsters and the cannibals. Some stayed and some came back, then left again. They were primarily teens with no parents and no place to go, but the intense jungle that had suddenly surrounded and engulfed the town freaked them out and most left. They liked concrete and danger better. It put him in mind of *The Jungle Book* he kept in his ragged backpack. His parents were long dead now but they used to read from that book sometimes, together at night when he was little and dreaming about living in a jungle someday and here he was. The Revolution had taken his parents but given him back the jungle. He kept a picture of another jungle at his sleeping space. He'd stolen it from the library. The picture also showed some terrible animals attacking each other. What if this jungle would summon such creatures? He began considering the possibility such wild beasts might arrive and decided he would always be ready. He kept his pocketknife, a sharp stick and a hammer always handy.

Not long ago there was a group that rode into town who seemed nice at first and then turned deadly. He had had little to no interaction with those just passing through Mud Creek, but these people laughed and danced and sang a lot. They built a big bonfire and ate rabbits and squirrel they shared with him. They made a game out of chasing a big beach ball one of them blew up and threw around like it was something special. Then one of the women got angry, the red-headed leader and her man who had a long black beard. They fought like feral cats and it scared him. He crawled back home when they started killing each other.

The next day, when he went to see if their camp in the parking lot of the abandoned police station was still there, he found it abandoned. Gone from Mud Creek. He was relieved and sad at the same time.

— ◆ —

"Good riddance to bad rubbish," Sleepy Sam had said when Jim told him and his son. Cranky Dan'l, who rarely spoke, nodded his head.

"Dey kilt my hog, Billy. I hate dem," Dan'l said.

"They be lost wanderers, those gypsy kind. They don't care about nothing but getting high and eatin' all they can, stealin' all they can and fightin' about what they didn't eat and didn't steal," Sleepy Sam said.

"But they danced. They sang songs. They seemed real happy and they just went crazy."

"I know. But the whole world be crazy now, son. Just keep clear of weirdos."

Jim took the advice and a hat full of eggs and left.

— ◆ —

Mud Creek was just a little town near the Rockets now. Weeds and grass grew in the cracks of the streets, curbs and sidewalks. The windows of most buildings no longer were glass. Most of the stores had been looted and truthfully, Jim had done his share of looting before going away to hide, but after most of the people left, he found it just wasn't as much fun doing it alone.

Jim knew there was still much to be had for one man and he shouldn't act like a kid, afraid of the ghosts in the stores. If he needed something now, he just took it like a man. Jim knew he had to act like a man now, not a little boy. The encounter with the ugly man had taught him that, as much as his own Jungle dreams which sometimes included a sad faced girl with big eyes and soft pink lips.

He wondered where everyone had gone to after they left Mud Creek and what in the Sam Hill could be better out there? He envisioned only the worst. All of them gone crazy and eating one another like sharks with blood in the water.

The town provided most of his needs and the library had provided books that taught him about things like sharks that he had never seen except in pictures, and about bears and such, the monkey, the lion, the birds. From Sleepy Sam and Cranky Dan'l, he also learned about how to plant the seeds from the stores, and because he planted them behind the garage, he survived because he didn't have to depend on Sleepy Sam or on anyone. He even bartered with his extras, sometimes with an old lady who made beeswax candles. She sold them in the center of town along with some moonshine her old man made, but she frightened him. She always made awful cannibal jokes.

"I got me a hankering for boy today. My stomach aches to eat me some boy. You know some boy I can eat? What's pink and white and et' all over?" she'd laugh.

"Raw boy," Jim would have to say or she wouldn't exchange her candle for what scavenged item he was proffering, usually some stolen book, unbroken crockery or beans. Mr.'s moonshine wasn't too bad and it was cheap. A book of matches and Jim was set with a jar full of amber fire. He didn't drink it, though. He used it to clean stuff.

— ◆ —

Their set-up was in an old gasoline station that smelled funny. He avoided Mr. and Mrs. (they had no other names that Jim knew of). He preferred the Rockets.

He had even come to like the quiet, the sky and the moon, the stars at night. The sun in the daytime. The rain. He had a good shelter not far from the SUV where he hid things and sometimes slept when he wasn't too scared. It was inside one of the old Rockets and it was roomy in there and the power that ran the lights never went down. It was not bad at all. He felt safe there, protected.

Being alone was not bad until he saw the girl. Saw her one day in town while he was hunting for things to barter with to go with what he grew. Saw her scrounging through an old Wal-Mart store, dressed only in a pink tee-shirt, flip-flops and boy's underwear. He saw her. She saw him. And she ran. And in that moment he knew he did not truly like being alone or with farts like Sleepy Sam and his dumb son.

After that, he thought of her often. Her long blonde hair and the way she looked in that underwear.

He knew about girls—and women like Mrs. and the insane warrior woman and her maniac man who fought till they died. Girls were better. There had been girls when there was a school, but after the Revolution there were few more girls to see, just some guys. The girls often fled to the cities. He assumed some girls lived nearby, he'd just never seen any. He thought most went into hiding because of the monsters who enjoyed taking women to their masters, so he thought they were all gone and he figured cannibals liked girl meat even more than boy meat. He liked to watch the old movies Sleepy Sam had on videos and DVDs. Sleepy Sam had quite a stash and Jim had loved watching the *Star Wars* series over and over but Sam always demanded payment. Jim had swiped the first *Star Wars* movie and watched it several times on a small battery powered DVD player he had found in some rich person's house but the battery went dead and he hadn't found another battery that would work. After awhile, though, he just got tired of the movies, especially the porno films Sleepy Sam adored. Too many pretty women in the movies.

It was better to know you were alone, and just be alone, and learn to like it. If you didn't, you thought too much, and if you thought too much, you hurt too much, and that led to wondering too much about imagined things that could not be. Then, if you held yourself in your hand at night and made pleasure come, it became a mean, hollow pleasure that only made you want the other and that made you feel just how lonely and alone you truly were.

If you didn't watch the DVDs and the jerky videos, then you didn't think about it so much.

Not so much.

Not as much.

But, once he knew the girl existed, he could not rest. He could no longer be alone and like it.

— ◆ —

Alone was no longer the absence of others. It was a hollow ache, a hole that couldn't be plugged and had no bottom. Then he asked Sleepy Sam what he did to get over being lonesome.

"I just never think about it none."

"What about Dan'l's mom?"

"She died."

"Well, how'd you get over it?"

Sleepy Sam attacked the dirt with his hoe. "You just don't."

"Well, then how do you stand it?"

"You just do."

Not much help. Jim supposed the two were his best friends in the universe but they weren't really very bright. He guessed he would have to find the girl. He needed to talk to her.

— ◆ —

On another day, as the year wound down and summer died out and the cool winds came in, bringing the first rains of the winter to come, he went back to town and scrounged about for some canned goods. He found some canned meat, and was happy even if the expiration date had come and gone years ago. He thought pork and beans and tuna and Spam would just make Mr. and Mrs. the happiest souls on the planet. And the tin of sardines, even if slightly spoiled, would make Sleepy Sam laugh. He also found a Corning Ware lid in excellent condition. That should be worth three candles at least. If he had a gun he might shoot something fresh to eat, but he had only seen a few crows and scrawny squirrels.

All the guns in town had been taken; the stores looted of them and their ammunition. So that was out. He fished from time to time with a pole, cord, and hook made from a paper clip. Worms he dug out of the ground for bait. Sometimes he used crickets. But finding the canned meat was a good thing. He had thought it was all gone, but there were several cans in a store he thought he had checked out. They were stashed under a tarpaulin inside an old standing fridge.

It was the store where he had first seen the girl. He was hoping she might be there.

She wasn't.

He took the meat back to the rocket ship and ate the Spam with some fresh carrots and enjoyed it, but it didn't stop him from thinking about the girl, and he couldn't be happy alone anymore.

—◆—

The boy had long dark hair. He kept it tied back with a strip of black leather. He acted tough, like he owned Mud Creek and he made her so angry. He stole her stash of food that she'd found the day before. She watched him cram everything into a kid's backpack. Her stomach growled. He was like a monster, one of those creeps that stole her family. She hated him and yearned for him at the same time. She decided to stalk him, pretend he was a beast she could capture and roast over a slow fire for dinner. A little garlic made anything edible. She carried a jar of garlic powder, pepper and salt with her at all times. Her mother had taught her how to cook when she was six years old. That was how old she was when the rockets came and the Revolution began.

The monsters. The cannibals. The robots.

How long had it taken her to reach Mud Creek? "Get to Mud Creek," were her mother's last words before the fire and the screams sent her running into the forest straight into the claws of a monster. She had told her the coordinates every night before bedtime and what to do when she got inside one of the spaceships. "Go home," her mother said. Sally didn't know where home was. She had to find out though.

She followed him quietly, like an Indian. Mother was an Indian. Maybe. Actually, Sally was not sure what Mother was, just that she was alone and much older than six.

And now seeing her reflection always disturbed her. How did she get so big? Her body had betrayed her. She even bled once a month and that meant she could have a baby. She saw a monster take a baby once. And she didn't want to know what it did with it. It frightened her. How she wanted to rip it from its claws and protect it.

That was when she got the dog. The dog, a shaggy, golden retriever became her friend and loyal companion. She knew his breed because her mother once showed her a dog book with wonderful pictures. When she saw him scavenging for food on the outskirts of a city, she called to him with a pang of longing sweeping through her: "Little One!" He came to her as if he had always known her. They slept together at night, Sally's hand often resting on his head. It was better than being alone. But the dog couldn't talk. She wished it could talk, explain to her what had gone so terribly wrong with the world that they had been forced to live like this, so alone, so horribly, hideously alone.

She called the dog *Little One* even though he wasn't exactly little because someone had once called her that. Maybe her mother or her father had whispered those words—his face was an even more distant memory than her mom's, featureless with two dark smudges for eyes and a mouth that never opened except to say, "Good bye." She was not sure. Maybe she didn't even have a dad.

Sally tracked the boy to the library, a place of rotting books and broken computers, several times. It took all her courage to confront him on the third visit. He rummaged in the librarian's office, squatting in front of an old DVD player. "If I could just figure out how to make a battery or make a generator. I really should study on it some. I think I could do it..." he said out loud, as if he knew she was standing behind him.

"I hate you," she finally said to force him to turn around, her shadow almost touching his. Of course he knew she was there. The light in her lantern glowed.

"Say what?" he turned slowly and looked at her.

"Won't do no good," she said, "—that thing can't hear you scream when I kill you.

"I've decided to roast you well done with wild onion and garlic or make me some boy jerky that will last me a year or more. How'd that be? You scared yet?" She set the lantern down with one hand. In the other she held a Glock 19, something she stole from the last cannibal she'd killed.

"I don't think you want to do that," the boy said, eyes wide. The gun always frightened the country boys.

Sally smiled. "Maybe. Maybe not. If you got a knife, show it now. Toss it over here or I'll shoot you right between the eyes."

The knife slid between her feet. "I'm unarmed now. You got me dead to rights. But are you sure you want to kill and eat me? You don't look like a cannibal."

"There ain't much meat on you, I do confess. Some fat makes for better eating when it comes to roast meat."

"I got some carrots, onions, potatoes and I can get some eggs. Wouldn't that taste better?"

"Yeah and I bet you've got some Spam, pork and beans and sardines. Am I right, you lousy, no good, asshole THIEF?"

"And you got a cute T-shirt and some Hanes underwear I think I might like to have. Fair exchange?"

"Not on your life," Sally said, trying to keep a smile from flickering across her lips. The fall weather meant her legs were cold. And the T-shirt wasn't enough to protect her against the cold to come.

"And tea. I got tea back at my sleeping space. Lipton or some Stash spice tea I've been keeping for just the right time. I'll share it with you if you don't kill me. That's a fine piece of gun you got there. I don't reckon I've seen one of them guns before. Not in these parts, anyway. You from the city?"

"I want my food back."

"I'll give it to you, just put the gun away. Okay? Let's be friends."

Her dog, Little One, had done nothing. He had stood beside her, didn't growl and his tail began wagging.

"Nice dog. What's its name?"

"Little One."

"He's not very little."

"I know and if you are mean to me, one word and you're dead meat."

"Okay."

"So—do you want to go shopping with me? I need me some clothes." Mother and Sally used to go shopping. She would never forget shopping. That was another word for scavenging now.

"Only if you don't kill me if we don't find much. There is this little clothes place that still has some wearable stuff. I bet you're kind of cold."

Sally looked at her torn, smelly T-shirt. "Yeah, I am. Lead the way."

The boy stood. He was a young man with long legs in worn jeans. The bare chest that showed through the opening of his button-less flannel shirt had brown hair on it while his shirt had sleeves that were far too short for his arms. He had some hair on his face, too, not a lot but enough to scare her just a little bit. At least it wasn't a lot and it looked kind of fine. Sally also realized he was a lot taller than she was. She followed him cautiously.

He led her out of the library and down about three blocks or so, to a small department store. A few mannequins still stood in one display, miraculously sporting the latest in pre-Revolution, post-Republic of Texas fashion, cobwebby and filthy. But the shoes looked intact—sturdy black shoes that might fit. Hands slightly shaking, she snatched them and tried them on. He threw her some socks. She put them on and then tried the shoes. They fit. "This is good," she said. She didn't know how long they'd last but she'd take them.

"The best clothes are at the back in a storeroom most looters miss," the young man said.

"Okay. What's your name?"

"Jim, James Leroy Carver. What's yours?"

"Sally Louise Alice Mistral Corabeth Angelique Kiki Anne Robinson Lewis Thompson Johnson Mason Something or Other. In other words, I haven't the vaguest clue but I think my Mother called me Sally."

"Well, dang, that's a mouthful, Sally." He smiled.

Sally felt suddenly weak. He held out his hand. "Let's get you some new clothes. I could use some new trousers myself. These jeans are getting too tight."

They were tight, she noticed but didn't think that was such a bad thing.

In the storeroom, the lantern came in handy. They tried on clothes, backs turned, used to nudity and unaware that seeing each other might provoke some strange feelings.

She looked at him like a wolf looked at a wounded pig when his pants slipped to the floor so he could try some gray silky suit pants.

"You don't got any underwear on. How come?"

He seemed stunned and uncomfortable. "Just don't see the point."

"Oh." She pulled on a short red skirt. "This is cute but I guess I need me some pants, too."

He threw her some jeans. She tried them and grinned. "I can wear these. They fit. I want me a shirt with pockets. And a jacket and sweater, too."

He grinned.

"I need me a back pack better'n that thing of yours. How come you carry such a little baby backpack? Don't you need a bigger one now? You're a man, not a kid."

"I guess I should. Never thought about it, really."

"Hey, thanks."

"Don't mention it."

"What do you mean?"

"I guess we're friends now."

She tried on a jacket after shaking the dust out of it. "This could do with a wash in the creek. Mud Creek has a creek, doesn't it?"

"Sort of. We can go bathe in the creek, if you'd like, but you can't swim with a gun."

"I'd like that, Jim. But I want my food back first or I'm telling you I'll kill you and roast you for supper." She waved the Glock 19.

"Put that away or we can't be friends," he said.

— ◆ —

Jim had done more talking with Sally than he'd ever done with another human being. She talked so much that it shocked him. He talked so much he got hoarse. They talked at the creek before they got naked and jumped in. He had never seen such a pretty girl in his life, certainly not one his own age and certainly not one with a gun.

He really wanted to look at the gun up close but she wouldn't let him. She made her dog sit on it while they swam.

Jim wanted to touch her so badly he actually ached. It hurt to watch her breasts bob in the water. They swam closer and closer to each other. He shook the cold water out of his ears when he came up for air after a few strokes that brought him right next to her. He suddenly had to do something or burst. He grabbed her and kissed her. She resisted at first and then she kissed him back. They were kind of sloppy at kissing.

It took a few tries before it felt right.

They kissed a lot and then she got scared and swam away. She got into her clothes, whistled to her dog and left. Jim treaded water for awhile and then he got out before his skin got all wrinkled. The sun was going down and the warmth of the moment had vanished

He waited for her to come back and get the food he'd stolen from her but she didn't. He didn't want to go all the way back into town to the SUV so instead he went to the rocket ship where he hid things.

That night he sat alone outside the Rocket, and looked at the stars and wondered what she thought about their kisses. Way out in the distance, coming from the mountains, he could see light. Fires. Someone was up there. He wondered if one of the lights belonged to the girl. He wondered if she were still alive or if some other man had her and was enjoying her.

It was not a thing he liked to think about for very long. Then he thought about the ridge and the giant faces.

He told himself that she was most likely not that far away. The lights from the fires looked near, but they were not. Maybe the beasts of the jungle were coming or the monsters or the cannibals. He wondered if they would come to the Rocket and find him. He feared that. He knew that he could stay inside his hiding place and finally figure how to close it up, and it would be impossible for them to come in after him, with him way up high, the hatch closed and air-tight. No one could ever get to him in here.

Maybe that girl Sally had become a cannibal. Let her have that damn Glock 19 and that dog she liked to sleep with. Maybe she had fleas. Maybe if he slept with her he'd get fleas and they'd scratch themselves to death. If he did not get caught outside, nothing could happen. That was the thing to watch out for, not getting caught out where there was a chance of being hurt, captured, killed and eaten. Or maybe just his supplies taken, his rocket ship stolen by a girl who could grow up to be like, well, Mrs.

There were other rockets. Someone like that girl could come along and move in next door. There could be a lot of people living in the rockets. They could call it Rocket City on Wuthering Heights Street. They could borrow tools and plant gardens and share and work their way straight into a Post-Revolution civilization. They could get that dang DVD player working again and the electric plant and make new Spam and pork and beans that never rotted.

It was a pretty thought, but he knew it was just a thought. If more men and women like Sally came with guns, they would most likely kill him. They had formed their packs, and the packs were what they protected. If you were outside the pack, they wanted you dead; they wanted to eat you.

He wondered if he would eat a human being, and knew, if there was no other food available, he would—easily— with or without potatoes. Sally had mentioned garlic. He liked garlic.

He remembered his garden behind the garage growing in the moonlight. It was fat with vegetables, and he was pleased by the thought of the coming harvest. If he didn't go check on it, what would happen? The garden needed watering.

Seemed like several days went by and he got bored waiting to see if Sally would come find him. She didn't so he decided to go into Mud Creek to just see what she was up to and check on his garden but he was afraid. What if she laughed at him?

He lingered in the rocket ship, at the doorway after checking his clothes and looked out, hoping she'd still come so he wouldn't have to search for her. He had slept poorly the night before, and while it was dark he had released the hatch and sat with his feet dangling out of the opening. Just sat there watching at the sunrise, as bright as red orange trumpet flowers opening in the morning air.

The air smelled rich with oxygen and the trees around him were bright green and the mountains in the distance shimmered a blue violet capped with white snow. He thought going to the mountains might be nice. It was cold up in the mountains and the air might be thin, still he might be able to breathe better, think better. The beauty might be enough to soothe his itch.

But he decided he had a better chance of coming home if he went into town, and even that was not smart.

He went anyway. He went back to the store where he first saw her.

—◆—

Sally hid behind a stack of hardware when she heard him enter the store.

He looked about, didn't see her. It was a large store. She knew he was looking for her. The store, an old Wal-Mart, had mostly been looted, but there were still tools lying about, and any one of them might make a good weapon.

He didn't pick one up. Maybe he didn't want to look aggressive. Still she couldn't be sure it was safe to be his friend. Could humans be friends now? Was she human?

Could anyone be trusted after the Revolution? She crept backwards, trying to reach a back room.

"I'm just lonely," he said out loud and that surprised her."—I've seen you in your underwear, and you've seen me in less than that. We kind of know each other." He laughed. "We should at least be friends."

And then she stood, at the back, just behind a door. But the door had not pulled back far enough. It had swollen and would only go so far, and he could see her right elbow poking out.

"Look. I don't have a weapon. I know where you are. I don't want to hurt you. Wouldn't you like someone to talk to some more, Sally?"

He stood still, waiting.

She did not move.

He said, "I have more fresh food. I could share it. I have some cocoa powder, too. I have a nice safe place to stay in the Rockets. I don't want to hurt you."

—◆—

The elbow moved.

An arm appeared. Sally waved. "Hi, Jim."

"Hi," he said.

They embraced. She shivered in his heat.

—◆—

He took her not to the Rockets, but to the ridge. He wanted her to see the stone faces staring up into the stars that night they finally satisfied their hunger.

The faces watched them make a fire. They ate and they mated like the animals in the jungle. He felt almost safe in her arms. Then he became frightened. Towards the chill of dawn he slipped from her sleeping form, gently disengaging her arms from his waist and pulling his blue blankie over her to keep her warm. Little One took his place. Sally moaned in her dreams but didn't awaken. He crept to the Rocket where he hid things, where he felt truly safe. He fell asleep curled around his ratty backpack, *The Jungle Book* on his bare chest.

Morning came. Jim rubbed his eyes as he heard something rustling. The hatch he had not been able to secure had betrayed him. She had found a way inside.

Sally stood over him with her Glock 19.

"I should kill you now, but I won't."

Jim tried to snatch the gun. She drew back. Little One growled.

"Go away!" Jim said.

"I intend to do just that."

"Go!" he said.

"Well, I am. But do you want to go with me?" Her large eyes blinked away tears.

Jim shook his head, confused. "This is my Rocket. You leave, now!"

"Jim, please—don't you understand? I'm taking this spaceship. I know how to activate it and I'm going home. The second I saw it, I remembered everything I'm supposed to do. Maybe my mother told me or something or somebody else. All I know is I've got to get out of here, now! I'm leaving this awful place. It's programmed to take us home."

"Us? Home?"

"We don't belong here, you know. We never did. We just got stuck here, that's what Mother said before she died."

"No."

"Yes. Now you must decide. You can either get out of this Rocket or I'll kill you and throw you out and let what's left of the damn humans eat you for dinner."

Jim pulled out his pocket knife.

Sally pointed her gun.

Little One whimpered behind her.

Sally put one hand on a dull panel that burst into violet and orange hues that pulsated and hummed. "L21—00-systems go," she whispered.

The Rocket thrummed louder, a high-pitched keening. The long dead Rocket had come to life, a silver bullet primed to erupt into the heavens.

"You've got to get out if you're staying. You've got to decide. You're either in or you're out."

Jim got to his knees and dropped his knife. He couldn't hurt her. "But this is my home. It's not yours."

"Why can't it be mine, too? Why can't we just share it?"

"You're stealing my safe place, my *home*—" Jim tried to knock the gun out of her hand and she hit him. He grabbed her wrist.

"How *dare* you?" she said. Who *are* you?"

They struggled for possession of the gun.

She kicked him where it hurt the most. He let go, groaning. He had kissed her. He had—loved her? Love. What did that word *mean*? Hell what if she wasn't even human? Was she a lost wanderer? A gypsy? An alien monster?

"I'm sorry. Oh, Jim, did I hurt you?" The gun slid down to the smooth reflective surface and they saw their own scared faces. She kicked the gun and the knife out of the hatch. Their reflections shimmered.

"Yes, you did—but I hurt you first, didn't I?" Then he understood. If Sally was a lost wanderer, maybe he was too.

"I don't want to be alone. I just want to go home."

The hatch slid into place. The strangers stared at each other while the dog licked Jim's hand.

"But where is home? Where *are* we going?"

Sally didn't know.

He didn't either.

Maybe it was better that way.

At least they could be alone together.

And as far as *home* went, they'd figure that one out when they got there.

Sally reached for Jim's hand, the one free of dog slobber. A half smile touched her lips. Jim sighed as his fingers curled around hers. Maybe they were already there.

Home.

The Events Concerning a Nude Fold-Out Found in a Harlequin Romance

L ooking back on it, I wouldn't have thought something as strange as all this, full of the real coincidence of life, would have begun with a bad circus, but that's how it started, at least for me.

My luck had gone from bad to worse, then over the lip of worse, and into whatever lower level it can descend into. My job at the aluminum chair plant had played out and no rich relatives had died and left me any money. Fact was, I don't think the Cooks, least any that are kin to me, have any money, outside of a few quarters to put in a jukebox come Saturday night, maybe a few bucks to waste on something like pretzels and beer.

Me, I didn't even have money for beer or jukeboxes. I was collecting a little money on unemployment, and I was out beating the bushes for a job, but there didn't seem to be much in the way of work in Mud Creek. I couldn't even get on at the feed store carrying out bags of fertilizer and seed. All the sixteen-year-olds had that job.

It looked like I was going to have to move out of Mud Creek to find work, and though the idea of that didn't hurt my feelings any, there was Jasmine, my teenage daughter, and she still had a year of high school to finish before she went off to Nacogdoches to start her degree in anthropology at Stephen F. Austin State University, and I planned to follow her over there and find a place of my own where we could be near, and improve our relationship, which overall was all right to begin with. I just wanted more time with her.

Right then Jasmine lived with her mother, and her mother doesn't care a damn for me. She wanted to marry a guy that was going to be a high roller, and believe me, I wanted to be a high roller, but what she got was a guy who each time at the mark throws craps. No matter what I do, it turns to shit. Last break I felt I'd had in life was when I was ten and fell down and cracked my ankle. Well, maybe there was one good break after all. One that wasn't a bone. Jasmine. She's smart and pretty and ambitious and the love of my life.

But my marital problems and life's woes are not what this is about. I was saying about the circus.

It was mid-June, and I'd tried a couple places, looking for work, and hadn't gotten any, and I'd gone over to the employment office to talk to the people there and embarrass myself about not finding any work yet. They told me they didn't have anything for me either, but they didn't look embarrassed at all. When it's you and the employment office, better known as the unemployment office, feeling embarrassed is a one-way street and you're the one driving on it. They seem almost proud to tell you how many unemployment checks you got left, so it can kind of hang over your head like an anvil or something.

So, I thanked them like I meant it and went home, and believe me, that's no treat.

Home is a little apartment about the size of a washroom at a Fina Station, only not as nice and without the air-conditioning. The window looks out over Main Street, and when a car drives by the window shakes, which is one of the reasons I leave it open most of the time. That and the fact I can hope for some sort of breeze to stir the dead, hot air around. The place is over a used bookstore called MARTHA'S BOOKS, and Martha is an all right lady if you like them mean. She's grumpy, about five hundred years old, weighs two-fifty when she's at her wrestling weight, wears men's clothing and has a bad leg and a faint black mustache to match the black wool ski cap she wears summer or winter, on account of her head is as bald as a river stone. I figure the cap is a funny sort of vanity, considering she doesn't do anything to get rid of that mustache. Still, she always does her nails in pink polish and she smokes those long feminine cigarettes that some women like, maybe thinking if the weeds look elegant enough they won't give them cancer.

Another thing about Martha, is with that bad leg she has a limp, and she helps that along with a golf putter she uses as a cane, putter-side up for a handle. See her coming down the street, which isn't often, you got to think there's not much you could add to make her any more gaudy, unless it's an assful of bright tail feathers and maybe some guys to follow her playing percussion instruments.

I liked to go down to Martha's from time to time and browse the books, and if I had a little spare change, I'd try to actually buy something now and then, or get something for Jasmine. I was especially fond of detective books, and Jasmine, bless her little heart, liked Harlequin Romances. She'd read them four or five a weekend when she wasn't dating boys, and since she was dating quite regularly now, she'd cut back mostly to one or two Harlequins a weekend. Still, that was too many. I kept hoping she'd outgrow it. The romance novels and the dates. I was scared to death she'd fall in love with some cowboy with a cheek full of snuff and end up ironing Western shirts and wiping baby asses before she was old enough to vote.

Anyway, after I didn't find any jobs and nobody died and left me any money, I went home and brooded, then went downstairs to Martha's to look for a book.

Jasmine had made out a list of the titles she was looking to collect, and I took the list with me just in case I came across something she needed. I thought if I did, I might buy it and get her a detective book too, or something like that, give it to her with the romance and maybe she'd read it. I'd done that several times, and so far, to the best of my knowledge, she hadn't read any of the non-romance novels. The others might as well have been used to level a vibrating refrigerator, but I kept on trying.

The stairs went down from my place and out into the street, and at the bottom, to the left of them, was Martha's. The store was in front and she lived in back. During business hours in the summer the door was always open since Martha wouldn't have put air-conditioning in there if half the store had been a meat locker hung with prize beef. She was too cheap for that. She liked her mustache sweat-beaded, her bald head pink beneath her cap. The place smelled of books and faintly of boiled cabbage, or maybe that was some soured clothing somewhere. The two smells have always seemed a lot alike to me. It's the only place I know hotter and filthier than my apartment, but it does have the books. Lots of them.

I went in, and there on the wall was a flyer for a circus at three o'clock that day. Martha had this old post board just inside the door, and she'd let people pin up flyers if they wanted, and sometimes she'd leave them there a whole day before she tore them down and wrote out the day's receipts on the back of them with a stubby, tongue-licked pencil. I think that's the only reason she had the post board and let people put up flyers, so she'd have scratch paper.

The flyer was for a circus called THE JIM DANDY THREE RING CIRCUS, and that should have clued me, but it didn't. Truth is, I've never liked circuses. They depress me. Something about the animals and the people who work there strike me as desperate, as if they're living on the edge of a cliff and the cliff is about to break off. But I saw this flyer and I thought of Jasmine.

When she was little she loved circuses. Her mother and I used to take her, and I remembered the whole thing rather fondly. Jasmine would laugh so hard at the clowns you had to tell her to shut up, and she'd put her hands over her eyes and peek through her fingers at the wild animal acts.

Back then, things were pretty good, and I think her mother even liked me, and truth to tell, I thought I was a pretty good guy myself. I thought I had the world by the tail. It took me a few years to realize the closest I was to having the world by the tail was being a dingle berry on one of its ass hairs. These days, I felt like the most worthless sonofabitch that had ever squatted to shit over a pair of shoes. I guess it isn't hip or politically correct, but to me, a man without a job is like a man without balls.

Thinking about my problems also added to me wanting to go to the circus. Not only would I get a chance to be with Jasmine, it would help me get my mind off my troubles.

I got out my wallet and opened it and saw a few sad bills in there, but it looked to me that I had enough for the circus, and maybe I could even spring for dinner afterwards, if Jasmine was in the mood for a hot dog and a soda pop. She wanted anything more than that, she had to buy me dinner, and I'd let her, since the money came from her mother, my darling ex-wife, Connie—may she grow like an onion with her head in the ground.

Mommy Dearest didn't seem to be shy of the bucks these days on account of she was letting old Gerald the Oil Man drop his drill down her oil shaft on a nightly basis.

Not that I'm bitter about it or anything. Him banging my ex-wife and being built like Tarzan and not losing any of his hair at the age of forty didn't bother me a bit.

I put my wallet away and turned and saw Martha behind the counter looking at me. She twisted on the stool and said, "Got a job yet?"

I just love a small town. You fart and everyone looks in your direction and starts fanning.

"No, not yet," I said.

"You looking for some kind of a career?"

"I'm looking for work."

"Any kind of work?"

"Right now, yes. You got something for me?"

"Naw. Can't pay my rent as it is."

"You're just curious, then?"

"Yeah. You want to go to that circus?"

"I don't know. Maybe. Is this a trick question too?"

"Guy put up the flyer gave me a couple tickets for letting him have the space on the board there. I'd give them to you for stacking some books. I don't really want to do it."

"Stack the books or give me the tickets?"

"Neither one. But you stack them Harlequins for me, I'll give you the tickets."

I looked at my wrist where my watch used to be before I pawned it. "You got the time?"

She looked at her watch. "Two o'clock."

"I like the deal," I said, "but the circus starts at three and I wanted to take my daughter."

Martha shook out one of her delicate little cigarettes and lit it, studied me. It made me feel funny. Like I was a shit smear on a laboratory slide. Most I'd ever talked to her before was when I asked where the new detective novels were and she grumped around and finally told me, as if it was a secret she'd rather have kept.

"Tell you what," Martha said, "I'll give you the tickets now, and you come back tomorrow morning and put up the books for me."

"That's nice of you," I said.

"Not really. I know where you live, and you don't come put up my romance novels tomorrow, I'll hunt you down and kill you."

I looked for a smile, but I didn't see any.

"That's one way to do business," I said.

"The only way. Here." She opened a drawer and pulled out the tickets and I went over and took them. "By the way, what's your name, boy? See you in here all the time, but don't know your name."

Boy? Was she talking to me?

"Plebin Cook," I said. "And I've always assumed you're Martha."

"Martha ain't much of a name, but it beats Plebin. Plebin's awful. I was named that I'd get it changed. Call yourself most anything and it'd be better than Plebin."

"I'll tell my poor, old, gray-haired mother what you said."

"You must have been an accident and that's why she named you that. You got an older brother or sister?"

"A brother."

"How much older?"

Earning these tickets was getting to be painful. "Sixteen years."

"What's his name?"

"Jim."

"There you are. You were an accident. Jim's a normal name. Her naming you Plebin is unconscious revenge. I read about stuff like that in one of those psychology books came in. Called KNOW WHY THINGS HAPPEN TO YOU. You ought to read it. Thing it'd tell you is to get your name changed to something normal. Right name will give you a whole nuther outlook about yourself."

I had a vision of shoving those circus tickets down her throat, but I restrained myself for Jasmine's sake. "No joke? Well, I'll see you tomorrow."

"Eight o'clock sharp. Go stacking 'em after nine, gets so hot in here you'll faint. A Yankee visiting some relatives came in here and did just that. Found him about closing time over there by the historicals and the Gothic Romances. Had to call an ambulance to come get him. Got out of here with one of my Gothics clutched in his hand. Didn't pay me a cent for it."

"And people think a job like this is pretty easy."

"They just don't know," Martha said.

I said thanks and goodbye and started to turn away.

"Hey," Martha said. "You decide to get your name changed, they'll do stuff like that for you over at the court house."

"I'll keep that in mind," I said.

— ◆ —

I didn't want any more of Martha, so I went over to the drug store and used the payphone there and called Jasmine. Her mother answered.

"Hi, Connie," I said.

"Get a job yet?"

"No," I said. "But I'm closing in on some prospects."

"Bet you are. What do you want?"

"Jasmine in?"

"You want to talk to her?"

No, I thought. Just ask for the hell of it. But I said, "If I may."

The phone clattered on something hard, a little more violently than necessary, I thought. A moment later Jasmine came on the line. "Daddy."

"Hi, Baby Darling. Want to go to the circus?"

"The circus?"

"The Jim Dandy Circus is in town, and I've got tickets."

"Yeah. Really." She sounded as if I'd asked her if she wanted to have her teeth cleaned.

"You used to like the circuses."

"When I was ten."

"That was just seven years ago."

"That's a long time."

"Only when you're seventeen. Want to go or not? I'll even spring for a hot dog."

"You know what they make hot dogs out of?"

"I try not to think about it. I figure I get some chili on it, whatever's in the dog dies."

"Guess you want me to come by and get you?"

"That would be nice. Circus starts at three. That's less than an hour away."

"All right, but Daddy?"

"Yeah."

"Don't call me Baby Darling in public. Someone could hear."

"We can't have that."

"Really, Daddy. I'm getting to be a woman now. It's… I don't know… kind of…."

"Hokey?"

"That's it."

"Gottcha."

— ◆ —

The circus was not under the big top, but was inside the Mud Creek Exhibition center, which Mud Creek needs about as much as I need a second dick. I don't use the first one as it is. Oh, I pee out of it, but you know what I mean.

The circus was weak from the start, but Jasmine seemed to have a pretty good time, even if the performing bears were so goddamned old I thought we were going to have to go down there and help them out of their cages. The Tiger act was scary, because it looked as if the tigers were definitely in control, but the overweight Ringmaster got out alive, and the elephants came on, so old and wrinkled they looked like drunks in baggy pants. That was the best of it. After that, the dog act, conducted by Waldo the Great, got out of hand, and his performing poodles went X-rated, and the real doo-doo hit the fan.

Idiot trainer had apparently put one of the bitches to work while she was in heat, and in response, the male dogs jumped her and started poking, the biggest male finally winning the honors and the other five running about as if their brains had rolled out of their ears.

Waldo the Great went a little nuts and started kicking the fornicating dogs, but they wouldn't let up. The male dog kept his goober in the slot even when Waldo's kicks made his hind legs leave the ground. He didn't even yip.

I heard a kid behind us say, "Mommy, what are the puppies doing?"

And Mommy, not missing a beat, said, "They're doing a trick, dear."

Children were screaming. Waldo began kicking at the remaining dogs indiscriminately, and they darted for cover. Members of the circus rushed Waldo the Great. There were disappointed and injured dogs hunching and yipping all over the place. Waldo went back to the horny male and tried once more to discourage him. He really put the boot to him, but the ole boy really hung in there. I was kind of proud of him. One of the other dogs, innocent, except for confusion, and a gyrating ass and a dick like a rolled-back lipstick tube, made an error in geography and humped air past Waldo and got a kick in the ass for it.

He sailed way up and into the bleachers, went so high his fleas should have served cocktails and dinner on him. Came down like a bomb, hit between a crack in the bleachers with a yip. I didn't see him come out from under there. He didn't yip again.

The little boy behind me, said, "Is that a trick too?"

"Yes," Mommy said. "It doesn't hurt him. He knows how to land."

I certainly hoped so.

Not everyone took it as casually as Mommy. Some dog lovers came out of the bleachers and there was a fight. Couple of cowboys started trying to do to Waldo what he had done to the poodles.

Meanwhile, back at the ranch, so to speak, the two amorous mutts were still at it, the male laying pipe like there was no tomorrow.

Yes sir, a pleasant afternoon trip to the circus with my daughter. Another debacle. It was merely typical of the luck I had been experiencing. Even a free ticket to the circus could turn to shit.

Jasmine and I left while a cowboy down from the bleachers was using Waldo the Great as a punching bag. One of the ungrateful poodles was biting the cowboy on the boot.

— ◆ —

Me and Jasmine didn't have hot dogs. We ended up at a Mexican place, and Jasmine paid for it. Halfway through the meal Jasmine looked up at me and frowned.

"Daddy, I can always count on you for a good time."

"Hey," I said, "what were you expecting for free tickets? Goddamn Ringling Brothers?"

"Really, Daddy. I enjoyed it. Weirdness follows you around. At Mom's there isn't anything to do but watch television, and Mom and Gerald always go to bed about nine o'clock, so they're no fun."

"I guess not," I said, thinking nine o'clock was awful early to be sleepy. I hoped the sonofabitch gave her the clap.

After dinner, Jasmine dropped me off and next morning I went down to Martha's and she grunted at me and showed me the Harlequins and where they needed to go, in alphabetical order, so I started in placing them. After about an hour of that, it got hot and I had to stop and talk Martha into letting me go over to the drugstore and buy a Coke.

When I came back with it, there was a guy in there with a box of Harlequin Romances. He was tall and lean and not bad-looking, except that he had one of those little pencil-line mustaches that looked as if he'd missed a spot shaving or had a stain line from sipping chocolate milk. Except for a black eye, his face was oddly unlined, as if little that happened to him in life found representation there. I thought he looked familiar. A moment later, it came to me. He was the guy at the circus with the performing dogs. I hadn't recognized him without his gold lamé tights. I could picture him clearly now, his foot up in the air, a poodle being launched from it. Waldo the Great.

He had a box of books on the desk in front of Martha. All Harlequin Romances. He reached out and ran his fingers over the spines. "I really hate to get rid of these," he was saying to Martha, and his voice was as sweet as a cooing turtle dove. "Really hate it, but see, I'm currently unemployed and extra finances, even of a small nature, are needed, and considering all the books I read, well, they're outgrowing my trailer. I tell you, it hurts me to dispense with these. Just seeing them on my shelves cheers me…. Oh, I take these books so to heart. If life could be like these, oh what a life that would be. But somebody always messes it up." He touched the books. "True love. Romance. Happy endings. Oh, it should be that way, you know. We live such a miserable existence. We—"

"Hey," Martha said. "Actually, I don't give a shit why you want to get rid of them. And if life was like a Harlequin Romance, I'd put a gun in my mouth. You want to sell this crap, or not?"

Martha always tries to endear herself to her customers. I reckon she's got a trust fund somewhere and her mission on earth is to make as many people miserable as possible. Still, that seemed blunt even for her.

"Well, now," Waldo said. "I was merely expressing a heartfelt opinion. Nothing more. I could take my trade elsewhere."

"No skin off my rosy red ass," Martha said. "You want, that man over there will help you carry this shit back out to the car."

He looked at me. I blushed, nodded, drank more of my Coke.

He looked back at Martha. "Very well. I'll sell them to you, but only because I'm pressed to rid myself of them. Otherwise, I wouldn't take twice what you want to give for them."

"For you, Mister Asshole," Martha said, "just for you, I'll give you half of what I normally offer. Take it or leave it."

Waldo, Mr. Asshole, paused for a moment, studying Martha. I could see the side of his face, and just below his blackened eye there was a twitch, just once, then his face was smooth again.

"All right, let's conduct our business and get it over with," he said.

Martha counted the books, opened the cash register and gave Waldo a handful of bills. "Against my better judgement, there's the whole price."

"What in the world did I ever do to you?" Waldo The Great, alias, Mr. Asshole, said. He almost looked really hurt.

It was hard to tell. I'd never seen a face like that. So smooth. So expressionless. It was disconcerting.

"You breathe," Martha said, "that's enough of an offense." With that, Waldo, Mr. Asshole, went out of the store, head up, back straight.

"Friend of yours?" I asked.

"Yeah," Martha said. "Me and him are fuckin'."

"I thought the two of you were pretty warm."

"I don't know. I really can't believe it happened like that."

"You weren't as sweet as usual."

"Can't explain it. One of those things. Ever had that happen? Meet someone right off, and you just don't like them, and you don't know why."

"I always just shoot them. Saves a lot of breath."

She ignored me. "Like it's chemistry or something. That guy came in here, it was like someone drove by and tossed a rattlesnake through the door. I didn't like him on sight. Sometimes I think that there's certain people that are predators, and the rest of us, we pick up on it, even if it isn't obvious through their actions, and we react to it. And maybe I'm an asshole."

"That's a possibility," I said. "You being an asshole, I mean. But I got to tell you, I don't like him much either. Kind of makes my skin crawl, that unlined face and all."

I told her about the circus and the dogs.

"That doesn't surprise me any," Martha said. "I mean, anyone can lose their cool. I've kicked a dog in my time—"

"I find that hard to believe."

"—but I tell you, that guy hasn't got all the corn on his cob. I can sense it. Here, put these up. Earn your goddamn circus tickets."

I finished off the Coke, got the box of Harlequins Waldo had brought in, took them over to the romance section and put them on the floor.

I pulled one out to look at the author's name, and something fell out of the book. It was a folded piece of paper. I picked it up and unfolded it. It was a magazine fold-out of a naked woman, sort you see in the cheaper tits and ass magazines. She had breasts just a little smaller than watermelons and she was grabbing her ankles, holding her legs in a spread eagle position, as if waiting for some unsuspecting traveler to fall in. There were thick black paint lines slashed at the neck, torso, elbows, wrist, waist, knees and ankles. The eyes had been blackened with the marker so that they looked like nothing more than enormous skull sockets. A circle had been drawn around her vagina and there was a big black dot dead center of it, like a bulls eye. I turned it over. On the back over the printing there was written in black with a firm hand: Nothing really hooks together. Life lacks romance.

Looking at the photograph and those lines made me feel peculiar. I refolded the fold-out and started to replace it inside the book, then I thought maybe I'd throw it in the trash, but finally decided to keep it out of curiosity.

I shoved it into my back pocket and finished putting up the books, then got ready to leave. As I was going, Martha said, "you want a job here putting up books I'll take you on half a day five days a week. Monday through Friday. Saves some wear on my bad leg. I can pay you a little. Won't be much, but I don't figure you're worth much to me."

"That's a sweet offer, Martha, but I don't know."

"You say you want work."

"I do, but half a day isn't enough."

"More than you're working now, and I'll pay in cash. No taxes, no bullshit with the employment office."

"All right," I said. "You got a deal."

"Start tomorrow."

—◆—

I was lying naked on the bed with just the nightlight on reading a hard-boiled mystery novel. The window was open as always and there was actually a pretty nice breeze blowing in. I felt like I used to when I was twelve and staying up late and reading with a flashlight under the covers and a cool spring wind was blowing in through the window screen, and Mom and Dad were in the next room and I was loved and protected and was going to live forever. Pleasant.

There was a knock at the door.

That figured.

I got up and pulled on my pajama bottoms and put on a robe and went to the door. It was Jasmine. She had her long, dark hair tied back in a pony tail and she was wearing jeans and a shirt buttoned up wrong. She had a suitcase in her hand.

"Connie again?"

"Her and that man," Jasmine said as she came inside. "I hate them."

"You don't hate your mother. She's an asshole, but you don't hate her."

"You hate her."

"That's different."

"Can I stay here for a while?"

"Sure. There's almost enough room for me, so I'm sure you'll find it cozy."

"You're not glad to see me?"

"I'm glad to see you. I'm always glad to see you. But this won't work out. Look how small this place is. Besides, you've done this before. Couple times. You come here, eat all my cereal, start missing your comforts, and then you go home."

"Not this time."

"All right. Not this time. Hungry?"

"I really don't want any cereal."

"I actually have some lunch meat this time. It's not quite green."

"Sounds yummy."

I made a couple of sandwiches and poured us some slightly tainted milk and we talked a moment, then Jasmine saw the fold-out on the dresser and picked it up. I had pulled it from my pocket when I got home and tossed it there.

She opened it up and looked at it, then smiled at me. It was the same smile her mother used when she was turning on the charm, or was about to make me feel small enough to wear doll clothes.

"Daddy, dear!"

"I found it."

"Say you did?"

"Cut it out. It was in one of the books I was putting up today. I thought it was weird and I stuck it in my back pocket. I should have thrown it away."

Jasmine smiled at me, examined the fold-out closely. "Daddy, do men like women like this? That big, I mean?"

"Some do. Yes."

"Do you?"

"Of course not."

"What are these lines?"

"I don't know exactly, but that's what I thought was weird. It got my mind working overtime."

"You mean like the 'What If' game?"

The "What If" game was something Jasmine and I had made up when she was little, and had never really quit playing, though our opportunities to play it had decreased sharply over the last couple of years. It grew out of my thinking I was going to be a writer. I'd see something and

I'd extrapolate. An example was an old car I saw once where someone had finger-written in the dust on the trunk lid: THERE'S A BODY IN THE TRUNK.

Well, I thought about that and tried to make a story of it. Say there was a body in the trunk. How did it get there? Is the woman driving the car aware it's there? Did she commit the murder? That sort of thing. Then I'd try to write a story. After fifty or so stories, and three times that many rejects, I gave up writing them, and Jasmine and I started kicking ideas like that back and forth, for fun. That way I could still feed my imagination, but I could quit kidding myself that I could write. Also, Jasmine got a kick out of it.

"Let's play, Daddy?"

"All right. I'll start. I saw those slashes on that fold-out, and I got to thinking, why are these lines drawn?"

"Because they look like cuts," Jasmine said. "You know, like a chart for how to butcher meat."

"That's what I thought. Then I thought, it's just a picture, and it could have been marked up without any real motive. Absentminded doodling. Or it could have been done by someone who didn't like women, and this was sort of an imaginary revenge. Turning women into meat in his mind. Dehumanizing them."

"Or it could be representative of what he's actually done or plans to do. Wow! Maybe we've got a real mystery here."

"My last real mystery was what finished your mom and I off."

That was the body in the trunk business. I didn't tell it all before. I got so into that scenario I called a friend of mine, Sam, down at the cop shop and got him geared up about there being a body in the trunk of a car. I told it good, with details I'd made up and didn't even know I'd made up. I really get into this stuff. The real and the unreal get a little hard for me to tell apart. Or it used to be that way. Not anymore.

Bottom line is Sam pursued the matter, and the only thing in the trunk was a spare tire. Sam was a little unhappy with me. The cop shop was a little unhappy with him. My wife, finally tired of my make-believe, kicked me out and went for the oil man. He didn't make up stories. He made money and had all his hair and was probably hung like a water buffalo.

"But say we knew the guy who marked this picture, Daddy. And say we started watching him, just to see—"

"We do know him. Kind of."

I told her about Waldo the Great and his books and Martha's reaction.

"That's even weirder," Jasmine said. "This bookstore lady—"

"Martha."

"—does she seem like a good judge of character?"

"She hates just about everybody, I think."

"Well, for 'What If's' sake, say she is a good judge of character. And this guy really is nuts. And he's done this kind of thing to a fold-out because... say... say...."

"He wants life to be like a Harlequin Romance. Only it isn't. Women don't always fit his image of what they should be—like the women in the books he reads."

"Oh, that's good, Daddy. Really. He's gone nuts, not because of violent films and movies, but because of a misguided view about romance. I love it."

"Makes as much sense as a guy saying he axed a family because he saw a horror movie or read a horror novel. There's got to be more to it than that, of course. Rotten childhood, genetic makeup. Most people who see or read horror novels, romance novels, whatever, get their thrills vicariously. It's a catharsis. But in the same way a horror movie or book might set someone off who's already messed up, someone wound-up and ready to spring, the Harlequins do it for our man. He has so little idea what real life is like, he expects it to be like the Harlequins, or desperately wants it to be that way, and when it isn't, his frustrations build, and—"

"He kills women, cuts them up, disposes of their bodies. It's delicious. Really delicious."

"It's silly. There's a sleeping bag in the closet. Get it out when you get sleepy. Me, I'm going to go to bed. I got a part-time job downstairs at Martha's, and I start tomorrow."

"That's great, Daddy. Mom said you'd never find a job."

On that note, I went to bed.

—◆—

Next morning I went down to Martha's and started to work. She had a storeroom full of books. Some of them were stuck together with age, and some were full of worms. Being a fanatic book-lover, it hurt me, but I got rid of the bad ones in the dumpster out back, then loaded some boxes of good-condition books on a hand truck and wheeled them out and began putting them up in alphabetical order in their proper sections.

About nine that morning, Jasmine came down and I heard her say something to Martha, then she came around the corner of the detective section and smiled at me. She looked so much like her mother it hurt me. She had her hair pulled back and tied at her neck and she was starting to sweat. She wore white shorts, cut a little too short if you ask me, and a loose red tee-shirt and sandals. She was carrying a yellow pad with a pencil.

"What you doing?" I asked.

"Figuring out what Waldo the Great's up to. I been working on it ever since I got up. I got lots of notes here."

"What'd you have for breakfast?"

"Same as you, I bet. A Coke."

"Right. It's important we pay attention to nutrition, Baby Darling."

"You want to hear about Waldo or not?"

"Yeah, tell me, what's he up to?"

"He's looking for a job."

"Because he got fired for the dog-kicking business?"

"Yeah. So, he's staying in the trailer park here, and he's looking for a job. Or maybe he's got some savings and he's just hanging out for a while before he moves on. Let's just say all that for 'What If's' sake."

"All right, now what?"

"Just for fun, to play the game all the way, let's go out to the trailer park and see if he's living there. If he is, we ought to be able to find him. He's got all these dogs, so there should be some signs of them, don't you think?"

"Wait a minute. You're not planning on checking?"

"Just for the 'What If' game."

"Like I said, he could have moved on."

"That's what we'll find out. Later, we can go over to the trailer park and look around, play detective."

"That's carrying it too far."

"Why? It's just a game. We don't have to bother him."

"I don't know. I don't think so."

"Why not?" It was Martha. She came around the corner of the bookshelves leaning on her golf putter. "It's just a game."

"Aren't you supposed to be counting your money, or something?" I said to Martha. "Kill some of those roaches in your storeroom. That club would be just the tool for it."

"I couldn't help but overhear you because I was leaning against the other side of the bookshelf listening," Martha said.

"That'll do it," I said, and shelved a Mickey Spillane.

"We've spoke, but I don't think we've actually met," Jasmine said to Martha. "I'm his daughter."

"Tough to admit, I'm sure," Martha said.

Jasmine and Martha smiled at each other and shook hands.

"Why don't we go over there tonight?" Martha said. "I need something to do."

"To the trailer park?" I asked.

"Of course," Martha said.

"Not likely," I said. "I've had it with the detective business, imaginary or otherwise. It'll be a cold day in hell when I have anything else to do with it, in any manner, shape or form. And you can take that to the bank."

— ◆ —

That night, presumably an example of a cold day in hell, around nine-thirty, we drove over to the only trailer park in Mud Creek and looked around.

Waldo hadn't moved on. Being astute detectives, we found his trailer right away. It was bright blue and there was red lettering on the side that read: WALDO THE GREAT AND HIS MAGNIFICENT CANINES. The trailer was next to a big pickup with a trailer hitch and there were lights on in the trailer.

We were in Martha's old Dodge van, and we drove by Waldo's and around the loop in the park and out of there. Martha went a short distance, turned down a hard clay road that wound along the side of the creek and through a patch of woods and ended up at the rear of the trailer park, about even with Waldo's trailer. It was a bit of distance away, but you could see his trailer through the branches of the trees that surrounded the park. Martha parked to the side of the road and spoke to Jasmine. "Honey, hand me them binoculars out of the glove box."

Jasmine did just that.

"These suckers are infra-red," Martha said. "You can see a mole on a gnat's ass with one of these dead of night during a blizzard."

"And why in the world would you have a pair?" I asked.

"I used to do a little surveillance for a private investigation agency in Houston. I sort of borrowed these when I left. You know, boss I had hadn't been such a dick, I'd have stayed with that job. I was born to it."

"Sounds exciting," Jasmine said.

"It beat smelling book dust, I'll tell you that." Martha rolled down her window and put the glasses to her face and pointed them at Waldo's trailer.

"He's at the window," she said.

"This has gone far enough," I said. "We're not supposed to be doing this. It's an invasion of privacy."

"Settle down. He ain't got his pecker out or nothing" Martha said. "Wish he did, though. He's an asshole, but he ain't bad-looking. I wonder what kind of rod he's got on him?"

I looked at Jasmine. She looked a little stunned. "Listen here," I said. "My daughter's here."

"No shit," Martha said. "Listen, you stuffy old fart. She's grown up enough to know a man's got a hooter on him and what it looks like."

Jasmine's face was split by a weak smile. "Well, I know what they are, of course."

"All right, we're all versed in biology," I said. "Let's go. I've got a good book waiting at home."

"Hold the goddamn phone," Martha said. "He's coming out of the trailer."

I looked, and I could see Waldo's shape framed in the trailer's doorway. One of the poodles ran up behind him and he back-kicked it inside without even looking, went down the metal steps and closed and locked the trailer, got in his pickup and drove away.

"He's off," Martha said.

"Yeah. Probably to a fried chicken place," I said.

Martha lowered the binoculars and looked over her seat at me. "Would you quit fucking up the game? 'What If' is going on here."

"Yeah, Daddy," Jasmine said. "We're playing 'What If.' "

Martha cranked the van and followed the clay road as it curved around the park and out into the street. She went right. A moment later, we saw the back of Waldo's pickup. He had an arm hanging out the window and a cigarette was between his fingers and sparks were flaring off of it and flickering into the night.

"Smokey Bear'd come down on his ass like a ton of bricks, he seen that," Martha said.

We followed him to the end of the street and out onto the main drag, such as it is in Mud Creek. He pulled into a fried chicken joint.

"See," I said.

"Even murderers have to eat," Martha said, and she drove on by.

—◆—

My plan was to end the business there, but it didn't work that way. I pulled out of it and let them stay with it. All that week Martha and Jasmine played "What If." They pinned up the fold-out in my apartment and they wrote out scenarios for who Waldo was and what he'd done, and so on. They drove out to his place at night and discovered he kept weird hours, went out at all times of the night. They discovered he let the poodles out for bathroom breaks twice a night and that there was one less than there had been during the circus act. I guess Mommy had been wrong when she told her kid the poodle knew how to land.

It was kind of odd seeing Jasmine and Martha become friends like that. Martha had struck me as having all the imagination of a fencepost, but under that rough exterior and that loud mouth was a rough exterior and a loud mouth with an imagination.

I also suspicioned that she had lied about not being able to pay her rent. The store didn't make that much, but she always seemed to have money. As far as the store went, it got so I was running it by myself, fulltime, not only putting up books, but waiting on customers and closing up at night. Martha paid me well enough for it, however, so I didn't complain, but when she and Jasmine would come down from my place talking about their "killer," etc., I felt a little jealous. Jasmine had moved in with me, and now that I had my daughter back, she spent all her time with a bald-headed, mustached lady who was her father's boss.

Worse, Connie had been on my case about Jasmine and how my only daughter was living in a shit hole and being exposed to bad elements. The worst being me, of course. She came by the apartment a couple of times to tell me about it and to try and get Jasmine to go home.

I told her Jasmine was free to go home anytime she chose, and Jasmine explained that she had no intention of going home. She liked her sleeping bag and Daddy let her have Coke for breakfast. I sort of wish she hadn't mentioned the Coke part. She'd only had that for breakfast one morning, but she knew it'd get her mother's goat, and it had. Only thing was, now Connie could hang another sword over my head. Failure to provide proper nutrition for my only child.

Anyway, I was working in the store one day—well, working on reading a detective novel—when Martha and Jasmine came in.

"Get your goddamn feet off my desk," Martha said.

"Glad to see you," I said, lowering my feet and putting a marker in the book.

"Get off my stool," Martha said. "Quit reading that damn book and put some up."

I got off the stool. "You two have a pleasant day, Massah Martha?"

"Eat shit, Plebin," Martha said, leaning her golf club against the counter and mounting her stool.

"Daddy, Martha and I have been snooping. Listen what we got. Martha had this idea to go over to the newspaper office in LaBorde and look at back issues—"

"LaBorde?" I said.

"Bigger town. Bigger paper," Martha said, sticking one of her dainty cigarettes into her mouth and lighting it.

"We went through some older papers," Jasmine said, "and since LaBorde covers a lot of the small towns around here, we found ads for the Jim Dandy Circus in several of them, and we were able to pinpoint on a map the route of the circus up to Mud Creek, and the latest paper showed Marvel Creek to be the next stop, and—"

"Slow down," I said. "What's the circus got to do with your so-called investigation?"

"You look at the papers and read about the towns where the circus showed up," Martha said, "and there's in every one of them something about a missing woman, or young girl. In a couple cases, bodies have been found. Sometimes they were found a week or so after the circus came to town, but most of the news articles indicate the missing women disappeared at the time of the circus."

"Of course, we determined this, not the papers," Jasmine said. "We made the connection between the circus and the bodies."

"In the case of the bodies, both were found after the circus passed through," Martha said, "but from the estimated times of death the papers gave, we've been able to figure they were killed about the time the circus was in town. And my guess is those missing women are dead too, and by the same hand."

"Waldo's?" I said.

"That's right," Martha said.

I considered all that.

Jasmine said, "Pretty coincidental, don't you think?"

"Well, yeah," I said, "but that doesn't mean—"

"And the two bodies had been mutilated," Martha said. She leaned against the counter and reached into her shirt pocket and pulled out the fold-out I had found. She smoothed it out on the counter top. "Body parts were missing. And I bet they were cut up, just like this fold-out is marked. As for the missing body parts, eyes and pussies, I figure. Those are the parts he has circled and blacked out."

"Watch your language," I said to Martha.

No one seemed to take much note of me.

"The bodies were found in the town's local dump," Jasmine said.

"It's curious," I admitted, "but still, to accuse a man of murder on the basis of circumstantial evidence."

"One more thing," Martha said. "Both bodies had traces of black paint on them. Like it had been used to mark the areas the killer wanted to cut, and I presume, did cut. That's certainly a lot of goddamn circumstantial evidence, isn't it?"

"Enough that we're going to keep an eye on Waldo," Jasmine said.

—◆—

I must admit right now that I didn't think even then, after what I had been told, there was anything to this Waldo the Great as murderer. It struck me that murders and disappearances happen all the time, and that if one were to look through the LaBorde paper carefully, it would be possible to discover there had been many of both, especially disappearances, before and after the arrival of the circus. I mean that paper covered a lot of small towns and communities, and LaBorde was a fairly large town itself. A small city actually. Most of the disappearances would turn out to be nothing more than someone leaving on a trip for a few days without telling anyone, and most of the murders would be committed by a friend or relative of the victim and would have nothing to do with the circus or marked-up fold-outs.

Of course, the fact that the two discovered bodies had been mutilated gave me pause, but not enough to go to the law about it. That was just the sort of half-baked idea that had gotten my ass in a crack earlier.

Still, that night, I went with Martha and Jasmine out to the trailer park.

It was cloudy that night and jags of lightning made occasional cuts through the cloud cover and thunder rumbled and light drops of rain fell on the windshield of Martha's van.

We drove out to the road behind the park about dark, peeked out the windows and through the gaps in the trees. The handful of pole lights in the park were gauzy in the wet night and sad as dying fireflies. Their poor, damp rays fell against some of the trees—their branches waving in the wind like the fluttering hands of distressed lunatics—and forced the beads of rain on the branches to give up tiny rainbows. The rainbows rose up, misted outward a small distance, then once beyond the small circumference of light, their beauty was consumed by the night.

Martha got out her binoculars and Jasmine sat on the front passenger side with a notepad and pen, ready to record anything Martha told her to. They felt that the more documentation they had, the easier it would be to convince the police that Waldo was a murderer.

I was in the seat behind theirs, my legs stretched out and my back against the van, looking away from the trailer most of the time, wondering how I had let myself in on this. About midnight I began to feel both sleepy and silly. I unwrapped a candy bar and ate it.

"Would you quit that goddamn smacking back there," Martha said. "It makes me nervous."

"Pardon me all to hell," I said, and wadded up the wrapper noisily and tossed it on the floorboard.

"Daddy, would you quit?" Jasmine said.

"Now we got something," Martha said.

I sat up and turned around. There were no lights on in the trailers in the park except for Waldo's trailer; a dirty, orange glow shone behind one of his windows, like a fresh slice of smoked cheese. Other than that, there was only the pole lights, and they didn't offer much. Just those little rainbows made of bad light and rain. Without the binoculars there was little to observe in detail, because it was a pretty good distance from where we were to Waldo's trailer, but I could see him coming out of the door, holding it open, the whole pack of poodles following after.

Waldo bent down by the trailer and pulled a small shovel out from beneath it. The poodles wandered around and started doing their bathroom business. Waldo cupped his hands over a cigarette and lit it with a lighter and smoked while he noted the dog's delivery spots. After a while he went about scooping up their messes with his shovel and making several trips to the dumpster to get rid of it.

Finished, he pushed the shovel beneath the trailer and smoked another cigarette and ground it hard beneath his heel and opened the trailer door and called to the dogs. They bounded up the steps and into the trailer like it was one of their circus tricks. No poodle tried to fuck another poodle. Waldo didn't kick anybody. He went inside, and a moment later came out again, this time minus the poodles. He was carrying something. A box. He looked about carefully, then placed the box in the back of his pickup. He went back inside the trailer.

"Goddamn," Martha said. "There's a woman's leg in that box."

"Let me see," I said.

"You can't see it now," she said. "It's down in the bed of the truck."

She gave me the binoculars anyway, and I looked. She was right. I couldn't see what was in the bed of the truck. "He wouldn't just put a woman's leg in the back of his pickup," I said.

"Well, he did," Martha said.

"Oh God," Jasmine said, and she flicked on her pen light and glanced at her watch and started writing on her notepad, talking aloud as she did. "Twelve-o-five, Waldo put woman's leg in the bed of his truck. Oh, shit, who do you think it could be?"

"One could hope it's that goddamn bitch down at the county clerk's office," Martha said. "I been waiting for something to happen to her."

"Martha!" Jasmine said.

"Just kidding," Martha said. "Kinda."

I had the binoculars tight against my face as the trailer door opened again. I could see very well with the infra-red business. Waldo came out with another box. As he came down the steps, the box tilted slightly. It was open at the top and I could see very clearly what was in it.

"A woman's head," I said. My voice sounded small and childish.

"Jesus Christ," Martha said. "I didn't really, really, believe he was a murderer."

Waldo was back inside the trailer. A moment later he reappeared. Smaller boxes under each arm.

"Let me see," Jasmine said.

"No," I said. "You don't need to."

"But…." Jasmine began.

"Listen to your father," Martha said.

I handed the binoculars back to Martha. She didn't look through them. We didn't need to try and see what was in the other boxes. We knew. The rest of Waldo's victim.

Waldo unfolded a tarp in the back of his pickup and stretched it across the truck bed and fastened it at all corners, then got inside the cab and cranked the engine.

"Do we go to the police now?" Jasmine said.

"After we find out where he's taking the body," Martha said.

"You're right," I said. "Otherwise, if he's disposed of all the evidence, we've got nothing." I was thinking too of my record at the police station. Meaning, of course, more than my word would be needed to start an investigation.

Martha cranked the van and put on the park lights and began to ease along, giving Waldo the time he needed to get out of the trailer park and ahead of us.

"I've got a pretty good idea where he's going," Martha said. "Bet he scoped the place out first day he got to town."

"The dump," Jasmine said. "Place they found those other bodies."

We got to the street and saw Waldo was headed in the direction of the dump. Martha turned on the van's headlights after the pickup was down the road a bit, then eased out in pursuit. We laid back and let him get way ahead, and when we got out of town and he took the turn off to the dump, we passed on by and turned down a farm to market road and parked as close as we could to a barbed wire fence. We got out and climbed the fence and crossed a pasture and came to a rise and went up that and poked our heads over carefully and looked down on the dump.

There was smoke rising up in spots, where sounds of burning refuse had been covered at some point, and it filled the air with stink. The dump had been like that forever. As a little boy, my father would bring me out to the dump to toss our family garbage, and even in broad daylight, I thought the place spooky, a sort of poor-boy, blue-collar hell. My dad said there were fires out here that had never been put out, not by the weight of garbage and dirt, or by winter ice or spring's rain storms. Said no matter what was done to those fires, they still burned. Methane maybe. All the stuff in the dump heating up like compost, creating some kind of combustible chemical reaction.

Within the dump, bordered off by a wide layer of scraped earth, were two great oil derricks. They were working derricks too, and the great rocking horse pumps dipped down and rose up constantly, night or day, and it always struck me that this was a foolish place for a dump full of never-dying fires to exist, next to two working oil wells. But the dump still stood and the derricks still worked oil. The city council had tried to have the old dump shut down, moved, but so far nothing had happened. They couldn't get those fires out completely for one thing. I felt time was against the dump and the wells. Eventually, the piper, or in this case, the pipeline, had to be paid. Some day the fires in the dump would get out of hand and set the oil wells on fire and the explosion that would occur would send Mud Creek and its surrounding rivers and woodlands to some place north of Pluto.

At night, the place was even more eerie. Flames licking out from under the debris like tongues, the rain seeping to its source, making it hiss white smoke like dragon breath. The two old derricks stood tall against the night and lightning wove a flickering crown of light around one of them and went away. In that instant, the electrified top of the derrick looked like Martian machinery. Inside the derricks, the still-working well pumps throbbed and kerchunked and dipped their dark, metal hammerheads then lifted them again. Down and up. Down and up. Taking with them on the drop and the rise, rain-wet shadows and flickers of garbage fire.

Waldo's truck was parked beside the road, next to a mound of garbage the height of a first-story roof. He had peeled off the tarp and put it away and was unloading his boxes from the truck, carrying them to a spot near one of the oil derricks, arranging them neatly, as if he were being graded on his work. When the boxes were all out, Waldo stood with his back to us and watched one of the derrick's pumps nod for a long time, as if the action of it amazed or offended him.

After a time, he turned suddenly and kicked at one of the boxes. The head in it popped up like a Mexican jumping bean and fell back down inside. Waldo took a deep breath, as if he were preparing to run a race, then got in his truck, turned it around, and drove away.

"He didn't even bother to bury the pieces," Jasmine said, and even in the bad light, I could see she was as white as Frosty the Snowman.

"Probably wants it to be found," Martha said. "We know where the corpse is now. We have evidence, and we saw him dispose of the body ourselves. I think we can go to the law now."

—◆—

We drove back to town and called Sam from Martha's bookstore. He answered the phone on the fifth ring. He sounded like he had a sock in his mouth.

"What?"

"Plebin, Sam. I need your help."

"You in a ditch? Call a wrecker, man. I'm bushed."

"Not exactly. It's about murder."

"Ah, shit, Plebin. You some kind of fool, or what? We been through this. Call some nuthouse doctor or something. I need sleep. Day I put in today was bad enough, but I don't need you now and some story about murder. Lack of sleep gives me domestic problems."

"This one's different. I've got two witnesses. A body out at the dump. We saw it disposed of. A woman cut up in pieces, I kid you not. Guy named Waldo did it. He used to be with the circus. Directed a dog act."

"The circus?"

"That's right."

"And he has a dog act."

"Had. He cut up a woman and took her to the dump."

"Plebin?"

"Yes."

"I go out there, and there's no dead body, I could change that, supply one, mood I'm in. Understand?"

"Just meet us at the dump."

"Who's us?"

I told him, gave him some background on Waldo, explained what Martha and Jasmine found in the LaBorde newspapers, hung up, and me and my fellow sleuths drove back to the dump.

—◆—

We waited outside the dump in Martha's van until Sam showed in his blue Ford. We waved at him and started the van and led him into the dump. We drove up to the spot near the derrick and got out. None of us went over to the boxes for a look. We didn't speak. We listened to the pumps doing their work inside the derricks. Kerchunk, kerchunk, kerchunk.

Sam pulled up behind us and got out. He was wearing blue jeans and tennis shoes and his pajama top. He looked at me and Jasmine and Martha. Fact is, he looked at Martha quite a while.

"You want maybe I should send you a picture, or something?" Martha said.

Sam didn't say anything. He looked away from Martha and said to me, "All right. Where's the body?"

"It's kind of here and there," I said, and pointed. "In those boxes. Start with the little one, there. That's her head."

Sam looked in the box, and I saw him jump a little. Then he went still, bent forward and pulled the woman's head out by the hair, held it up in front of him and looked at it. He spun and tossed it to me. Reflexively, I caught it, then dropped it. By the time it hit the ground I felt like a number one horse's ass.

It wasn't a human head. It was a mannequin head with a black paint mark covering the stump of the neck, which had been neatly sawed in two.

"Here, Jasmine," Sam said. "You take a leg," and he hoisted a mannequin leg out of another box and tossed it at her. She shrieked and dodged and it landed on the ground. "And you that's gonna send me a picture. You take an arm." He pulled a mannequin arm out of another box and tossed it at Martha, who swatted it out of the air with her putter cane.

He turned and kicked another of the boxes and sent a leg and an arm sailing into a heap of brush and old paint cans.

"Goddamn it, Plebin," he said. "You've done it again." He came over and stood in front of me. "Man, you're nuts. Absolutely nuts."

"Wasn't just Plebin," Martha said. "We all thought it. The guy brought this stuff out here is a weirdo. We've been watching him."

"You have?" Sam said. "Playing detective, huh? That's sweet. That's real sweet. Plebin, come here, will you?"

I went over and stood by him. He put an arm around my shoulders and walked me off from Jasmine and Martha. He whispered to me.

"Plebin. You're not learning, man. Not a bit. Not only are you fucking up your life, you're fucking up mine. Listen here. Me and the old lady, we're not doing so good, see."

"I'm sorry to hear it. Toni has always been so great."

"Yeah, well, you see, she's jealous. You know that."

"Oh yeah. Always has been."

"There you are. She's gotten worse too. And you see, I spend a lot of time away from the home. Out of the bed. Bad hours. You getting what I'm saying here?"

"Yeah."

He pulled me closer and patted my chest with his other hand. "Good. Not only is that bad, me spending those hours away from home and out of the bed at bedtime, but hey, I'm so bushed these days, I get ready to lay a little pipe, well, I got no lead in the pencil. Like a goddamn spaghetti, that's how it is. Know what I'm saying?"

"Least when you do get it hard, you get to lay pipe," I said.

"But I'm not laying it enough. It's because I don't get rest. But Toni, you know what she thinks? She thinks it's because I'm having a little extracurricular activity. You know what I mean? Thinks I'm out banging hole like there's no tomorrow."

"Hey, I'm sorry, Sam, but…."

"So now I've got the rest problem again. I'm tired right now. I don't recover like I used to. I don't get eight hours of sack time, hey, I can't get it up. I have a bad day, which I do when I'm tired, I can't get it up. My shit comes out different, I can't get it up. I've gotten sensitive in my old age.

Everything goes straight to my dick. Toni, she gets ready for me to do my duty, guess what?"

"You're too tired. You can't get it up."

"Bingo. The ole Johnson is like an empty sock. And when I can't get it up, what does Toni think?"

"You're fucking around?"

"That's right. And it's not bad enough I gotta be tired for legitimate reasons, but now I got to be tired because you and your daughter and Ma Frankenstein over there are seeing heads in boxes. Trailing some innocent bystander and trying to tie him in with murder when there's nobody been murdered. Know what I'm saying?"

"Sam, the guy looks the part. Acts it. There's been murders everywhere the circus goes...."

"Plebin, ole buddy. Hush your mouth, okay? Listen up tight. I'm going home now. I'm going back to bed. You wake me up again, I'll run over you with a truck. I don't have a truck, but I'll borrow one for the purpose. Got me?"

"Yeah."

"All right. Good night." He took his arm off my shoulders, walked back to his car and opened the door. He started to get inside, then straightened. He looked over the roof at me. "Come by and have dinner next week. Toni still makes a good chicken-fried steak. Been a while since she's seen you."

"I'll keep it in mind. Give her my love."

"Yeah. And Plebin, don't call with any more murders, all right? You got a good imagination, but as a detective, you're the worst." He looked at Jasmine. "Jasmine, you stick with your mother." He got in his car, backed around and drove away.

I went over and stood with my fellow sleuths and looked down at the mannequin head. I picked it up by the hair and looked at it. "I think I'll have this mounted," I said. "Just to remind me what a jackass I am."

— ✦ —

Back at the apartment I sat on the bed with the window open, the mannequin head on the pillow beside me. Jasmine sat in the dresser chair and Martha had one of my rickety kitchen chairs turned around backwards and she sat with her arms crossed on the back of it, sweat running out from under her wool cap, collecting in her mustache.

"I still think something funny is going on there," Jasmine said.

"Oh, shut up," I said.

"We know something funny is going on," Martha said.

"We means you two," I said. "Don't include me. I don't know anything except I've made a fool out of myself and Sam is having trouble with his sex life, or maybe what he told me was some kind of parable."

"Sex life," Jasmine said. "What did he tell you?"

"Forget," I said.

"That Sam is some sorry cop," Martha said. "He should have at least investigated Waldo. Guy who paints and cuts up mannequins isn't your everyday fella, I'd think. I bet he's painting and sawing them up because he hasn't picked a victim yet. It's his way of appeasing himself until he's chosen someone. Akin to masturbation instead of real sex."

"If we could see inside his trailer," Jasmine said, "I bet we'd find evidence of something more than mannequins. Evidence of past crimes maybe."

"I've had enough" I said. "And Jasmine, so have you. And Martha, if you're smart, so have you."

Martha got out one of her little cigarettes.

"Don't light that in here," I said.

She got out a small box of kitchen matches.

"I can't stand smoke," I said.

She pulled a match from the box and struck it on her pants leg and lit up, puffed, studied the ceiling.

"Put it out, Martha. This is my place."

She blew smoke at the ceiling. "I think Jasmine's right," she said. "If we could divert him. Get him out of the trailer so we could have a look inside, find some evidence, then maybe that small town idiot cop friend of yours would even be convinced."

"Waldo's not going to keep a human head in there," I said.

"He might," Martha said. "It's been known to happen. Or maybe something a victim owned. Guys like that keep souvenirs of their murders. That way they can fantasize, relive it all."

"We could watch his place tomorrow," Jasmine said, "then if he goes out, we could slip in and look around. We find something incriminating, something definite, there's a way to cue the police in on it, even one as stubborn and stupid as Sam."

"I'm sure Waldo locks his doors," I said.

"That's no trouble," Martha said. "I can pick the lock on Heaven's door."

"You're just a basket of fine skills," I said.

"I used to work for a repo company, years back," Martha said. "I learned to use lock jocks and keys and picks on car doors and garage doors. You name it, I can get in it, and in a matter of moments."

"Listen, you two," I said, "leave it be. We don't know this guy's done anything, and if he is a murderer, you damn sure don't need to be snooping around there, or you may end up on the victim list. Let's get on with our lives."

"Such as yours and mine is," Martha said. "What have I got to look forward to? Selling a few books? Meeting the right man? Me, a gargoyle with a golf club?"

"Martha, don't say that," Jasmine said.

"No, let's call a spade a spade here," Martha said. She snatched off her wool cap and showed us her bald head. I had seen a glimpse of it a time or two before I went to work there, when she was taking off and adjusting her cap or scratching her head, but this was the first time I'd seen it in all its sweaty, pink glory for more than a few moments. "What's gonna pull a mate in for me? My glorious head of hair. I started losing it when I was in my twenties. No man would look twice at me. Besides that, I'm ugly and have a mustache."

"A mate isn't everything," I said.

"It's something," Martha said. "And I think about it. I won't kid you. But I know it isn't possible. I've been around, seen some things, had some interesting jobs. But I haven't really made any life for myself. Not so it feels like one. And you know what? After all these years, Jasmine and you are my only real friends, and in your case, Plebin, I don't know that amounts to much."

"Thanks," I said.

"You could get a wig," Jasmine said.

"I could have these whiskers removed," Martha said. "But I'd still be a blimp with a bum leg. No. There's nothing for me in the looks department. Not unless I could change bodies with some blonde bimbo. Since that isn't going to happen, all I got is what I make out of life. Like this mystery. A real mystery, I think. And if Waldo is a murderer, do we let him go on to the next town and find a victim? Or for that matter, a victim here, before he leaves?

"We catch this guy. Prove he's responsible for murders, then we've actually done something important with our lives. There's more to my life than the bookstore. More to yours Plebin than a bad name and unemployment checks. And… well, in your case Jasmine, there is more to your life. You're beautiful, smart, and you're going places. But for all of us, wouldn't it be worthwhile to catch a killer?"

"If he is a killer," I said. "Maybe he just hates mannequins because they look better in their clothes than he does."

"Women's clothes?" Jasmine said.

"Maybe it's women's clothes he likes to wear," I said. "Thing is, we could end up making fools of ourselves, spend some time in jail, even."

"I'll chance it," Jasmine said.

"No you won't," I said. "It's over for you, Jasmine. Martha can do what she wants. But you and me, we're out of it."

Martha left.

Jasmine got out her sleeping bag and unrolled it, went to the bathroom to brush her teeth. I tried to stay awake and await my turn in there, but couldn't. Too tired. I lay down on the bed, noted vaguely that rain had stopped pounding on the apartment roof, and I fell immediately asleep.

—◆—

I awoke later that night, early morning really, to the smell of more oncoming rain, and when I rolled over I could see flashes of lightning in the west.

The west. The direction of the dump. It was as if a storm was originating there, moving toward the town.

Melodrama. I loved it.

I rolled over and turned my head to the end table beside the bed, and when the lightning flashed I could see the mannequin head setting there, its face turned toward me, its strange, false eyes alight with the fire of the western lightning. The paint around the manikin's neck appeared very damp in that light, like blood.

I threw my legs from beneath the covers and took hold of the head. The paint on its neck was wet in my hands. The humidity had caused it to run. I sat the head on the floor where I wouldn't have to look at it, got up to go to the bathroom and wash my hands.

Jasmine's sleeping bag was on the floor, but Jasmine wasn't in it. I went on to the bathroom, but she wasn't in there either. I turned on the light and washed my hands and felt a little weak. There was no place else to be in the apartment. I looked to see if she had taken her stuff and gone home, but she hadn't. The door that led out to the stairway was closed, but unlocked.

No question now. She had gone out.

I had an idea where, and the thought of it gave me a chill. I got dressed and went downstairs and beat on the bookstore, pressed my face against the windows, but there was no light or movement. I went around to the rear of the building to beat on the backdoor, to try and wake Martha up in her living quarters, but when I got there I didn't bother. I saw that Martha's van was gone from the carport and Jasmine's car was still in place.

I went back to my apartment and found Jasmine's car keys on the dresser and thought about calling the police, then thought better of it. Their memory of my body in the trunk stunt was a long one, and they might delay. Blow off the whole thing, in fact, mark it up to another aggravation from the boy who cried wolf. If I called Sam it wouldn't be any better. Twice in one night he'd be more likely to kill me than to help me. He was more worried about his pecker than a would-be killer, and he might not do anything at all.

Then I reminded myself it was a game of "What If" and that there wasn't anything to do, nothing to fear. I told myself the worst that could happen would be that Jasmine and Martha would annoy Waldo and make fools of themselves, and then it would all be over for good.

But those thoughts didn't help much, no matter how hard I tried to be convinced. I realized then that it hadn't been just the rain and the humidity that had awakened me. I had been thinking about what Martha said. About Waldo picking a victim later on if we didn't stop him. About the mannequins being a sort of warm-up for what he really wanted to do and would do.

It wasn't just a game anymore. Though I had no real evidence for it, I believed then what Jasmine and Martha believed.

Waldo the Great was a murderer.

—◆—

I drove Jasmine's car out to the trailer park and pulled around where we had parked before, and sure enough, there was Martha's van. I pulled in behind it and parked.

I got out, mad as hell, went over to the van and pulled the driver's door open. There wasn't anyone inside. I turned then and looked through the bushes toward the trailer park. Lightning moved to the west and flicked and flared as if it were fireworks on a vibrating string. It lit up the trailer park, made what was obvious momentarily bright and harsh.

Waldo's truck and trailer were gone. There was nothing in its spot but tire tracks.

I tore through the bushes, fought back some blackberry vines, and made the long run over to the spot where Waldo's trailer had been.

I walked around in circles like an idiot. I tried to think, tried to figure what had happened.

I made up a possible scenario: Martha and Jasmine had come out here to spy on Waldo, and maybe Waldo, who kept weird hours, had gone out, and Jasmine and Martha had seen their chance and gone in.

Perhaps Waldo turned around and came back suddenly. Realized he'd forgotten his cigarettes, his money, something like that, and he found Jasmine and Martha snooping.

And if he was a murderer, and he found them, and they had discovered incriminating evidence....

Then what?

What would he have done with them?

It struck me then.

The dump. To dispose of the bodies.

God, the bodies.

My stomach soured and my knees shook. I raced back through the tangled growth, back to Jasmine's car. I pulled around the van and made the circle and whipped onto the road in front of the trailer park and headed for the dump at high speed. If a cop saw me, good. Let him chase me, on out to the dump.

Drops of rain had begun to fall as I turned on the road to the dump. Lightning was crisscrossing more rapidly and more heatedly than before. Thunder rumbled.

I killed the lights and eased into the dump, using the lightning flashes as my guide, and there, stretched across the dump road, blocking passage, was Waldo's trailer. The truck the trailer was fastened to was off the road and slightly turned in my direction, ready to leave the dump. I didn't see any movement. The only sounds were from the throbbing thunder and the hissing lightning. Raindrops were falling faster.

I jerked the car into park in front of the trailer and got out and ran over there, then hesitated. I looked around and spotted a hunk of wood lying in some garbage. I yanked it out and ran back to the trailer and jerked open the door. The smell of dogs was thick in the air.

Lightning flashed in the open doorway and through the thin curtains at the windows. I saw Martha lying on the floor, face down, a meat cleaver in the small of her back. I saw that the bookshelves on the wall were filled with Harlequin romances, and below them nailed onto the shelves, were strange hunks of what in the lightning flashes looked like hairy leather.

Darkness.

A beat.

Lighting flash.

I looked around, didn't see Waldo hiding in the shadows with another meat cleaver.

Darkness again.

I went over to Martha and knelt beside her, touched her shoulder. She raised her head, tried to jerk around and grab me, but was too weak. "Sonofabitch," she said.

"It's me," I said.

"Plebin," she said. "Waldo... nailed me a few times.... Thinks I'm dead.... He's got Jasmine. Tried to stop him.... Couldn't.... You got to. They're out... there."

I took hold of the cleaver and jerked it out of her back and tossed it on the floor.

"Goddamn," Martha said, and almost did a push up, but lay back down. "Could have gone all day without that... Jasmine. The nut's got her. Go on!"

Martha closed her eyes and lay still. I touched her neck. Still a pulse. But I couldn't do anything now. I had to find Jasmine. Had to hope the bastard hadn't done his work.

I went out of the trailer, around to the other side, looked out over the dump. The light wasn't good, but it was good enough that I could see them immediately. Jasmine, her back to me, upside down, nude, was tied to the inside of the nearest derrick, hung up like a goat for the slaughter. Waldo stood at an angle, facing her, holding something in his hand.

Lightning strobed, thunder rumbled. The poodles were running about, barking and leaping. Two of the dogs were fucking out next to the derrick, flopping tongues. The great black hammerhead of the oil pump rose up and went down. Fires glowed from beneath debris and reflected on the metal bars of the derrick and the well pump, and when the rain hit the fires beneath the garbage they gave up white smoke and the smoke rolled in the wind like great balls of cotton, tumbled over Jasmine and Waldo and away.

Waldo swung what he had in his hand at Jasmine. Caught her across the neck with it. Her body twitched. I let out a yell that was absorbed by a sudden peal of thunder and a slash of lightning.

I started running, yelling as I went.

Waldo slashed at Jasmine again, and then he heard me yelling. He stepped to the side and stared at me, surprised. I ran up the little rise that led to the derrick before he could get it together, and as I ducked under a bar on the derrick, he dropped what he was holding.

A long paint brush.

It fell next to a can of dark paint. Rain plopped in the paint and black balls of paint flew up in response and fell down again. One of the dogs jumped the can of paint for no reason I could determine and ran off into the rain.

Jasmine made a noise like a smothered cough. Out of the corner of my eye I could see a strip of thick, gray tape across her mouth, and where Waldo had slashed her neck with the brush was a band of paint, dissolving in the rain, running down her neck, over her cheeks and into her eyes and finally her hair, like blood in a black-and-white movie.

Waldo reached behind his back and came back with a knife. The edge of the blade caught a flash of lightning and gave a wicked wink. Waldo's face was full of expression this time, as if he had saved all his passion for this moment.

"Come on, asshole," I said. "Come on. Cut me."

He leapt forward, very fast. The knife went out and caught me across the chest as I jumped back and hit my head on a metal runner of the derrick. I felt something warm on my chest. Shit. I hadn't really wanted him to cut me. He was a fast little bastard.

I didn't invite him to do that again.

I cocked my piece of wood and let him get as close as I could allow without fear taking over, then I ducked under the metal runner and he ducked under it after me, poking straight out with the knife.

I swung at him, and the wood, rotten, possibly termite ridden, came apart close to my hand and went sailing and crumbling across the dump.

Waldo and I watched the chunk of wood until it hit the dirt by the derrick and exploded into a half dozen fragments.

Waldo turned his attention to me again, smiled, and came fast. I jumped backwards and my feet went out from under me and dogs yelped.

The lover mutts. I had backed over them while they were screwing. I looked up between my knees and saw the dogs turned butt to butt, hung up, and then I looked higher, and there was Waldo and his knife. I rolled and came up and grabbed a wet cardboard box of something and threw it. It struck Waldo in the chest and what was in the box flew out and spun along the wet ground. It was half a mannequin torso.

"You're ruining everything," Waldo said.

I glanced down and saw one of the mannequin legs Sam had pulled from a box and tossed. I grabbed the leg and cocked it on my shoulder like a baseball bat.

"Come on, asshole," I said. "Come on. Let's see if I can put one over the fence with you."

He went nuts then, dove for me. The knife jabbed out, fast and blurry.

I swatted. My swing hit his arm and his knife hand went wide and opened up and the knife flew into a pile of garbage and out of sight.

Waldo and I both looked at where it had disappeared.

We looked at one another. It was my turn to smile.

He staggered back and I followed, rotating the leg, trying to pick my shot.

He darted to his right, dipped, came up clutching one of the mannequin's arms. He held it by the wrist and smiled. He rotated it the way I had the leg.

We came together, leg and arm swinging. He swung at my head. I blocked with the leg and swung at his knees. He jumped the swing, kicked beautifully while airborne, hit me in the chin and knocked my head back, but I didn't go down.

Four of the poodles came out of nowhere, bouncing and barking beside us, and one of them got hold of my pants leg and started tugging. I hit at him. He yelped. Waldo hit me with the arm across the shoulder. I hit him back with the leg and kicked out and shook the poodle free.

Waldo laughed.

Another of the poodles got hold of his pants legs.

Waldo quit laughing. "Not me, you dumb ingrate!"

Waldo whacked the poodle hard with the arm. It let go, ran off a distance, whirled, took a defiant stance and barked.

I hit Waldo then. It was a good shot, clean and clear and sweet with the sound of the wind, but he got his shoulder up and blocked the blow and he only lost a bit of shirt sleeve, which popped open like a flower blossoming.

"Man, I just bought this shirt," he said.

I swung high to his head and let my body go completely around with the swing, twisting on the balls of my feet, and as I came back around, I lowered the blow and hit him in the ribs. He bellowed and tripped over something, went down and dropped his mannequin arm. Three poodles leapt on his chest and one grabbed at his ankle. Behind him, the other two were still hung up, tongues dangling happily. They were waiting for the seasons to change. The next ice age. It didn't matter. They were in no hurry.

I went after Waldo, closing for the kill. He wiped the poodles off his chest with a sweep of his arm and grabbed the mannequin arm beside him, took it by the thick end and stuck it at me as I was about to lower the boom on him. The tips of the mannequin's fingers caught me in the family jewels and a moment later a pain went through me that wasn't quite as bad as being hit by a truck. But it didn't keep me from whacking him over the head with everything I had. The mannequin leg fragmented in my hands and Waldo screamed and rolled and came up and charged me, his forehead streaked with blood, a poodle dangling from one pants leg by the teeth. The poodle stayed with him as he leaped and grabbed my legs at the knees and drove his head into my abdomen and knocked me back into a heap of smoking garbage. The smoke rose up around us and closed over us like a pod and with it came a stink that brought bile to my throat and I felt heat on my back and something sharp like glass and I yelled and rolled with Waldo and the growling poodle and out of the corner of my eye, in mid-roll, I saw another of the poodles had caught on fire in the garbage and was running about like a low-flying comet. We tumbled over some more junk, and over again. Next thing I knew Waldo had rolled away and was up and over me, had hold of six feet of two-by-four with a couple of nails hanging out of the end.

"Goodnight," Waldo said.

The board came around and the tips of the nails caught some light from the garbage fires, made them shine like animal eyes in the dark. The same light made Waldo look like the devil. Then the side of my neck exploded. The pain and shock were like things that had burrowed inside me to live. They owned me. I lay where I was, unable to move, the board hung up in my neck. Waldo tugged, but the board wouldn't come free. He put a foot on my chest and worked the board back and forth. The nails in my neck made a noise like someone trying to whistle through gapped teeth. I tried to lift a hand and grab at the board, but I was too weak. My hands fluttered at my sides as if I were petting the ground. My head wobbled back and forth with Waldo's efforts. I could see him through a blur. His teeth were clenched and spittle was foaming across his lips.

I found my eyes drifting to the top of the oil derrick, perhaps in search of a heavenly choir. Lightning flashed rose-red and sweat-stain yellow in the distance. My eyes fell back to Waldo. I watched him work. My body started trembling as if electrically charged.

Eventually Waldo worked the nails out of my neck. He stood back and took a breath. Getting that board loose was hard work. I noted in an absent kind of way that the poodle had finally let go of his ankle and had wandered off. I felt blood gushing out of my neck, maybe as much as the oil well was pumping. I thought sadly of what was going to happen to Jasmine.

My eyelids were heavy and I could hardly keep them open. A poodle came up and sniffed my face. Waldo finally got his breath. He straddled me and cocked the board and positioned his features for the strike; his face showed plenty of expression now. I wanted to kick up between his legs and hit him in the balls, but I might as well have wanted to be in Las Vegas.

"You're dog food," Waldo said, and just before he swung, my eyes started going out of focus like a movie camera on the fade, but I caught fuzzy movement behind him and there was a silver snake leaping through the air and the snake bit Waldo in the side of the head and he went away from me as if jerked aside by ropes.

My eyes focused again, slowly, and there was Martha, wobbling, holding the golf club properly, end of the swing position. She might have been posing for a photo. The striking end of the club was framed beautifully against the dark sky. I hadn't realized just how pretty her mustache was, all beaded up there in the firelight and the occasional bright throb of the storm.

Martha lowered the club and leaned on it. All of us were pretty tuckered out tonight.

Martha looked at Waldo who lay face down in the trash, not moving, his hand slowly letting loose of the two-by-four, like a dying octopus relaxing its grip on a sunken ship timber.

"Fore, motherfucker," she said, then she slid down the golf club to her knees. Blood ran out from beneath her wool cap. Things went fuzzy for me again. I closed my eyes as a red glow bloomed to my left, where Waldo's trailer was. It began to rain harder. A poodle licked my bleeding neck.

— ◆ —

When I awoke in the hospital I felt very stiff, and I could feel that my shoulders were slightly burned. No flesh missing back there, though, just a feeling akin to mild sunburn. I weakly raised an arm to the bandage on my neck and put it down again. That nearly wore me out.

Jasmine and Martha and Sam came in shortly thereafter. Martha was on crutches and minus her wool cap. Her head was bandaged. Her mustache was clean and well groomed, as if with a toothbrush.

"How's the boy?" Sam said.

"You'd listened, could have been a lot better." I said.

"Yeah, well, the boy that cried wolf and all that," Sam said.

"Jasmine, baby," I said, "how are you?"

"I'm all right. No traumatic scars. Martha got us both out of there."

"I had to rest awhile," Martha said, "but all's well that ends well. You did nearly bleed to death."

"What about you?" I said. "You look pretty good after all that."

"Hey," Martha said, "I've got enough fat and muscle on me to take a few meat cleaver blows. He'd have done better to drive a truck over me. When he caught us sneaking around his trailer, he came up behind me and clubbed me in the head with a meat cleaver before I knew he was there, or I'd have kicked his ass into next Tuesday. After he hit me in the head he worked on me some more when I went down. He should have stuck to my head instead of pounding me in the back. That just tired me out for a while."

"Daddy, there were all kinds of horrid things in his trailer. Photographs, and… there were some pieces of women."

"Pussies," Martha said. "He'd tanned them. Had one on a belt. I figure he put it on and wore it now and then. One of those pervert types."

"What about old Waldo?" I asked.

"I made a hole-in-one on that sonofabitch," Martha said, "but looks like he'll recover. And though the trailer burned down, enough evidence survived to hang him. If we're lucky they'll give his ass the hot needle. Right, Sam?"

"That's right," Sam said.

"Whoa," I said. "How'd the trailer burn down?"

"One of the poodles caught on fire in the garbage," Jasmine said. "Poor thing. It ran back to the trailer and the door was open and it ran inside and jumped up in the bed, burned that end of the trailer up."

"Ruined a bunch of Harlequin Romances," Martha said. "Wish the little fuck had traded those in too. Might have made us a few dollars. Thing is, most of the photographs and the leather pussies survived, so we got the little shit by the balls."

I looked at Jasmine and smiled.

She smiled back, reached out and patted my shoulder. "Oh, yeah," she said, and opened her purse and took out an envelope. "This is for you. From Mama."

"Open it," I said.

Jasmine opened it and handed it to me. I took it. It was a get well card that had been sent to Connie at some time by one of her friends. She had blatantly marked out her name, and the senders name, had written under the canned sentiment printed there, "Get well, SLOWLY."

"I'm beginning to think me and your Mom aren't going to patch things up," I said.

"Afraid not," Jasmine said.

"Good reason to move then," Martha said. "I'm getting out of this one-dog town. I'll level with you. I got a little inheritance I live off of. An uncle left it to me. Said in the will, since I was the ugliest one in the family, I'd need it."

"That's awful," Jasmine said. "Don't you believe that."

"The hell it's awful," Martha said. "I didn't have that money put back to live on, me and those damn books would be on the street. Ugly has its compensations. I've decided to start a bookstore in LaBorde, and I'm gonna open me a private investigations agency with it. Nice combo, huh? Read a little. Snoop a little. And you two, you want, can be my operatives. You fulltime, Plebin, and Jasmine, you can work part-time while you go to college. What do you think?"

"Do we get a discount on paperbacks?" I asked.

Martha considered that. "I don't think so," she said.

"Air-conditioning?"

"I don't think so."

"Let me consider it," I said.

Suddenly, I couldn't keep my eyes open.

Jasmine gently placed her hand on my arm. "Rest now," she said.

And I did.

(For Roman Ranieri)

The Gentleman's Hotel

A little dust devil danced in front of Jebidiah Rain's horse, twisted up a few leaves in the street, carried them skittering and twisting across the road and through a gap made by a sagging wide door and into an abandoned livery stable. Inside, the tiny windstorm died out suddenly, dropping the leaves it had hoisted to the ground like scales scraped from a fish. Dust from the devil puffed in all directions and joined the dirt on the livery floor.

Jebidiah rode his horse to the front of the livery, looked inside. The door groaned on the one hinge that held it, moved slightly in the wind, but remained open. The interior of the livery was well lit from sunlight slicing through cracks in the wall like the edges of sharp weapons. Jebidiah saw a blacksmith's anvil, some bellows, a few old, nasty clumps of hay, a pitchfork and some horse tackle gone green with mold draped over a stall. There were no human footprints in the dirt, but it was littered with all manner of animal prints.

Jebidiah dismounted, glanced down the street. Except for an overturned stagecoach near a weathered building that bore a sign that read: GENTLEMAN'S HOTEL, the street was as empty as a wolf's gut in winter. The rest of the buildings looked equally as worn, and one, positioned across the street from the hotel, had burned down, leaving only blackened ruins and a batch of crows that moved about in the wreckage. The only sound was of the wind.

Jebidiah thought: Welcome to the town of Falling Rock.

He led his horse inside the livery, looked about. The animal tracks were what you would expect. Possum. Coon. Squirrel. Dog and cat. There were also some large and odd tracks that Jebidiah did not recognize. He studied them for a while, gave up on their recognition. But he knew one thing for sure. They were not human and they were not truly animal tracks. They were something quite different.

This was the place. Any place where evil lurked was his place. For he was God's messenger, that old celestial sonofabitch. Jebidiah wished he were free of him, and even thought sometimes that being the devil's assistant might be the better deal. But he had once gotten a glance at hell, and it was well short of appealing. The old bad devil was one of God's own, because God liked hell as much as heaven. It was God's game, heaven and hell, good and evil. That's all it was, a game, and Jebidiah despised, and feared God because of it. He had been chosen to be God's avenger against evil, and he couldn't give the job back. God didn't work that way. He was mighty mean spirited. He created man, then gave him a choice, but within the choice was a whore's promise. And instead of making it easy for man, as any truly kind spirit might, he allowed evil and sin and hell and the devil to exist and blamed it all on man. God's choice was simple. Do as I say, even if I make it hard on you to do so. It didn't make sense, but that's how it was.

Jebidiah tied his horse in one of the stalls, took the pitchfork and moved the old hay about. He found some good hay in the middle of the stack, forked it out, shook the dust from it and tossed it to his horse. It wasn't the best there was, but it would do, along with the grain he carried in a bag on his saddle. While the horse ate, Jebidiah put the fork aside, went into the stall and loosened the saddle, slid it off and hung it over the railing. He removed the bridle and reins, briefly interrupting his horse's feed, slung it over the stall, went out and shut the gate. He didn't like leaving his horse here in this bleak, unattended stable, but he had come up on another of life's evils and he had to be about his business. He didn't know the particulars, but he could sense evil. It was the gift, or the curse, that God had given him for his sins. And this sense, this gift, had come alert the minute he had ridden into the ghost town of Falling Rock. His urge was to ride away. But he couldn't. He had to do whatever it was that needed to be done. But for the moment, he needed to find water for his horse and himself, grain the horse, then find a safe place to bed down. Or as safe a place as possible.

Jebidiah walked down the street, and even though it was fall, he felt warm. The air was humid and the wind was hot. He walked until he came to the end of the street, finally walked back toward the Gentleman's Hotel. He paused for a brief look at the overturned stage coach, then turned and went into the hotel.

He saw immediately from the look of it that it had been a brothel. There was a bar and there were a series of stalls, not too unlike horse stalls. He had seen that sort of thing once before, in a town near Mexico. Women worked the stalls. Once there might have been curtains around the stalls, which would have come to the women's waist. But business would have been done there in each of them, the women hiking up their dresses so that cowboys, at two-bits a pop, could clean their pipes and happy up their spirits, be cheered on by their comrades as they rode the whores like bucking horses. Upstairs, in the beds, the finer girls would work, bringing in five Yankee dollars per roll on the sheets.

Jedidiah slid in behind the bar, saw that on the lower shelf were all manner of whiskey bottles. He chose one, held it up to the light. It was corked and full. He sat it on the bar and found some beer bottles with pry up pressure caps. He took a couple of those as well. Clutching it all in his arms, he climbed the stairs. He kicked a few doors open, found a room with a large bed covered in dust. He placed the bottles on a night table, pulled the top blanket back, shook the dust onto the floor. After replacing the blanket, he went to the window and pushed it up. There wasn't much air, and it was warm, but it was welcome in comparison to the still humidity of the room.

Jebidiah had found his camp. He sat on the bed and opened one of the beers and took a cautious sip. It was as flat as North Texas. He took it and the other beer, which he didn't bother to open, and tossed them out the window, sent them breaking and splattering into the dry, dirt street below. He wasn't sure what had possessed him to do such a thing, but now it was done and he felt better for having done it.

He went back to the nightstand, tugged the cork from the whisky with his teeth. He took a swig. The whiskey was warm both in temperature and spirit, and he could have cleaned his pistols with it, but it did the trick. He felt a comfortable heat in his throat and his stomach, a wave of relaxation soaking into his brain. It wasn't food, and it wasn't water, but it beat nothing in his stomach at all. After a moment, and a few more swigs, the whisky warmed him from head to toe, set a bit of a fire in his balls.

He sat on the bed and took several sips before returning the cork to the bottle and going downstairs. He went out into the street again, still looking for some place with water. He glanced at the stagecoach lying on its side, horseless, and noted something he had not noted before. The runner to which the horses would be hooked, was dark with blood. Jedidiah examined it. Dried gore was all along the runner. And now he noted there were horse hooves, bits of hair, even a gray horse ear, and what looked like a strip of skin lying in the street. Not to mention a hat and a shotgun. There was a smell too. Not just the smell of dried blood, but a kind of wet stink smell in the air. Jebidiah was sure the source was not from the blood or the horse remains. It was the stink of evil, and the smell of it made him absently push back his long black coat and touch the revolvers in their holsters.

He heard a moan. It was coming from the stage coach. Jebidiah scampered onto the runner and onto the side of the coach, moved along to the door with its cut away window, looked down and inside. Lying against the far side door that lay on the ground, was a woman. Jebidiah reached through the open gap, grabbed the interior latch, swung the door open and climbed inside. He touched the woman's throat. She moved a little, groaned again. Jebidiah turned her face and looked at it. She was a handsome woman with a big, dark bruise on her forehead. Her hair was as red as a campfire. She wore a tight fitting green dress, some fancy green shoes. She wore a lot of makeup. He lifted her to a sitting position. She fluttered her eyes open, jumped a little.

Jebidiah tried to give her a smile, but he was no good at it. "It's okay, lady" he said. "I am here to help."

"Thanks. But I need you to let me lift my ass. I'm sitting on my umbrella."

—◆—

Jebidiah helped her out of the stagecoach, into the hotel and upstairs. He put her on the bed he had shaken the dust from, gave her a snort of the whisky, which she took like a trooper. In fact, she took the bottle from him and took a long deep swig. She slapped the umbrella, which had a loop for her wrist against the bed.

"Damn, if that don't cut the dust," she said.

Jebidiah pulled a chair beside the bed and sat. "What's your name?" he said.

"Mary," she said disengaging herself from the umbrella, tossing it onto the end of the bed.

"I'm Jebidiah. What happened? Where are the stage horses?"

"Eat up," she said. "Them, the driver, and the shotgunner too."

"Eaten?"

Mary nodded.

"Tell me about it."

"You wouldn't believe me if I told you."

"You might be surprised."

And then, after another shot of whisky, she told it.

— ◆ —

"I'm a working girl, as you may have already noticed. I am late of Austin, Texas and Miss Mattie Jane's establishment. But Mattie met a man, got married, sold her place, made a deal with the madam here in Falling Rock for my services, as well as the remaining girls. I was the only one that took her up on the deal. The others spread out across Texas like prairie chickens.

"Must say, I thought there would be more to Falling Rock than this. Thought it would be a sizable town. And maybe it was. I figure what ever got the driver and shotgunner, as well as a whisky drummer in the coach with me, got most of the town too. Hadn't been for my umbrella, I'd be dead. I was surprised at how well I was able to protect myself with it.

"We came into town late last night, me ready to start my job here at the Gentleman's Hotel, ready to buck pussy, when a strange thing occurred. No sooner had the stage entered the town, then a shadow, heavy as if it had weight, fell across the place, and sort of lay there. You could see the moon, you could see the town, but the shadow flowed between buildings and into the stage coach. It became hard to breath. It was like trying to suck down flannel instead of air. Then the stage shadow flowed away and the stage rolled on, stopped in front of the hotel. The stage shook real hard and then I heard a noise. A kind of screech, unlike anything I had ever heard. Then I remembered one of my old johns telling about being in an Indian fight, and that it had been close and hand to hand, and the horses had been wounded, and there had been a fire in a barn that the Indians set, and the horses inside burned alive. He said the horses screamed. Somehow, I knew that was what I was hearing. Screaming horses. Except there wasn't any fire to burn them. But something was scaring them, causing them pain.

"The stage coach shook and tumbled over. I heard the shotgun go off a couple of times, and next thing I knew the driver and the shotgunner were yelling. The whisky drummer stuck his head out of the overturned window, jerked it back again. He turned and looked at me. His face, even in the night, was as white as the hairs on an albino's ass. He pulled a derringer, then there was a face at the window. I ain't never seen a face like it. I couldn't place it. My mind wouldn't wrap around it.

"The drummer fired his derringer, and the face jerked back, then it filled the window again. An arm, a hairy arm with what looked like hooks on it snapped through the window and caught the drummer in the face, peeled him from his left ear to the side of his lip. I remember seeing his teeth exposed through a gap in his jaw. Then the hairy, hooked hand had him by the throat. The drummer fought, slamming the derringer into the thing's face, pounding on its hands with the butt of the gun. He was snatched through the window in a spray of blood.

"I didn't know nothing but to grab up my umbrella. It's all I had. Then the face was there again, tugging at the door, about to pull it off, I figured, so I jumped forward and stabbed out with the tip of the umbrealla and got the thing in the eye. It let out a horrible howl, moved away. But two more ugly, hairy faces took its place. Yellow eyes glowing, and all those teeth, dripping spit. I'm not brave, but fear drove me to jump at them and stab into them, and I got one of them, and it, he, whatever it was, jumped back and went away.

"I don't think I scared them, I just think they sort of, well, got bored or something. Or more likely...full. Cause I could hear them prowling around and around the stage, and I could hear other things, snapping sounds, gnawing sounds, a kind of excitement that sounded like miners at a free lunch.

"They climbed up on the stage and looked in the window a few times, and I struck at one of them, missed. The thing almost swatted me with that hairy arm, those big claws, then there was pink light through the window, and it went silent outside. I considered coming out, but couldn't. I was too frightened. I was exhausted too. More than I realized. I dreamed I was awake. I had no idea I had fallen asleep until you came. Good thing I dropped my umbrella while I slept, otherwise you would have found it in your ribs, your eye, some place."

Jedidiah picked up the umbrella and looked at it. It was ragged and broken in spots, tipped with wood. He touched it with his fingers. Oak. He gave it to her. "The tip is sharp," he said.

"I broke it off some time ago. Never did get another."

"Good thing," Jebidiah said. "The broken tip made a good weapon."

Mary looked at the window. "It's growing dark. We need to leave this town."

Jebidiah shook his head. "No. I have to be here. But you should leave. I'll even give you my horse to do it."

"I don't know why you have to stay, that's your business, but I won't lie. I'm ready to go. And I'll tell you, I was just lucky. I think the day light ran them. Had it been earlier in the night, I wouldn't be here right now. I'd be some turd, digested and dropped on a hill somewhere, maybe drawing flies in an alley. I'll take you up on that horse, mister. But I'd like to do it now. And I'm telling you, you damn sure don't need to be here afoot. Or on horseback, or in a stage, or no kind of way. You need to ride on out with me."

"I'll leave when my job is done."

"What job?"

"His job...God."

"You some kind of preacher?"

Some kind."

"Well, sir, that's your business if you say so. I don't pray to God much. He ain't never answered any of my prayers."

"I don't know that he's answered anyone's," Jebidiah said.

—◆—

Darkness was edging into the street when Jebidiah and Mary left the hotel, began to walk briskly toward the barn. The oppressive humidity was gone, and now there was a chill in the air. By the time they reached the livery and Jebidiah had saddled his horse, the night had slipped in smooth and solid.

Outside the livery, leading the horse, Jebidiah looked toward the woods that lay beyond the town, saw that they were holding thick shadows between leaves and limbs.

"I'm not going anywhere," Mary said. "I've waited too long. Bad enough it's dark, but me out there without anyone to help, damn if I will. I'd rather stay here till morning. Provided I'm here in the morning."

"You are probably right," Jebidiah said. "It wouldn't be good for you to go now. It's best to go back to the hotel."

They started back down the street, Jebidiah leading his horse, and as they went, a kind of dark cloud fled out of the woods and covered the quarter moon and fell on the town and came apart, shadows skittering in all directions.

"What in hell is that?" Mary said.

"The mantle of darkness," Jebidiah said, and picked up his pace. "It sometimes comes when a place is full of evil."

"It's cold."

"Odd, isn't it? Something from the devil, from the bowels of hell, and it's cold."

"I'm scared," Mary said. "I don't normally scare up easy, but this shit is making my asshole pucker."

"Best not to think about being scared," Jebidiah said. "Best to think about survival. Let's get back to the hotel."

—◆—

When they got to the hotel it was full of ghosts.

Jebidiah tried to lead his horse inside. It pulled at the reins, not wanting to enter.

"Easy, boy," Jebidiah said to the horse, stroked its nose, and the horse settled down, slightly. Jebidiah continued to soothe the horse as he and Mary watched the ghosts move about. There were many ghosts and they seemed not to notice Jebidiah and Mary at all. They were white and thin as clean smoke, but were identifiable shapes of cowboys and whores, and they moved across the floor and into the stalls. Women hiked their ghostly dresses, and ghostly men dropped their trousers and entered them. The bartender behind the bar walked up and down its length. He reached and took hold of bottles that were not bottles, but shapes of bottles that could be seen through. At a piano a ghostly presence sat, hatless, in striped shirt and suspenders, all of which could be seen through. The ghost moved his hands over the keys but the keys didn't move, but the player seemed to move as if he heard the music. A few cowboys and whores were dancing about to the lively tune that was heard to them, but not the living.

"My God," Mary said.

"Funny how he always gets mentioned," Jebidiah said.

"What?"

"Nothing. Don't fear these. They can't hurt you. Most of them don't even know you're here."

"Most?"

"They are spirits of habit. They do this over and over. It was what they were doing, or wanted to do before they died. But that one—"

Jebidiah pointed to a ghostly, but much more distinct shape sitting in a chair against the far wall. He was a stubby cowboy in a big ghostly hat. He was almost solid, but the wall and the furniture could be seen through him. "He knows we're here. He sees us as we see him. He has been here a while. He has begun to accept his death."

At that statement, the ghostly figure Jebidiah referred to, rose and crossed the room toward them, walking, but not quite touching the floor.

Mary moved toward the door.

Jebidiah grabbed her arm. "Best not. The street will be a far less welcome place shortly, perhaps already. There's more out there than an oppressive cloud."

"Will he hurt us?" Mary asked.

"I don't think so."

The ghost sauntered toward them, and as he neared, he showed a lopsided grin, stopped, stood directly in front of Jebidiah. Beside him, Mary shook like a leaf in a high wind. Jebidiah's horse tugged at the reins, Jebidiah pulled the horse forward slightly, glanced at it. Its visible eye rolled in its head. "Easy, boy," Jebidiah said to the horse, then turned to the ghost, said, "Can you speak?"

"I can," said the spirit, and the voice was odd, as if it were climbing up to them from the bottom of a deep, dark well.

"How did you die?"

"Must I answer that?"

"You are bound to answer nothing at all, or anything you wish," Jebidiah said. "I have no control over you."

"I want to pass on," the ghost said, "but for some reason, I can not. I am here alone, because the others, they don't know they're dead. This town, it holds us. But I seem to be the only one that knows what has happened."

"Evil has claimed it," Jebidiah said. "When that happens, all manner of things can occur. Not always the same, but always evil. You have decided to embrace the truth, they have not. But in time, they must."

"I'm not evil. I'm just a cowpoke that got dead."

"The evil is what's holding you," Jebidiah said.

The cowboy nodded. "Them."

"The hairy ones," Mary said.

"Yes, the hairy ones," the ghost said. "What they did left me in this place. There are other places, places I would like to move to, but I can't, and it's because of them, who they are and what they are."

"It's the way you died," Jebidiah said. "You are caught in one of God's little jokes."

The ghost twisted its head to the side like a curious dog.

"What kind of joke?" the cowboy said, "because I assure you, I don't find it all that funny."

"And, in time, you will find it less and less humorous, and then you will get angry, and then you will react, and your reactions will not be of the best nature."

"I have no intent of haunting anyone," said the ghost.

"Time and frustration turns the spirit dark," Jebidiah said. "But I can help you pass on."

"You can?"

"I can."

"Then do it, for Christ's sake."

"The evil must be destroyed."

"Do it."

"I would ask a small favor of you, first."

"Of me?"

"Tell me about this town. What happened to you. If I know about it, I can fight what's here, and I can help you pass on. That is my promise."

"Oh, you can't fight what's here. Soon, you and her will be like me."

"Perhaps," Jebidiah said.

"I don't like the sound of that," Mary said.

"First things first," Jebidiah said. "I don't want to stand here with my horse and my back against the door."

"Understood," said the ghost.

—◆—

Jebidiah found a big room, a kind of sitting room, and that was where he put his horse, fed it grain that he poured out onto the hardwood floor. Then, as the ghost watched, he pushed a long cabinet across the doorway and pulled the curtains on the window. He and Mary took a seat on a kind of settee that was before the large window with the pulled curtains. There was no light inside, and Jebidiah did nothing to find one, though an oil lamps stood out from the wall in brass fixtures. They sat in the dark, it being nothing to the ghost. Jebidiah and Mary's eyes adjusted in time, enough to make out shapes, and of course the ghost was forever constant, white and firm.

Once seated, the Reverend pulled both his revolvers

and laid them on his thighs. Mary sat tight against him. The ghost took a chair as he might have in real life. He pulled a ghostly chaw from his pocket and put it in his jaw. The room grew darker and the night grew more still.

"There's no taste," the ghost said after a few jaw movements. "It's just the idea of a chaw. It's there, and I can put it in my mouth, but it's like the liquor the bartender serves, it's not really there. Thing that makes me feel a bit better about that is the fact the money I pay him, it ain't there either. Ain't nothing really there but my urges."

"So the bartender knows you're here?" Jebidiah said.

"Sometimes. Sometimes not."

"I'm sure it is a misery," Jebidiah said. "But now, if I'm to help you, help us. I feel that we are short of time. Already the street is full of the night, and the great shadow lays heavy on the town. I can taste it when I breathe."

"You talk funny."

"I was educated funny."

The ghost nodded. "That shadow comes down on the town before they do. It comes, they are not far behind. When they show up, and that's at the beat of twelve," and with that the ghost nodded toward a big grandfather clock in the near corner of the room, "that's when things get hairy, so to speak."

Jebidiah struck a match and leaned it in the direction of the clock. It said seven p.m.

"Then we have some time," Jebidiah said, shaking out the match.

"So maybe we can and should get out of town now," Mary said.

The ghost shook its head. "Nope. You don't want to go out there. They don't get serious until midnight, but being out in the street, under that big ole shadow, that ain't the place to be. The things to worry about the most ain't gonna be here for awhile, but, still, there's things out there under and in that shadow, and you don't want no part of that. I'm dead, and I don't want no part of it. And besides, time ain't the same here. Take a look at the clock."

Jebidiah struck another match, held it up. The clock had moved a full fifteen minutes. Jebidiah shook out his match.

"It's messed up," Mary said.

The ghost shook its head.

Jebidiah said, "The devil's time is different from mine and yours." Jebidiah turned to the ghost. "Do you have some helpful advice for us? I believe we could use any you might possess, and considering your situation, you are bound to have experiences that we do not."

"And if you're lucky," said the ghost, "you'll never have them. Let me tell you, this ain't no dosey-do, being dead, being hung up between here and wherever."

The ghost paused for a moment, as if gathering his energies, and in fact, he seemed to become brighter, more solid, and as he did, he leaned forward and told his story.

—◆—

"My name was Dolber Gold, but everyone called be Dol when I was alive. Me and all these cowboys and whores once lived in, or worked in, or passed through this town. And this here establishment, which could be called a kind of house of pleasure, a sure enough Gentleman's hotel, minus the goddamn gentleman, was always packed and full of piano music and dancing, and if you'll pardon me, ma'am, the riding of asses and the drinking of liquor.

"Mine has been ridden plenty," Mary said. "I'm a working girl. So no begging your pardon is necessary."

"I thought as much," Dol said, "and I mean that with no disrespect. My favorite women were always of the loose nature, and I respect the job they do and the pleasure they give. And if I were able, I'd be glad to lay coins down to buck a bit with you."

"Tell your story," Jebidiah said.

"The hairy ones," Dol said. "That's your problem."

Dol nodded at the grandfather clock. "Go outside now you'll be covered in a kind of sickness, a feeling that will make you weak. It's them a'comin'. There's bad things in that shadow in the street, but it ain't nothing to what's gonna be here when that clock hits high midnight. "

"You've said as much," Jebidiah said, throwing a glance at the clock. His eyes had adjusted enough he could make out the fact that the hands had moved again. Another fifteen minutes. There were still time, but it was best to be prepared, and have time to do it. Dol was as chatty as a squirrel, and no where near on point.

"Me and some of the boys got liquored up and rode out to the old graveyard for some fun. I didn't have no respect, cause I was full of rotgut to the gills. We rode out there with bad intentions. Graveyard there is what used to be for all them folks settled here, but there was graves older than that on top of the hill, lost in amongst the trees. And it was said Conquistadors come through here, gave trouble to the Indians. Story went that they come through this part of East Texas, up the Sabine River, searching for gold. Course, wasn't none. But they searched anyway. These woods, deep as they are now, were deeper then, and there was things in there from times before we know'd about time. Conquistadores began to die out, and the six that was left, they camped here a'bouts, and in the night, a hairy one came. Maybe he was an Indian. Who knows? The Indians tell the story. But he was hairy and he came into the center of them and killed the lot of them, tore them up. Their bones were left to rot on the hill. But Indians said them Conquistadores, ever full moon, gathered flesh and hair on their bones, and come into camp searching for food and fun killin'. It was said this thing that killed them had passed along a piece of himself to them, making them like him. Wolves that walked like men. Indians finally captured these six and even the original hairy one, who they claimed came from some hole in the ground, came up to plague man and spread evil. But they captured them somehow, and buried them deep and pinned them to the ground."

"Pinned them?" Jebidiah said.

"Comin' to that," Dol said. "So me and my buddies, we thought it might be fun to dig up them old graves. We wasn't worried about no curse, but we figured there might be something inside them graves worth somethin', if it was no more than just a look. Armor, maybe. Swords. Might even have been something in there worth a few dollars. Truth is, we didn't figure there really was no Conquistadores buried there. But, you get bottle smart when you've drunk enough, and we'd drunk enough, and we rode up there and found some old, unmarked mounds at the top of the hill, trees and vines grown up on and around them. There was a big old stick, like a limb, stuck down in one of the mounds. It looked fresh, like it had just been put there."

"What kind of limb?" Jebidiah asked?

"What?"

"What sort of wood was it?"

"Hell, I don't know. I think it was hickory or something like that."

"Oak?"

"Could have been," Dol said. "I ain't for certain, but I sure wish I could remember, and maybe figure on what kind of trees grew around there and the name of all the plants and birds and such. What is wrong with you fella? Who gives a shit?"

"My guess is it was oak," Jebidiah said. "Like the tip of Mary's umbrella."

The ghost just looked at him.

"Never mind," Jedidiah said. "Go on with your story."

"Tim, he'd brought some shovels and he passed them out, and we started digging. I remember we come to this stick in the ground, a stick carved on with symbols and such, and I pulled it out and tossed it, and, well, drunk like we was, we didn't last too long. But before we passed out, we did make some progress on one of them mounds, enough to open it. But I don't remember much about that. Next thing I knowed, I was on my back looking up at the full moon shining down through the trees. I got up on one elbow, and that's when I seen it. It was the grave we had dug into. There was a hairy arm pushing up out of the ground, and then this long snout sheddin' dirt, and then this thing pulled its way out of the hole and wobbled up there on the edge of the grave. It was about seven feet tall. It was like a wolf, only it had a long snout and ten times the teeth. Them teeth hung out and twisted ever which way, and tall as it was, it was still bent some, and its paws was tipped out with long, shiny claws. But the eyes, that was the worst. They was as yellow as old custard, except when they rolled, cause then they showed a kind of bloody white around them.

"I tried to get up. But I couldn't move at first. Drunk and scared like I was, kind of going in and out of being awake. This thing bent over and started digging in the ground, and pretty soon it was tearing at the dirt and tossing it all over the place. It didn't seem to take no time at all before it had dug into a hole and pulled out another stick like that one I pulled, and then up come another of them things, and he went on to do this time and again, and I tried to get up, tried to shake one of my buddies awake, but he wouldn't budge. Got my gun out and shot at it, but it ignored me. It just went on getting them others out of the ground until there were six. Well, even drunk like I was, by this time I knew I wasn't having no dream, and I was scared sober.

"One of them things picked up one of my buddies by the ankle, held him up high and bit into his head, started slurping at the brain. Well, I'll tell you, I was up then and running. I heard one of my buddies scream up there on the hill, then after that I was running so fast through the trees, getting hit in the face by limbs and such, I didn't hear nor notice nothing. It come to me that I might have been better to have grabbed up my horse, but I don't remember if it was even around no more. Good as it was about being trained to stand, I had either forgotten it, or it had run off first sight of that thing comin' out of the ground.

"I ran and I ran, thought I was making pretty good time and doing well, then I seen a shadow moving through the woods, and pretty soon it was everywhere. It made me feel sick and weak, like I'd walked into a cloud of poison. Then there was these other shadows that come out of the darker shadow, and they moved, and they changed, took shape. It was them hairy things, kind of wolf like they were. I got my brains back for a moment, started firing my six gun, but it wasn't doing no good. I'd have done about as much good to try and stop them by peeing on them. But I didn't even have that kind of ammunition, having already peed all over myself from being so scared. And I guess, since I've gone this far, got to say I messed myself to. I was so scared my goose bumps had goose bumps.

I ran and ran, then come to a break in the woods, climbed to the top of a hill, and then I heard them growl, and they was on me. It happened faster than you can skin your foreskin back for a soapin'.

"But they didn't kill me. Not right off. They slapped me around, bit on me some. Finally one of them threw me over his shoulder like I was a sack of taters, carried me off. I tell you, I was one scared cowpoke. Didn't know if they was gonna eat me or stick their pecker's in my asshole. What they did was carry me to the woods and they brought me back to where we had been, up the top of the graveyard. As they carried me I tried to take note of things, see where I was goin', thinking maybe I stayed alert I had a chance. But there wasn't no chance. They got to the graveyard they threw me down and one of them stood there with his big paw on my chest, the claws cutting into me like knives, and the others took to digging. Down on their knees, digging like dogs, or wolves, or whatever they was, and soon they had a big hole dug out and they pulled this big run of bones out of the ground, and yanked a long, carved, stick out of between its forehead, which wasn't nothin' but a skull, and while I'm lookin', I seen the moonlight come down on that head and I seen that hole in the head seal up, then I seen flesh start to run over them bones, and then I seen it get pink with blood and the chest start to breathe, and then hair started to grow, in patches at first, then finally all over, and when it was thick as wild prairie grass, the thing sat up, and finally stood up. It was a male, that was obvious. Male like all the others, cause the thing that let me know they was all male was hanging out for all to see, long as a razor strap, thick as my ankle. And then it looked right at me.

"Well now, this is the ugly part, and I start to almost feel humanly sick when I think about it, even though I'm deader than Custer and his whole outfit. Still feel the fear, dead or not, thinking back on it. This thing, it come at me slow and easy, pulled its lips back on that long old snout and showed me all them teeth, and I went to screamin', just like a little girl who's seen a spider. And boy, that thing liked that. It pulled those lips back even more and spit started dripping off its teeth, and then it crouched like, and finally I realized I was screamin', cause at first I was just doin' it, not knowing I was, you know, and I heard the quality of it, and I thought, well, 'You go to hell', I ain't screamin' another sound. And I shut my mouth and went quiet and made to go like a man...Only, I didn't. He started to move fast then, a funny kind of move, like some of the moves was left out, and then just before he had me his pecker got stiff, like he was gonna do some business, and maybe he was I thought, and I screamed again. Big and loud and I couldn't stop till he stopped me, his teeth in my throat. I don't remember much after that, but the next thing I knowed I was here in this hotel, and thinkin' I'd dreamed. But I couldn't get nobody to see me. And then gradually, there was more spirits like me, cause that cloud come through the street every night, and then them wolves would come. Kind of folded out of the shadows. Caught everyone here eventually. Before they did, they once got trapped in the old hotel across the street. The real hotel. And the folks in the town burned in down. And them things, they come out of there afire, their hair and flesh growing back fast as bullets fly. They went on a rampage, and then there wasn't no one left in this town but ghosts, like me. They took to eating horses and cats and rats and dogs, whatever stray animal might wander in. After that, there wasn't nothing. And then they kept coming around. Kept waiting for something. More meat I guess. I don't know why they didn't go off somewhere else, but they didn't. Maybe far as the trees where me and my poor pals found them was as far as they could go, cause I know one night I seen the big one up there on the hill, howling at the moon. I figure it was cause he was so hungry his stomach thought its throat was cut."

"They're confined to this area," Jebidiah said. "The cloud is part of the evil that came out of the graves. They were held there by the sharp ends of the oak. Some evil can't stand oak. And this, obviously, is that evil. Unfortunately, you released them."

"Unless it's hickory," Dol said. "Or some kind of other tree. Ain't nothing says it's oak. I didn't tell you it was oak. I don't remember."

"You have a point," Jebidiah said, "but from my experience, I'm betting on oak."

"It's your bet," Dol said.

"I don't understand," Mary said. "He bit you, like he bit them Spaniards so long ago. They become wolves until the Indians killed them…Or held them down with the sticks. But you got bit, the others got bit, why ain't you and them wolf-things?"

Dol shook his head. "Ain't got a nugget on that. Nothin'."

"Because," said Jebidiah, "the leader, he is one, and they are six, and together they are seven."

"Well now, that clears it right up," Dol said.

"Satan's minions, that's what they are. And there is one directly from Satan, and there are six that he made. That allows seven. They can kill others, but they can only make so many, and seven is their number. If they were vampires, or ghouls, they could make more, but the hairy things, they can only make seven."

"Who made that rule?" Mary said.

"My guess is the gentleman in charge," Jebidiah said.

"God?" Dol said.

"He likes his little games," The Reverend said. "They have no rhyme of reason to us, or perhaps to him, but, they are his games and they are real and they effect us all. Seven. That is the number for the hairy ones."

"How do you know that?" Mary asked.

"I've seen more than I would like, read tomes that are not that delightful to read."

"So you seen it, or you read about it?" Mary said.

"In this case, I read about it."

"So you ain't had no practical experience on the matter?" Mary said.

"On this, no. On things like it, yes."

"Well, Mary said, "I hope this is some like them other things, or otherwise, we can bend over now and look up between our legs and piss on ourselves."

— ◆ —

The night grew heavy and the shadow fled through all parts of the town. In the hotel, and in the other buildings, it was nothing more than a dark, cool, fog, a malaise that swept over Jebidiah and Mary. Jebidiah removed the barrier from the setting room door, and as he did, the clock ticked eight thirty. Dol and the other ghosts returned to what substituted for lives; the limbo of the hotel; the existence of the not quite gone and the not quite present.

Jebidiah led his horse out of the sitting room, into the saloon. In there they watched the ghosts for a moment, and then Jebidiah took a candle from one of the tables where it was melted to a saucer, broke the saucer free, and put the candle in his pocket. He found two kerosene lamps with kerosene still in them, and gave those to Mary to carry. He and Mary went up the stairs to the hotel room where Jebidiah's whisky resided. Jebidiah led his horse up there with him. The animal was reluctant at first, but then made the stairs easily and finally arrived at the landing, snorting in protest.

When Jebidiah looked down on the hotel, the dark fog had laid down on the floor like a black velvet carpet, was slowly seeping out of sight into the wood.

"You don't go far without that horse, do you?" Mary said, causing Jebidiah to turn his head and look.

"I'll save him if I can. No use leaving him to be eaten.

He's the best horse I ever had. Smart. Brave. Worth more than most humans."

"That may be true, but he just shit on the floor. And it smells like a horse stall now."

"We'll live with it."

The went into the bedroom, Jebidiah leading his horse. He let go of the animal and took Mary's umbrella off the bed and pulled out his pocket knife, and began to whittle pieces off of it.

"I'm glad you got a hobby," Mary said. "Me, I'm scared shitless."

"And so am I. Whittling relaxes me. Especially when it has a purpose."

"What purpose?"

"These little shards of oak. For it to effect the wolves, it has to bear some of the wood's insides. Oak itself, that doesn't do it. Shaved oak. Sharpened oak. Anything that takes the husk off and shows the meat of the tree."

"What you gonna do, chase them down and poke them with that little stuff? I don't see you're doing no good."

"I'm going to take these little fragments, and I'm going to make them smaller. Then I'm going to take my bullets, use my pocket knife to noodle a small hole in the tips of the loads. I'm going to put wood fragments in those little holes, then, I'm going to take this—"

He produced the candle from his pocket. "I'm going to seal the little wood shaving stuffed holes with wax. When I shoot these guns, the oak goes into the wolves along with the bullets."

"Ain't you the smart one?" Mary said, and she took a swig from Jebidiah's bottle.

He took it from her. "No more. We had best have our wits about us."

Mary said, "You want, you could knock you off a piece. No charge."

"I would hardly have my wits about me doing that? Now would I?"

"Reckon not. Just a friendly offer."

"And a fine one. But I fear I'll have to pass."

Jebidiah went back to whittling, but not before he waved a match under the bottom of the candle and stuck it up on the nightstand and lit the wick. When he finished whittling, the wax was soft. He went to work inserting the miniature wood shavings, sealing them with wax. Mary helped.

Howls came down from the piney hills and filled the streets and filled the Gentleman's hotel.

"They're coming," Jebidiah said.

— ◆ —

Jebidiah went out on the landing, looked down. The ghosts had gone, except Dol, and he had wandered behind the bar and laid down flat on the floor. The wolves couldn't hurt him, but Jebidiah assumed he didn't want to see them. Dead or not, he still knew fear. Jebidiah watched his silent, still, white figure for a while, then returned to the room and closed the door. He hefted the revolvers in their holsters. They were packing his special prepared bullets. He had done the same for his Winchester ammunition. And he had done it for his gun belt reloads until the wax ran out. The umbrella he had whittled on was little more now than a thin, sharp stick, as Jebidiah had torn off the umbrella itself, and worked on the shaft with his knife.

Mary sat in the center of the bed. He had given her the rifle.

She said, "You know, I can't hit the back end of an elephant with a tossed shot glass."

"Wait until they're close."

"Jesus," Mary said.

"He'll be of no help," Jebidiah said. "Put your faith in that Winchester."

"Maybe they won't know we're here," Mary said.

"They'll know. They're hungry. They can smell us."

The sound of Mary swallowing was as loud as a cough.

—◆—

Jebidiah sat in a chair by the window and watched Mary who had fallen asleep. He was surprised she could sleep. Every nerve in his body was crawling. He lit one of the lanterns and put it on the floor by his chair, then sat back down, took out his pocket watch. He popped the metal cover and looked at it. Even as he watched the hands crawled from eight-thirty to nine. He took a breath, shut his eyes, looked again. It had already moved five minutes past. He went to the window and looked out. Something moved across the street, through the low hanging shadow that had mostly seeped into the ground, like a dark oil of evil. Jebidiah had gotten only a glance, but it was something big and hairy, and it had moved from the far side of the street to the back of the hotel. His horse stirred in the corner of the room, where it had taken up residence by backing its ass against the wall.

Jebidiah took a breath and moved away from the window. He went over and stroked the horse's nose, then went to the door, opened it, stepped out on the landing.

It was dead dark down there and he couldn't see a thing. Not even Dol lying behind the bar; perhaps he had gone wherever the others had gone, some other part of the town, all scrunched up and wadded together in a mass of white mist in a closet somewhere. He could see that the door to the hotel was partially opened. When they had come into the hotel, he had closed it.

Jebidiah stood there for a long time, one hand on the

rail, looking down. Gradually his eyes became somewhat more adjusted. He thought he saw something moving near the bar.

There was a shape.

It was still.

Perhaps it was nothing.

All right, Jebidiah thought, it's not like they don't know we're here. He took a small bible from the inside of his coat pocket and tore off the front page and took out a wooden match, struck it, lit the paper and dropped it.

In the falling light of the paper, which lasted briefly, he saw the shape was not just a shadow, but was in fact a thing. Dark fur was glimpsed, hot, yellow eyes, teeth, and then the beast was moving, darting around the bar, heading for the stairs, climbing two or three steps at a bound. In that brief moment, Jebididah saw that there was another in the corner. A large beast with even larger, yellow eyes. That would be the King Wolf, the thought, the one who would command the others, the one who would send them on their missions.

Jebidiah stepped to the mouth of the stairway and pulled his revolver, pointed it casually and comfortably at the shape that was bounding up the stairs, its chest covered in a metal Spanish breast plate. In the darkness he could only tell it was there, couldn't make out features, could catch glimpses of that breast plate by the thin moonlight they came through the hotel windows. He aimed a little low, toward the groin, so that when he pulled the trigger on the Colt .45 it bucked and rode up, throwing the bullet into the upper part of the thing's body, clanging the armor, but traveling through it. The beast grunted, twisted slightly, kept coming. White smoke twisted up from its breast plate where the bullet had gone in, and from its back where it had come out.

Jebidiah cocked back the hammer again, thought, my God, I hit it straight on. A .45 slug should have knocked him down the stairs and on his ass, flat, breastplate or no breastplate.

The Colt jumped again, a burst of red flame coughed from the barrel, the bullet struck the beast in the face just as it reached the top of the stairs and was within six inches of Jebidiah's gun barrel. There was a barking sound. The beast twisted and slammed against the wall and rolled down the stairs, smashed through the railing, bounced onto the bar and lay silent and dark in the shadows.

One, thought Jebidiah.

He looked down into the shadows, but couldn't really make out much. He thought he still saw the shape lying there, but he wasn't for sure. He glanced toward the corner of the room. The King Wolf moved. And it was like Dol said. It seemed to move with some of the moves torn out. One moment it was in the corner, the next it was consumed by shadows.

Okay. One down. Maybe.

He squinted and looked again. He couldn't be sure what was down there. He had hit it solid, and with the oak in the bullet, so he thought perhaps he had done the old boy in.

The front door of the hotel burst open wider and in came four hairy black shapes, moving so fast it was hard to realize at first what they were. They leaped about, two hitting the stairs and coming up fast, another striking the wall, moving along the side of it, scuttling there with its claws like a giant, hairy roach. The fifth was running on all fours up the railing.

Jebididah shot at the one on the railing, hit it in the head and saw it fall, but now the others were coming at top speed. Jedidiah felt his nerves grow taut, about to snap.

Red flames and a loud bark came from his left and one

of the wolves on the stairway fell and hit the other and they both went tumbling through the already damaged railing. One hit the floor and didn't move, the other scrambled, ran in a circle like a frightened dog.

Jebidiah glanced left. It was Mary with the rifle. He grabbed her elbow and twisted her and pushed her through the open doorway and into the room and slammed the door even as the beast running alongside the wall—causing plaster and wood to fly every which way from its claws—climbed to the ceiling, turned upside down and scuttled across that. They heard the creature drop to the floor outside the doorway, heard its breathing, loud as the pumping of blacksmith bellows.

Then it hit the door, knocking a large gap in it. But as it did it screeched and drew back its paw. There was a roar and the sound of something clambering wildly on the landing.

Inside the room, the horse reared and came down hard on the floor with its hooves. Jebidiah feared he had made a mistake bringing the horse up there with them. It could do as much damage to them as the wolves if it became frightened.

Well, maybe not that much.

Mary stood staring at the gap in the door. "What happened?"

"The door is oak. He snagged his arm on it, a sharp piece of wood."

"Then they can't come through?"

"I think they can, just not easily."

"Did I kill the one I shot?"

"I don't know. I think the bullet still has to strike a vital organ, and if it does, the oak splinter in it should act like poison. But maybe it has got to be solid hit. Not just a leg, a shoulder. But the heart. The brain. Liver. Something like that. Looked to me you had a good shot, right in the head.

But it was dark. It happened so fast...I can't say for sure."

Jebidiah went over and took his horse's reins and pulled at them gently and stroked the horse's nose. Its eyes rolled wildly and it lifted its nose and dropped it back down, repeated the motion numerous times. Slowly the horse calmed.

They stood for a while, then sat on the edge of the bed, facing the door, guns in hand.

Nothing.

The night crawled on.

Mary said: "It couldn't have been midnight. Not already. My God, did you see those things?"

Jebidiah took out his watch, looked at it in the lantern glow. The hands indicated two a.m.

"I thought it was just after nine," he said. "Advantage to this limbo time is that it will be day soon, and then time will slow. They don't come out in the day."

"You know that for a fact?"

"No," Jebidiah said. "I don't."

—◆—

They had sat for only a moment when they heard a kind of scratching sound, coming from the street. Jebidiah went to the window to look out, saw nothing. But the sound increased. He leaned against the window glass and looked down. Something was coming up the side of the wall. He opened the window quickly, stuck his head out. A wolf was scratching its way up, moving fast, its head lifted to look up at Jebidiah. It was almost on him.

Jebidiah grabbed up the lantern, flung it out the window and down on the wolf. Flames burst in all directions and rose up on the thing's head like a dunce hat of flame, whipped about and caught the fur on fire. The beast let go with its front paws, slapped at the flames, held itself out from the side of the building with its back claws, then lost purchase, first one foot came loose, then the other, and it fell. It dropped in a twist of fire, hit the ground on its back, rolled on its belly. The flames licked down and along its spine and it screeched and crawled along the street, then went still in the middle of it. The flames lapped its fur clean and cooked the charred meat and the meat fell off in puddles, then there were only the bones, blackened and smoking. The eye sockets in the thick wolf skull chugged out wafts of dark smoke that rose up to the sky and made little black, dissipating mushroom shapes. The skull shifted and cracked and fell apart. Jebidiah blinked. It was the skeleton of a man now. The wolf bones had twisted and changed.

Jebidiah, trembling slightly, pulled his head in. "They don't like fire," he said. "That and oak splinters. Make a note."

Mary had moved to the window to stand beside him. She looked down at the bones in the street. "Noted," she said, but the word sounded as is she were clearing her throat.

—◆—

Jebidiah reloaded his six gun. "If I got one with a shot, and you got one, and now there's this dead one in the street, we've done all right so far."

"If? So we either have four left, or six," Mary said.

"That sounds about right," Jebidiah said. "And we haven't even seen the big boy, the pack leader. Least not well. He might be a whole different kettle of fish. One thing is for sure, he lets his boys do the dirty work."

"What time is it?"

Jebidiah looked. "Damn," he said.

"What?"

"The watch. It's moving backwards. It's midnight again."

—◆—

Jebidiah thought: If we can last until morning, it won't matter if we stop them all. Perhaps then I can catch them where they sleep, someplace dark and well hidden most likely. But if I can get them now, I can be sure, I won't have to search for them. Of course, there's the problem of time. It moves forward and backward. It could do that until we are hunted down, eaten, shat out brown and greasy on a distant hill.

He walked up and down the floor, stopping now and then to sooth the horse that now he wished he had not bothered with. Yet, the thought of leaving a fine animal to the monsters, that wasn't good, couldn't do that. Even God, the old sonofabitch, might appreciate a good horse.

He paced and he thought and he felt his nerves twist around inside of him, his feelings and impressions coming fast like rifle shots, jumping from one thought to another. Mary was sitting dead center in the bed, the rifle across her knees, watching the split in the door, turning her head now and then to look behind her, toward the open window, out into the night which seemed to have gone more dark and bleak than before, leaving only thin silver moonlight.

Jebidiah went to the window and looked out. The bones were still there.

He walked across the room, trying to make himself sit and rest. But he couldn't do it, felt like he had drank two or three pots of coffee. Shit. Coffee. That would be good right now. Some bacon and eggs. Hell, he was hungry enough to eat the ass out of a menstruating mule.

What was that? A flutter?

A moth beat at the window.

Okay. A moth. No problem there. It moved beneath the window and through the gap where Jebidiah had opened it to drop one of the lanterns. The remaining lantern hung from a hook in the ceiling and bled pollen-yellow light all over the place.

Jebidiah watched the moth. It was a big one and dark of wing and fuzzy. It flew into the room over the bed, up against the ceiling where it flittered about, the lantern light causing its shadow to flick and swell and flap along the wall. Jebidiah turned to look at the shadow and the shadow seemed larger than before. Jebidiah felt something move on the back of his neck, like prickly pear needles. It was his hair, standing on end. He turned to look at the moth again, up there on the ceiling, and it was a wolf; it had shifted shape. It clung upside down over the bed and Mary. Jebidiah wheeled, cross drew pistols and fired rapidly. One. Two. Three.

Mary was moving then, off the bed, running across the floor.

The wolf dropped, hit the bed, blew slats and frame in all directions, tossing fur and flesh, scattering dry bones. Then the door was hit, and Jebidiah caught a glimpse of a big yellow eye through the rent in the wood. He jerked off a shot. Mary wheeled toward the door, fired and cocked the rifle and fired and cocked the rifle and fired again, banging holes through the door. Outside the door came a noise like someone sticking a hot branding iron up a bull's ass.

The horse ran around the room, nearly knocking Jebidiah and Mary over. The door banged. Another bang, louder this time, and the frame cracked and the door came flying in. Two of the wolves bounded in.

The horse went wild. It reared. It slammed its hooves down on one of the wolves. The beast was driven beneath it. It latched its teeth into the horse's belly. The horse bolted toward the door, clattered through it, dragging the wolf beneath it as it went. Jebidiah could hear his mount clattering down the stairs, then there was a breaking sound, and Jebidiah knew the horse had lost its step and gone through the railing. He could hear a cracking sound as it fell, the horrible noise of a horse screaming.

He didn't have time to consider it. The other wolf was there. The revolvers bucked in his hands and the wolf took two shots in the teeth and the teeth flew like piano ivory. Mary, who had dropped to her knees was cocking and firing with amazing accuracy, hitting the staggering beast with shot after shot in the chest. One went low and took off his balls. The wolf fell backwards, skidded, hit the wall, slammed up against it in a sitting position. Immediately it transformed. Its characteristics changed. The snout dove back into its face. The ears shrunk. Hair dropped off. A moment later where the odd version of a wolf had been was a naked Conquistador. Flesh fell off its frame like greasy bacon and its bones clattered to the floor like a handful of dice.

They waited.

They breathed.

They continued to look toward the gaping doorway.

Nothing.

Just silence.

After a long time Jebidiah picked up the lantern and carried it out on the landing, pistol at the ready. Nothing jumped him.

He walked to the railing and dangled the lantern over it and looked down. His horse lay dead with its back broken across the bar. The wolf was not visible. Without fire or oak splinters, it had survived the fall.

He waved the lantern around, saw the bones of two other wolves. The ones he and Mary had shot on the stairway. All right, he thought, that's good. One in the street. Two in the room. And two out here. That's five. Two left. One of them the big guy.

Jebidiah saw movement. Something white. Or gray. It was Dol. He was gliding up the stairs.

"Why are you hiding?" Jebidiah said. "They can't hurt you now."

"It's a habit," Dol said, more or less standing on the landing beside Jebidiah. "I still think they can hurt me, even though I know they can't. There ain't no reason to it, but that's the way it is."

"So why did you come out now?"

"To tell you the big fella's coming. I can sense it. And he's mad. He ain't got but one wolf left. Thing is, he can make five others. That means you and her or two more. Least that's the way I see it from what you've told me. Long as there's six he can't make no more. But now for fresh meat. Fresh wolves. Put a gun in your mouth. Don't let him take you like he did them Conquistadores. You did them a favor. But don't let the big boy or the last wolf have you, boy. You won't like it."

"Thanks for the warning," Jebidiah said. "So there are just the two? We got the others?"

"Yep." Dol lifted his ghostly hat, slid past Jebidiah, across the floor and melted into the wall.

Jebidiah turned to see Mary in the doorway with the rifle.

"Dol," he said.

"I heard," she said. "Jeb?"

"Yeah," he said, as the two of them moved back inside the room.

"Looks like I ain't gonna make it...Shoot me."

"We'll make it."

"Promise. You'll shoot me."

"We'll make it."

"Promise."

"It looks bad, you got my word."

"And if I can, I'll do the same for you."

"Well, just do not be in any hurry. I am in no rush. Make damn sure the end is nigh."

—◆—

No sooner had they ceased speaking than they heard steps on the stairs. The lantern light gave the room a soft glow. A cool wind came through the open window and blew against their backs. Jebidiah said. "You turn, watch the window. See a moth, a bird, a bat, if you can hit it, shoot it."

"I can't hit it," she said. "I have to be standing right in front of it to hit it."

"You've done well enough tonight."

"Once with luck, once because no one could miss, not even a blind man."

"Well, if it's small, swat it."

They went silent again. Boards creaked on the landing.

Jebidiah wiped his hand on his coat, took hold of his revolver again. Then he did the same with the other hand. He pointed both revolvers in the direction of the door.

A slat of darkness fell into the room, but Jebidiah couldn't see its source in the hall. The shadowy slat began to move, a kind of oily thing that took shape, flowed over the floor, rose up large and solid.

It was a wolf thing with barred teeth. Jebidiah had been so amazed, he had done nothing, and now the wolf was on him. It came at him so hard it knocked him across the room, to the window, forcing him through the opening.

He fell. A boot caught on the window frame. The wolf leaned way out and grabbed him, pulled him up by his pants legs. Its mouth opened so wide Jebidiah felt as if he could see all the way to hell. Its breath was every dead thing and rotten thing that had ever existed. It was about to bite him in the crotch.

Mary's rifle cracked two times and the wolf let him go. Jebidiah fell, twisting to land on his back with a white puff of dust. He hit so hard the breath was knocked out and he was unconscious.

When he awoke, he realized he had only been out for moments. He could hear screaming in the room upstairs. He moved, and it hurt to do so. His back felt as if it were on fire. He eased to a sitting position and tried flexing his legs. They still worked. All of him worked. His head ached as if he had been on a ten day drunk.

He found his revolvers in the dust. Started back toward the hotel.

The screaming stopped with a loud shot. Jebidiah looked up. The wolf thing was at the window now, its snout dripping blood. It crawled out the window and scuttled down the side of the hotel toward Jebidiah.

Jebidiah opened fire. Hit the beast in the head the moment it dropped to the ground, a good shot just above the left eye.

The thing charged him. Jebidiah dropped the revolvers and grabbed at the wolf's shoulders, pushing away its head, its snapping teeth. He fell back, placing his boot in the creature's stomach, kicked up, launching the wolf.

When Jebidiah whirled to his feet and snatched up the revolvers, the wolf lay in the dirt. Not moving. Jebidiah realized his shots had been well placed, if slow in having effect.

The wolf lost fur, changed shape, shifted back to a naked Conquistador. The flesh fell of, and instantly it was nothing but bones scattered in the street.

—◆—

When Jebidiah had reloaded his revolvers, he walked around to the front door of the hotel, stood for a moment in the street. The door to the hotel was still wide open. He eased inside, pistols at the ready. He thought about Mary, took a deep breath, started up the stairs. Every step he took made a squeak. He thought he saw a shadow move on the landing. He squinted, saw nothing solid. But the wall paper appeared darkly stained in one spot, and he had a feeling that his huckleberry was there, part of the shadows, part of the wall paper.

Easing on up, he paused, turned his head like a curious dog. The spot on the wall moved, and as it did it swelled. It was the great wolf, easily eight feet tall. It clacked its claws as it walked. It bent slightly at the waist and stood at the top of the stairs.

"Could not wait, could you?" Jebididah said. "Too impatient."

The King Wolf's ears flicked, its tongue came out of its mouth and licked at the air and lapped across its own snout.

"You are not tasting me yet," Jebidiah said.

And then the King Wolf bent forward and came down on its front paws in a dive, came down the stairs at a run. Jebididah's pistols barked, once each, and then the King Wolf hit him and he went tumbling backwards, step by step, landing at the base of the stairs.

He looked up. Smoke was twisting out of the King Wolf's body where the bullets had struck and it seemed frozen on the stairs, and he could see the creature better. It was unlike the others. Not only bigger, but there was a peculiar countenance about the horror that made Jedidiah feel as if he were in the presence of Satan himself.

And unlike the others, the bullets had done damage, but the King Wolf had been able to take it. Jedidiah got to his feet in a kind of shuffle, backed toward the door, the pistols held before him, his back aching, his side on fire. So far he had fallen out of a window and been knocked down a flight of stairs and he could still walk, so he felt he was doing well enough. And he hadn't even added in the werewolves.

When he was in the street, the doorway of the Gentleman's Hotel filled with the King Wolf's shape. It stood on its hind legs and its cock and bulls swung about when it moved as if they were a clockwork mechanism. It bent its head to accommodate the doorway and moved out into the street, its teeth dripped saliva in thick strings.

"Guess it's you and me, Mr. Wolf. I know your boss. Both of them. One high, one low. I have not got such a great opinion of either."

The King Wolf charged off the hotel porch and into the street on its hind legs. Jebidiah fired with his revolvers, two shots, and though the shots had effect, they didn't stop the beast.

Jebidiah bolted and ran. He felt pain in every muscle, but fear of what was about to happen was stronger than pain. He ran. He ran fast. He was nearly to the overturned stage coach when he looked back to find that the King Wolf was loping along rapidly, closing the gap. He could feel its burning breath on the back of his neck.

Jebidiah jumped up on the stage, dove through the open side window, dropped down inside. The King Wolf's face dunked into the open space and it let out with a wild howl that shook Jebidiah already tormented insides.

Jebidiah let loose with both revolvers. Firing twice.

King Wolf jerked back. Jebidiah quickly began to reload. He had three bullets in one revolver when the thing showed itself again. Jebidiah fired a shot that hit the King Wolf solid in the forehead, made a hole and smoke twisted up from the hole, but the beast took the shot and didn't pull back. It stuck an arm through, caught Jebidiah by the ankle, jerked him up and out of the stage window, banging his head and causing him to drop one of his revolvers as he was pulled free.

King Wolf held Jebidiah high above the ground with one hand, its face easing closer toward him. Slowly. Making the triumphant moment last. The King Wolf's mouth opened wide.

Jebidiah jerked up the loaded revolver he still clutched

in his fists, and fired his last shots straight into the King Wolf's open mouth.

King Wolf snapped its mouth shut. Smoke came out of its nostrils. It stepped back a step. It opened its mouth so wide Jebidiah could hear the bones in its jaws pop. And then the King Wolf dropped Jebidiah on his head. The Reverend rolled and came up with the empty revolver. He supported himself on one knee, began reloading, glad he still had some wax and wood shaving shells left, not happy that it seemed to be taking him forever to fumble the bullets into the gun. He glanced up fearfully as he loaded. The King Wolf was stepping backwards, slowly. Then it paused, its head tilted...and fell off, splatting heavily into the street, rolling over and over, losing hair, showing nothing but a skull, white as purity.

The rest of the torso fell over.

Finally, thought Jebidiah, the accumulated bullets, the shavings, have done their duty.

The great cold shadow rose out of the ground and filled the street. Jedidiah stood. The shadow rose thick and to the height of his neck, then the shadow fled, and with its passing came a cool wind, and when the wind was gone, there was nothing in the street, not even the shadow which was melting into the tree line at the far end of the town.

The King Wolf was gone. There was only a twist of fur flying by. It clung to his cheek for a moment, then was blown away.

Out of the hotel came the white wraiths that had hidden there, among them the more solid Dol. All of the spirits rose up toward the sky, toward the stars, gathered into a fluffy, white formation that fled upward to join the Milky Way. In a moment they were all gone and the stars in the sky winked out like snuffed candles. The sun rose as if out of the ground and took a position at high noon immediately. The sky turned blue. White clouds boiled across it quickly, and then stopped, looking like mounds of mashed potatoes on a shiny blue, china plate.

Jebidiah turned his head toward a sound.

Birds chirping in a tree on the edge of the North end of the street. Brightly colored birds so thick that at first Jebidiah thought they were fall leaves gone red and yellow and blue and golden. The birds made a sudden burst to the sky, as if confetti had been tossed, and the sunlight behind them made them look strange and otherworldly.

—◆—

In the hotel room Jebidiah found Mary. She lay on the floor. She had the rifle under her chin. She had managed to pull the trigger, shooting herself. He could see why. She had been bit all over. Maybe she had been in time. He decided to make sure.

He took her body out to the street, then brought the mattress out. He broke up chairs from the hotel and made a bon fire and got it started and put the mattress on that, put Mary's body on top of the mattress. He leaned against the stage coach and watched her burn. When there was nothing left, he went up the hill to the trees where Dol had said the graveyard was. He saw it and walked among it, went up the hill and into the deeper trees where he found gutted graves. The wolves' graves. He used his pocket knife to shave off pieces of oak, and he made crosses from them, tying them together with strips of cloth from his shirt. One cross for each grave. Just in case. He tore pages out of his bible and put those in the graves with them. Another just in case.

He went back to the hotel and got his saddle and saddle bags off of his dead horse, threw it over his shoulder, went out into the street and started walking south.

A crow followed, flying just above him, casting a shadow.